life after

Genalea Barker

IMMORTAL WORKS
SALT LAKE CITY

Immortal Works LLC
1505 Glenrose Drive
Salt Lake City, Utah 84104
Tel: (385) 202-0116

© 2023 Genalea Barker
genalea.wordpress.com

Cover Art by Lenore Stutznegger
www.lenorestutz.com

All rights reserved, including the right to reproduce this book or portions thereof in any form whatsoever. For more information visit https://www.immortalworks.press/contact.

This book is a work of fiction. Names, characters, businesses, organizations, places, events and incidents either are the product of the author's imagination or are used fictitiously. Any resemblance to actual persons, living or dead, events, or locales is entirely coincidental.

ISBN 978-1-953491-49-7 (Paperback)
ASIN B0BRW6SM5F (Kindle)

For Kate, who believed in me long before I did.

Chapter 1

October

The voices aren't real.

I tell myself this over and over as I listen to the echoes of my past. Of a time when my home was little more than a parental war zone. Words weaponized like grenades, spewing hate like shrapnel through my fragile heart.

I've visited this night in my dreams dozens—maybe hundreds—of times. The scene never fails to rattle me. Never fails to trick me into believing I'm actually *there*. Even after a decade, I'm helpless against the visceral pull.

I try to comfort my seven-year-old self, to send a message to the poor girl I used to be. *Don't pay attention. Just close your eyes. It'll be okay*—a lie.

Life won't be okay. At least not yet. First, the poor girl will cry, shedding a little of her sadness in every tear until all that's left inside her is a dry well of rage. Eventually, rage will fizzle to mere cynicism, and she'll be fine. Mostly.

But not here. Not now. For that innocent child sitting alone on her bed, clutching her knees to her chest, *okay* is so distant, she can't sense it over the dreadful here and now.

Though I fight to remain the present version of myself and not get sucked down the rabbit hole, I converge with the helpless girl in my dream and become engulfed in the tragedy.

Angry voices move throughout the house. Tears fall heavy—*plop*—onto my periwinkle blue sheets.

They've fought before, intensity and frequency accumulating these last few weeks, but it's never been like *this*. Never has their fighting instilled such fear, such certainty that my world is crumbling around me.

I bury my face in my knees, pulling my shoulders up tight to muffle the screaming. I can't do this alone anymore. I need Benny. Why did our parents move him to his own room?

"You're growing up," they'd said. "You both need some privacy."

They'd forced this cruel independence on us before we were ready. Now everything is ending, and I need my brother here. His room seems worlds away. *How can I sneak past them and get to the basement without being seen?* Before I can devise a plan, he touches my shoulder.

My head snaps up. "Benny!" I cry in a whisper. He sits beside me, and we cling to each other in a way only twins can, two halves of the same soul, wound so tightly I'm not sure where I end and he begins. Benny gives the best hugs; they drive out the loneliness and pain.

"Gigi," he mumbles, "Gigi, I..." His babyish nickname for me and these tears—both clear signs I'm dreaming. Right. This isn't real. Maybe I can force myself to wake up from this nightmare.

"I don't think I can..." Benny tries again, and he sounds so helpless I know I can't leave him. I'll let this play out to the bitter end because, even in my dreams, I could never abandon my better half.

I know exactly what he needs right now, even if he's too proud to say it aloud. Unfortunately, our father holds these truths to be self-evident that Big Boys don't cry or get scared. Dream Benny is only seven; he doesn't understand how flawed our father is, he simply wants to please the man. But it's okay, because I can read Benny's mind so clearly, he doesn't need to ask.

"Stay here with me, Benny?" I plead, so he can be the hero. "Please?"

He squeezes my hand, choking over a sob, his feverish eyes burrowing into mine.

"I'll sing if you stay," I offer through tears.

He nods, wiping his face. His shoulders droop as he relaxes, and we both inhale, releasing a sigh in seamless, unplanned unison.

"Gigi," he whispers. "I'm scared."

I squeeze him tighter; he reciprocates. "Me, too."

Profane voices grow louder as our mother recounts her grievances. She's sick of being trampled on. Sick of watching life pass her by. She's sick—so sick—of doing *nothing* with her life, of suffocating here with him. With us. She was going to be famous. She was going to cut a record deal and rise to the top, except she got pregnant with us, settled down, and left those dreams untouched.

He offers her the world—anything she wants—if only she'll stay. But nothing here can satiate her. Nothing here is *enough*. And I feel myself draining, draining, draining, empty.

Not enough.

We are not enough for her. *I* am not enough.

Raised voices become shouts. Shouts became screams. Benny and I shudder as she slams the front door behind her.

I sing Benny's favorite tune, "Two Little Boys". Mom sang it to him—to us—since we were tiny, and it always brings him comfort. We're both breathing a little easier as I approach the first chorus.

Did you think I would leave you cryin'
When there's room on my horse for two?

The door flies open before I can get any further. My father rages into my bedroom, and a shrill noise releases from his lips.

What is that? A car alarm?

I try to respond, but nothing makes sense, and the noise keeps going and going and—*crap.* I get it now.

My hand fumbles around, searching for the source of the noise.

"*What* the actual—" My fist pounds against a clunky box and the buzzing stops.

"Happy birthday, Gus Gus!" Benny yells.

"You're the worst," I say. "Happy birthday."

My eyes open enough to see him standing in the doorway, hip against the wall, arms crossed, clearly pleased with himself. I glance over at Benny's old alarm clock, on *my* nightstand.

"Really, Benjamin?"

"You changed the password on your phone," he says. "I had to do something."

I hurl a pillow at his face, and he doesn't even flinch on impact.

"I deserved that," he says as the pillow falls to the floor.

"You deserve worse," I say, pulling the sheet over my head. "I changed the password so you'd quit doing crap like setting my *alarm!*"

"Where is your sense of adventure?" With true brotherly affection, he rips the blankets off my bed, discarding them onto the floor.

"I hate you." My hands muffle my words as I wipe my greasy face. "I'm returning your birthday present and spending the money on myself."

"Lighten up." He grabs my shoulders, shaking me gently. "I couldn't have you sleeping through all the excitement." I swat at him, and an amused grin dances across his face as he jumps back.

"You mean the entertainment portion of the morning where I behead you for waking me up? On a *bonus* Friday?" Granted, he pulled me from a nightmare. I *should* be thanking him, but I won't on principle.

Where does she get off hijacking my dreams? On my birthday, of *all* days. Dreams regarding my mother are only ever a response to stress, or a sign something horrible is about to go down. She's a bad reaction or a bad omen, never anything else.

"Come *oooon!*" Benny whines, rolling his dark eyes. "How often does your eighteenth birthday fall on a three-day weekend?

No school. No dance practice for you. No marching band competitions for me." He counts the reasons I should be excited on his fingers, inching closer to me all the while. "This is a golden goose, Gus!"

"*Sleep* was my golden goose, Benjamin. And you killed it." I sit up, wiping my eyes. He ignores my audible frustration and tugs on my arm until I stand. "How long have you been waiting to do this, anyway?"

He shrugs. "I may not have slept..."

"Figures. You're more annoying than usual."

"And you're more hostile than usual," he claps back.

"Fair," I sigh. "Sorry. Crappy dream."

He frowns. "Poor Gus. Come on. I'll make you breakfast," he offers sweetly, his hand beckoning me to follow him to the kitchen.

"Cold cereal doesn't count! Not after such debauchery."

"Ah. Well." He pauses, then waves again. "I'll figure something out. Now, move!"

"I said cold cereal didn't count," I state through a laugh, entering the kitchen a few minutes later. Benny's set the table with our "finest" placemat and bowl, only to dump Cheerios into it.

He pulls the chair out for me. "Ah, but I cut up a banana for you too. So, it required *some* effort."

I try to glare, but his sunny smile gets the better of me. I playfully ram into him and shove his alarm clock into his hands with enough force to convey a clear, *never again*.

The banana helps mask the staleness of the cereal, and the milk is at least fresh. Dale isn't the best at keeping a well-stocked fridge or pantry. Benny and I often do the grocery shopping in his stead. Depending on his mood, this often throws Dale into a tantrum.

I'm the father!

I'm the provider!

I mentally scream back, *Then* be *the father!* I'm never brave enough to say it out loud.

Benny props himself on a stool while I eat, his hands drumming a beat on the counter, his foot peddling the bass. He's never without a beat in his head.

"So why were you up all night, anyway?" I ask after a few bites.

He shrugs. "My brain wouldn't turn off."

"Oh?" I raise my eyebrows, inviting further explanation, but Benny divulges nothing. "Should I be worried?" I ask.

He blinks at the ceiling. His cadence slows as he grumbles under his breath.

"Benny? What's wrong?"

"Not *everything* is a crisis, August!"

My heart sinks as Benny's hands fall to his sides.

"I'm sorry," he whispers. "I shouldn't have snapped. I'm tired is all."

He stares at the countertop to conceal any secrets potentially hiding behind his eyes. It doesn't matter; eye contact or no, his anxiety may as well be my own.

"That bad?" I ask, but he just starts drumming again. Clearly, this is not a breakfast conversation. I take another bite and let it go. For now.

"I started a song," Benny says, perking up. "I'll play it for you later."

"Sure, sure. I wanna hear it." My words slur and weave around my breakfast. A drop of milk slides down my chin, and I wipe it away with the back of my hand. "Is it insanely depressing?"

He grins. "You know it."

We ease back into our natural rhythm, avoiding the inevitable a little longer.

"For someone so incessantly cheery, you write the saddest songs."

"It's a gift," he says, beaming.

"Didn't Warren stay over last night?" I ask, eyes wandering the house. Our mutual bestie had still been vegging on the basement couch when I went to bed last night. Why that boy willingly spends so much time *here* when he has such a stable home life waiting for him is beyond comprehension. Benny would probably blame it on me. He might not be entirely wrong.

"Left already. Soccer something or other? Or helping his mom?" He squints his eyes, cocking his head to one side, then shrugs. "I was in the composing zone; I can't remember. Wanna go hiking today? It's gorgeous outside." He continues drumming with his hands, tapping his foot.

"Gorgeous?" I frown, knit my brows. "Really?"

"Yes, Grumpy Gus, *gorgeous*." Closing his eyes, he focuses harder on his rhythm.

While I'll never understand his ability to be relentlessly chipper first thing in the morning, I'm grateful he's the sunshine to my grump.

"Fine," I relent, failing to suppress a smile. "You win. But can we not hike? My legs are screaming—practice was brutal this week. Besides, *gorgeous* this time of year can't exactly be trusted."

He tilts his head, thoughtful. "Solid point. Leave in the sunshine, come home in a blizzard."

Most Oregonians will tell you, *if you don't like the weather, wait five minutes*. La Grande is no exception.

I sigh, blowing my unkempt hair out of my face. "Can't we do the usual birthday stuff? Music? Movies? Ignore all responsibility for a day? Come on, I hate how quickly this year is flying by. We're technically adults now. *Adults*, Benjamin. Life choices—serious life choices abound." I grimace, abandoning my spoon to my bowl, still half-full. I've lost my appetite.

"Right?" His busy hands and feet still, his brown eyes grow a shade sadder. "If I'm being honest, it..."

"Kept you up all night?"

"Yeah," he breathes. "I need to get out of this house, Gus. I need *air*."

It's more than a plea; there's a gravity to his voice so thick, the words stop midair and circle around him like a dark cloud.

"Understood. Catherine Creek?" I suggest, then rinse my bowl in the sink. "But I'm driving. *Your* car."

Benny gasps. "You love your truck."

"I do, but it's our birthday, and I want to drive the 'Vette. Windows down, hugging the curves. You wanted air, right? Freedom?" Nothing says freedom like the 'Vette.

"*Yes*," he says, pumping a triumphant fist in the air. "Let's go!"

"Hell*ooo*, pajamas," I intone, gesturing to us both.

"Right. Public. Real clothes. Got it." He grins before skipping—literally skipping—away.

"Why are you like this?" I yell.

"Love you, too!" he answers.

Chapter 2

The park is quiet, save for the chirping of birds. A light layer of frost covers the grass and soggy leaves. We find a private nook. Beams of sunlight illuminate an array of boulders and stumps, perfect for lounging. Benny unlatches his guitar case and pulls out his no-frills, secondhand Washburn. He's already worlds away by the time I sprawl out a blanket and settle in against a wide stump.

I grab Susan Rosenberg's *Trisha Brown: Choreography as Visual Art* from my backpack. Kali, my coach, gave it to me earlier in the week. She called it a birthday present, but it felt a little like an assignment.

You're gifted, August. But learnin' doesn't only happen in the studio.

Bless that woman; she never lets me become complacent. Not on the dance floor.

I get through two pages of the introduction before words start blurring together and my lids droop. I rest the open book against my chest and blink up at the gray-blue sky. Trees boast leaves of every shape and color, dancing in the breeze. Benny's gentle guitar playing provides the perfect soundtrack to this scene.

He started as a drummer—still is, of course—but a few years back, he learned guitar and started writing his own songs. He's never had lessons; it all simply makes sense to him. I can strum a few basic chords, and I might be decent at it with practice. But Benny makes Shirley sing. Yes, the guitar has a name, and it's Shirley. I stopped asking why ages ago.

Benny's the musician in the family, and I'm the dancer, and I love how our interests overlap but don't collide. We each get to have our unique talent, even though other than that—aside from his incomprehensible love of mornings—we're essentially the same person. Dark mahogany eyes, soft cheekbones, and a coarse, raven mess atop our heads. Granted, he's got five inches on me, like maybe I was merely an echo born out of his shadow.

In sixth grade, Maribel Vasquez asked me if twins realize one of them is an accident. Maribel is a bit of a jerk, but that stuck with me. If one of us was an accident, it definitely wasn't Benny—it was me. He's better in every conceivable way, and I'm okay with that.

His shadow can exceed mine; I don't care. I get to be his sister, and that's enough. Because despite his endless fresh ways to irritate me or con me out of sleep, he is the best part of my life.

He glances beyond his guitar to me, offering a one-sided grin. We share a brief moment, like, *this is nice*, then retreat to our separate tasks.

Seamless chord progressions, Benny's soft humming, and the gentle flow of Catherine Creek echo in my mind as I turn my focus to Trisha Brown and dance—the one aspect of my life where I shine, and Benny doesn't. Liliana, my so-called mother, started me down that path. The way she told it, I danced before I walked.

The book thuds against my chest again as my mind anxiously sifts through memories, highlighting only the worst ones. One day I hope to think about Lilianna with anything other than disdain, but right now, I can't help it. The dream only added fuel to the fire.

Hesitantly, I interrupt Benny's music, softly calling his name.

"Hm?" He doesn't break focus. There's a guitar pick between his lips and he's staring intently at the fretboard. A clear sign he's learning something new. Guilt rains down, urging me to bury this conversation before it even starts, but I can't.

"What's really going on with you?"

His fingers still and the air swallows up the last echoes of his melody. He removes the pick from his mouth. "Nothing. Really. I'm fine."

I brace for impact as I spit the words out. "I had the dream again." More than ten years later, speaking *of* her in relation to that awful night stings.

"Oh." His gaze falls.

"Sorry. I know it sucks to bring it up. And on such a *gorgeous* day." It elicits the quiet laugh and eye roll I'd hoped for. "It's always a bad sign. And with the way you were talking this morning about needing out, about needing *air*..." My voice drifts away with the ripples of the creek.

"I thought that's what your 'crappy dream' this morning might have been about. I hoped I was wrong."

"Nope." I smack my lips on the *p*, and Benny sighs.

"Damn. Sorry, Gus. Sucks you have to keep reliving it like that."

"I can take it. So long as you're okay."

He scratches at his forehead, then ruffles his shaggy hair. "I'm okay. I promise."

"Benny, you couldn't lie convincingly to a stranger. Zero poker face, man."

"It's a problem," he concedes.

"It wouldn't matter with me, anyway."

"Yeah, there's always that."

"Question: does the freakish connection get more or less creepy over time?"

He twists his lips, tilts his head. "I think less. Though it's definitely annoying sometimes. I'd like my privacy." He scowls.

"Dude, please. You're not the only one." I glower back, pointing a judgmental finger. We break face simultaneously, cracking smiles and going about our business. I settle back against my stump, picking up my book.

After a lengthy, comfortable silence, Benny clears his throat.

"I keep getting this really weird feeling." His voice is low, tranquil. "Something about this," he gestures to me, then back to himself. "Eighteen, graduation, college—it's a lot. It's a lot for..."

"Dad," I finish, closing my book. Holding his gaze, I silently inquire if he wants to talk about it.

"Not really," he says. "But I guess it's inevitable." We share a lopsided smirk. "It's like he's not even registering *any* of it. It scares me. I want to get out of this place. I want to move on, do something with my life. But if we—if *I* leave him here—I'm not convinced he'll make it on his own." He mechanically plucks at the strings on his guitar.

"It worries me, too," I admit. Dale's not been the world's most attentive father, but we could have done a *lot* worse. He cares in his way, and he's usually approachable when we need anything. He's given us the chance to earn extra money at the garage, he's worked on our cars with us. Dale's been there for almost as much as he's missed. But he also relies on us. Not in the sense he needs us to *do* anything for him, more like if we aren't around, he might lose all reason to keep his life together.

Benny holds a long, innocent shrug. "I'm probably being dramatic." I don't buy it, and he knows this. "August, I swear, I'm fine."

Eventually, I cave. "Alright, alright. We don't have to talk about it anymore right now, but I'm not letting it go."

"Gus—"

"Benny, it's okay if you're not okay. I won't sit here trying to solve your problems when you're clearly done talking about them. But I won't forget about this, either. And I won't feel better until you do. Also, if I keep having that dream with no explanation on *my* part, I'll know it's because you need help, and I *will* come after you."

"I know you will," he assures me, wide-eyed. "I love you, August. More than any human in this or any other universe. But you need to stop worrying so much about me. Otherwise," he frowns, lowering his voice, "Warren and I are gonna have you committed."

"Worrying is what I do, Benny. I have *no* chill."

"You really don't."

I scrunch up my nose, then sigh. "I'll try to relax, though. I promise. But you know I hurt when you hurt."

He responds silently with a subtle grin, then returns his attention to Shirley, striking up a familiar chord. An unspoken invitation to drop the conversation and sing.

Revisiting this same old lullaby together never gets old. It's an outlet—a comfort. A reminder light once existed where emptiness now resides. A reminder that once, there was a woman we called *Mom* who tucked us in and kissed our noses, who rubbed our backs and bandaged *owies*.

She's gone now—a mere memory. And our father is the shell of who he used to be when she was around.

Benny sings along in a smooth, baritone harmony until the last few lines, leaving me to carry the tune alone. His face is sullen as he continues strumming long after my voice fades. He transitions to a lower key, his fingers fumbling over some fancy picking. Must be his new work in progress.

"It's so unfair you got saddled with that song," he says. "Kind of a crappy move, right? Leaving you with one lullaby to remember her by, about two boys?"

"Well, it's not like she was swimming in options. Brother songs? Sure. Sister songs? Plenty. Not a lot of songs specifically for boy-girl twin siblings."

"Then she should have written one," he nearly shouts, smiling.

"She lacked—lacks—your talent, Benny. Can't hold her to any higher of a standard than we do." Which is none. We hold her to *no* standard.

"Maybe I'll write one, then. Make millions." His maniacal laugh echoes through the park.

"Do it. But I get half."

"Clearly."

Forget Liliana. Forget the Dale we knew before things fell apart. I've got Benny. He's got me. We've got music, secret looks, laughter, inside jokes, and a weird, somewhat depressing song welding us together. What else do we need?

"Happy Birthday, brother," I say, resting my head against my stump, staring at the cloudy, graying sky.

"Happy Birthday, Gus Gus." I can hear his smile as clearly as the water lapping against stones or the crows seemingly laughing at a joke only they understand. "It's getting cold. If you want—"

"Nah. Let's stay a while," I say with finality. "Gorgeous day."

Chapter 3

It's midafternoon by the time we arrive home. We stayed at the creek for hours despite the chill in the air. We probably would have stayed longer if we'd packed sufficient snacks.

I sit holding the steering wheel, staring at a section of paint peeling on the side of our stucco house, right next to the bulky gas meter. Our house lacks plenty—curb appeal is the least of our worries.

"Felt like your tire alignment was a tad off during the drive," I mumble. "Might want to have it checked."

"My tires are fine. You're stalling."

He's right. I am. Besides, Dale and Benny both baby this machine. The idea anything might be wrong with it is laughable. Dale acquired the 'Vette five years ago in the only poker game he ever won against the guys at the garage. The car wasn't much when he towed it into the driveway. But through Dale and Benny's literal blood, sweat and tears, it now looks every bit the shiny, gorgeous treasure they'd seen it as from day one. Was I a little jealous of the bonding the two of them shared over this treasure hunt?

Perhaps.

"Come on, August. I'm sure he wants to do something together to celebrate. We shouldn't ignore him all day."

"Maybe he's forgotten again. We could catch a movie with Warren. Sneak in some junk food? You could invite Millie to come with us. Poor girl's *dying* for you to ask her out already."

His mouth gapes open, his eyes burrowing into me. "*What? How...*"

"I told you, Benny. You can't keep secrets from me. You're so into that sweet girl, and she's *hardcore* into you. Branch out, dude. I mean, I know I'm amazing, but you're allowed to do things that don't include me. Besides, I'd never forgive myself if you passed up something potentially wonderful because you felt guilty about having another girl in your life."

"Wow, Gus." He frowns. "I'm mildly jealous of your intuition."

"Naturally," I tease. "Now, I'm not kidding. Ask her out, or I'm not giving you your birthday present."

"Weren't you returning it and spending the money on yourself?"

I gasp, side-eyeing him. "How *dare* you use my own words against me!"

He chuckles. "You really think I should ask Millie out?"

"Heck *yes*! Right now. Let's go! Movies, junk food, birthday shenanigans."

"Hold up," he says, putting a hand over my forearm. "I promise I'll talk to her next week. But tonight, let's give Dale a chance. Maybe he'll remember. Maybe he won't. Maybe it'll be a letdown. But if we skip out, we won't know."

"Why are you so *nice?*" I whine.

"Come on. Besides, if it is a letdown, there's always tomorrow's dinner with the Mitchells."

"Bless them," I sigh. Warren's mom doesn't hover over us or anything, but she cares. She hosts a birthday dinner for us every year, always the day after our birthday, to allow for "family" time, but also to console us afterward, in case "family time" doesn't go so well.

"Gus, he came to Homecoming. Remember? He's trying this year."

I slump back against the seat, knowing Benny's right and I'm being petty. Dale had shown up to the Homecoming football game, where they honored the seniors on the team and in the marching band. Dale stood on the field next to Benny, who was all decked out in his Drum Major getup. I *think* Dale was even smiling. Hard to tell.

Dramatically rolling my eyes, I relent with a *"Fine-ah"* and open my door.

Distant noises trickle through the house as we enter. Nineties grunge music plays through the static-y speakers of the kitchen radio. Dale hums intermittently with Eddie Vedder, the old floorboards creaking under his movement. Then, almost in time with the music, *thud, thud, thud!*

Benny and I exchange curious, furrowed brows and edge closer.

"Dad?" he tries, cautious.

"There you two are!" Dale calls. We find him seasoning freshly tenderized steaks at the cluttered kitchen counter. "Worried you might miss your birthday dinner."

"Wow, Dad," I manage. "Those look..." *raw* is all that comes to mind. The meat isn't a great cut. Rather fatty. Probably the best he could afford, though. Benny's voice intrudes on my criticism. *He's trying.* And clearly, he is. "This is amazing, Dad," I try again. "Really. Should I put together a salad to go with it?"

"Nah. Picked up some tater salad from the deli," Dale says as he arranges raw beef in a glass baking dish, pouring marinade over the top. His thinning, salt and pepper hair falls in his eyes as he bobs his head in time to the music. "Not as good as yours, Goose, but it'll do."

I draw my head back, side-eyeing Benny. He returns a subtle shrug. Dale so rarely calls me anything other than *August* these days. I honestly don't remember the last time I heard *Goose*. At least three years? Maybe longer?

"Benjamin, hand your old man that roll of plastic wrap, will ya?"

DINNER IS DELICIOUS. Or maybe it seems delicious because Dale put so much effort into it. I don't remember the last time he tried this hard. Usually, if Dale cares enough to celebrate anything, we go out for pizza. Maybe order in—nothing requiring substantial preparation.

Benny and I start the meal chipper and grinning, having exchanged presents beforehand. He loves the desktop recording software I got him. I wish I could have afforded a quality mic, but he'll make do for now. As it was, the software cost half of last month's paycheck from the dance studio.

Benny's gift to me is a shadow box containing a pair of my old, tattered lyrical shoes. On the glass, vinyl letters illustrate a quote by Marilyn Monroe. "Give a girl the right shoes, and she can conquer the world." I have no idea how or when he found the energy to come up with it, but it's the most beautiful, badass gift I've ever received. If I were a person who cried, I would have. Instead, I bear-hugged him for a solid minute.

Dale is two beers in when he makes a quip about how we might not see another such hearty, seasoned cut of beef until our next birthday, so he hopes we enjoyed it.

Benny and I exchange nervous grins because we haven't told Dale our first choice for college *isn't* Eastern Oregon University, and we both plan to leave La Grande next fall. I fidget in my seat. Benny opens his mouth as though to speak but comes up silent.

Dale pieces it together with a heavy sigh.

"Oh," he starts, slicking his hair back with both hands. "I see."

"We won't go too far," Benny says. "But we've been kicking around the idea of Washington State or University of Oregon. We thought it might be good for us to gain a little independence. Maybe not rely on you so much."

Smooth, Benny. Real smooth. I silently pray Dale accepts his flattery.

Dale slaps a hand against the tabletop. "Don't patronize me."

Nope. Didn't take.

"You two can't wait to show me how much better off you'd be without me weighing you down."

"Dad," I stutter, "that's *not* what we're doing." *We just need some space from you before we suffocate.*

"Well," Dale says, "if you think I'm paying out-of-state tuition, you're nuts."

"We won't even go out of state unless we get enough scholarship and Pell Grant money to cover the bulk of tuition," I argue. Benny gives me a look from across the table, the equivalent of squeezing my arm and pulling me back from the ledge.

"Dad," he says, "we haven't turned in our applications yet." He keeps a calm, suave tenor, as though he doesn't feel the instantaneous rage I do every time Dale stomps out any light in our eyes. "We can talk about this more before we do. And August is right. Just because we apply somewhere doesn't mean we have to go if we're accepted."

Dale stares at his plate, chewing on the insides of his cheeks.

"The steak was really delicious, Dad," I squeak out. "Thank you for making dinner special."

He chugs down the rest of his beer before muttering something I don't entirely understand, then slumps to his recliner. He turns the TV on full volume and flips through channels. A subtle, *I can't hear you anymore* gesture.

Dinner is over.

Chapter 4

Our dinner with Dale may have crashed and burned, but I don't even care. As far as I'm concerned, the real party begins Saturday evening at the Mitchells' house.

We invite Dale to come, as we always do. And he turns us down, as he always does. I wave at Benny, encouraging him to hurry out the door with me, but he kneels next to Dale's recliner and asks again, gently.

"Please, Dad. They specifically invited *all* of us."

"I'm sure they meant you two," Dale says through a cough. "I'm fine where I am."

I have no doubt he is, as he spends almost every hour outside the garage in his chair. Some nights, he doesn't even bother moving to his bed to sleep. He rarely socializes with people outside work. I mean, he tried harder right after Liliana left, for our sake, but it didn't last long.

Sure, I wish he'd stepped up to become Super Dad when she left us. That he'd put in continual, substantial effort, never letting us down in the truly important ways. But I guess you can't ask such things of a man; he has to *want* it. Dale never has. Instead, he's left Liliana's role wide open for her all this time, maybe in hopes she might show up to reclaim it. She hasn't, and it's slowly tortured him, leaving him more reclusive and impenetrable with every passing year.

"Well, Dad..." Benny finally gives up, putting a hand on Dale's shoulder and standing. "If you change your mind, you're welcome to join us."

Dale grunts as Benny and I leave, not once looking up from the Auto Finder he holds in his calloused hands.

"Just once, I'd like him to surprise me," Benny grumbles, climbing into the passenger's seat of my truck. He's not usually one to begrudge Dale vocally. Even more out of character are his downcast eyes and trembling jaw. He slams the door a little too hard, then apologizes.

"It's okay," I whisper, resting my hand atop his shoulder.

"We know other single parents," he says, not looking at me. "None of them..."

"No," I agree. "They aren't. Not like him."

He turns to me then, his brown eyes heavy and glistening. "Why did he let it ruin him? Why does he *do* this?"

"I hate it, too." I do. So much. "But hey," I offer, my voice light and hopeful, "we've got the Mitchells."

Benny nods. "I know."

"They're pretty amazing, right?"

Benny breathes a weak chuckle. "Careful, don't let Warren hear you. He might take it to heart."

"Oh, Warren," I sigh, shaking my head.

He laughs again, more believably this time. "Poor, poor Warren. Senior year, you know. You sure it won't finally happen for you two?" he teases, knowing it won't. Can't.

"Janey—from dance class, remember her? She has a crush on him. Maybe it will be their year."

"He'd have to have eyes for someone other than you first. And I don't know if it's within his realm of possibility. Poor dude."

Warren's *crush* on me developed so long ago, I can't remember a time it wasn't a running joke. But because he's the world's best friend, he's never once pushed it. He doesn't try to hide it, but the moment I ask him to stop flirting, he does. He doesn't sulk or act offended because I don't love him in the way he wishes I did. He simply goes on, being there for me in all the ways that matter, and thankfully he does. I'm not exactly swimming in genuine friends, and I don't know what I'd do if I lost one.

⁓

Warren is an only child. Doted on and spoiled by his parents occasionally, but never obnoxiously. He even drives a piece of crap car he paid for himself, and he's insanely proud of that hunk of metal. Granted, the deal is if he maintains a 3.8 or higher GPA, his parents will buy him something newer—less mid-nineties death trap—for graduation.

Mrs. M tasks Warren and Benny to assemble a salad—which will likely be ready by next weekend—then entices me into conversation while I help her carry side dishes and place settings to the dining room.

"How's school going for you, honey?"

Mr. M is visible through the French doors, flipping meat over the smoking outdoor grill.

"It's going alright," I answer. "I think."

"Yeah? Tell me." She gestures for me to sit with her, gazing intently like I'm the most interesting person in the world. She props her elbow on the table, and her curly caramel hair frames her face as she rests her chin atop her fist. "Is it exciting?"

"I mean, who isn't excited about leaving high school?" I shrug. "Possibilities really do seem endless. The world may very well be my oyster."

She laughs at the seriousness of my tone. "Oh, you kill me, August. Really. Have you started on those pesky college applications yet? I've been bugging Warren to finish his."

"They are mildly overwhelming. But we've started." I realize I'm answering in terms of "we" and not "me" again. A common folly. "I mean, Benny and I. We're sort of doing it together because we're deciding, you know, if..."

Benny appears and sits beside me. "Will they brave living apart from one another, learning to function as individuals?" It's his corny game show host voice. "Are they truly *ready* for such a bold move?" Mrs. M throws her head back in a hearty laugh, and Benny grins, beaming. He snatches a baby carrot from the veggie tray in front of us, eats it with a loud crunch. Offers me one.

"Stay tuned for the exciting conclusion," I deadpan, accepting the carrot. "It's not really looking as though we will."

"Oh?" Mrs. M raises an eyebrow at us.

"We have the same top five choices," we mutter in unison. I hate when we do this. I also love when we do this.

"May I ask…?" she says.

"George Fox is number one," Benny says. "The 'if we win the lottery' fantasy."

"Then Washington State," I continue, "Willamette, U of Oregon, and U of Washington in Tacoma."

"All great choices," Mrs. Mitchell says. "All really *solid* choices."

"Thanks," I say, smiling. "But it doesn't mean we'll both be accepted to all of them. Or if we'll get the scholarships to afford them."

"We'll cross that bridge when we come to it," Benny says, gently nudging me.

Mrs. M sighs through a widespread grin. "I adore you two. Makes me wish Warren had a sibling."

Warren brings the salad to the table, looking curiously at his mother. "You rang?"

"No," she says, "merely discussing you. You need not participate." She winks.

"Gee, thanks, Ma." They share a secret look, which makes me smile and elicits a slight pang of envy.

"Warren has us," Benny says. "He's fine."

"This is true," she agrees. Warren looks back and forth between everyone, still confused. Mrs. M waves a dismissive hand at him, then touches my arm. "How is your dancing going?"

"Good. Busy. I've been hired to choreograph both a duet and a solo. I'm also teaching two competition teams. It's busy. But wonderful."

"Mercy! I don't know how your mind does it—creates such beautiful movements."

"Thanks," I say, feeling flush. "It's the one thing I'm really going to miss about this place—about high school, about La Grande. That studio is home. You know?"

Dancing is my *thing*. Always has been, ever since diapers. It came more naturally than walking, and it's the one thing I truly excel at. Dancing is what makes me special. What makes me August.

"I remember the woman who owns the studio. I was her agent when she bought the building years ago."

"Kali," I offer.

"Yes. Kali. Sweet gal. Is her hair still bright pink?"

"It changes with her moods," I say, laughing.

"She was one of my first clients after I got my license."

"She's amazing. If it weren't for her, I would have had to quit years ago."

"Oh?"

"Yeah. You know, my dad..." I pause, not wanting to say anything too degrading about him publicly. "Well, it was hard for him to keep up after my mom left. After I missed a couple of classes and Kali couldn't reach my mom, she came over to check on me and realized the situation. She arranged my rides to class until I was old enough to manage it alone."

She'd also forgiven the tardiness of my tuition multiple times without penalizing Dale. She realized it was a miracle he allowed me to continue dancing in the first place, considering my enrollment had been my mother's doing.

Mrs. M smooths my hair away from my face. Her glossy eyes reveal a quiet rage shrouded in sympathy—her typical response anytime the subject of my mother comes up.

"What a wonderful thing Kali did for you," she says after a quick hug and a sniffle. "Now, you make sure to tell me when your performances are. Every single one. I'll be at as many as I can, cheering embarrassingly loud."

"You don't need to do that, Mrs. M. It's really not—"

Autumn air wafts into the dining room as Mr. Mitchell comes inside with a platter of chorizo and burgers. "You're welcome," he announces to the room, closing the door behind him. Placing the platter in the middle of the table, he orders us to "Dig in!"

"Save room for cake!" Mrs. Mitchell adds. "Red velvet." She winks at me, knowing it's my favorite.

Chapter 5

After dinner, Mrs. Mitchell asks Benny to play a song for her and is crushed to learn he didn't bring his guitar along.

"What a shame. It's been too long since I heard you play. You and August sang the most beautiful duet—what was it called?"

"Oh, Benny's the one with the voice," I say. Benny narrows his eyes on me.

"I'll go grab Shirley right now, Mrs. M," he says. "August will sing you all the songs you want." On his way out, he tousles my hair a little too forcefully.

While Benny retrieves his guitar, Warren and I tackle kitchen clean up.

"Why do you always sell yourself short?" he asks me, breaking a comfortable silence.

"What are you talking about?"

"You know exactly what I mean."

I knit my brow, tilting my head. "I really don't."

"August, come on. I don't know anyone who gives themselves less credit than you do. Telling my mom she doesn't need to come to your dance performances and that crap about Benny being the one with the voice."

"Well, he is."

"Dude, I've *heard* you sing. You're such a freaking liar, always trying to pass yourself off as mediocre."

"On the contrary," I argue, tucking containers of leftovers away in the fridge. "Pretty sure I'm a massive snob. I think too highly of myself and judge others too harshly." I close the fridge door and meet his gaze, daring him to prove me wrong.

"Okay," he relents, smiling. "In some ways, yes, you *are* a snob."

"Thank you." I hold my hand to my heart. "Truly." He laughs, closing and starting the dishwasher.

"But in other ways, you're stupidly hard on yourself. You make Benny out to be the star, always averting the conversation to him or even me whenever someone asks you about your plans."

"Hey, I was open about my plans to keep dancing; I never sell myself short there. I know I can dance, and I know I'm good at it. Great, even. I work insanely hard and push myself to extremes to be great at it." I shiver, repulsed by my conceit. "See, told you I was a snob."

He braces himself against the counter; I brace myself opposite him. "Well, yeah, you're glad enough to talk about *that* because it's the one thing Ben doesn't also do. But if he showed up at your studio with a pair of tap shoes and took up the sport—yes, I admit, it's a sport. You've made that abundantly clear." I bite my lip, smiling as he references my many lectures on the topic. "You'd suddenly be second-guessing yourself. When people asked you how dance team was going, you'd say, 'Oh, fine, but Benny's the one with the coordination.'"

I stare, cold and hard, unable to say anything. Warren sighs, waving his arm as he pulls up a stool at the breakfast bar. His foot nudges the stool next to him. I shuffle over, accepting the silent invitation.

"I get you have to be this," he pauses, "hard shell. At least, you think you do. I don't know exactly why you're constantly on your guard, keeping people away. I mean, I can guess, but I don't understand. Not truly. And I don't have to; it's not my business."

"Warren, *what* are you *talking* about? Why is there a sudden need for this conversation? It's not like I'm a different person from the one I've always been. I honestly don't even know what you're trying to say, let alone *why*."

He throws up his hands. "To be honest, I'm not entirely sure. I like you the way you are, Gus. Of course, I do. We all do. It's just, tonight, I found myself a little annoyed. I wish you'd open up now and again. Enough so people could see you're special, and you're not blind to it."

"Look, Warren..." I have no reply. None of this makes sense. It's common knowledge Benny is the more talented and likable twin, and it's never bothered me. I know my personality is less than inviting. I keep people at a distance, and Warren is right; I have my reasons. I'm fully aware of my reserve around people, and Benny's ability to wear his heart on his sleeve means he'll always be more popular than me. I literally couldn't care less.

"Warren," I sigh, "I know I'm awesome." I flash a cocky smirk. He chuckles half-heartedly. "First of all, I'm a delight to be around." His head bobs as his laughter intensifies. "A *delight*. I'm smart *and* pretty. My talents are vast, and my potential limitless. I have moves like Jagger, baby." I shimmy my shoulders. "*Better* than Jagger. Jagger wishes he had moves like me. I. Am. *Outstanding*." He nudges me, still laughing. I let my voice break for a few seconds as I laugh with him. Then, more seriously, "I just don't care if anyone else knows it. It's not important to me. Not right now.

"Maybe I do give Benny a little too much credit sometimes, but he's the most important part of my life. I'm always going to be ridiculously proud of him, and I'll always have the compulsion to gush about how great he is. It's hard to explain. It's simply who I am and what matters most to me right now—to see Benny do well. Maybe I go a little Dance Mom sometimes; talk him up too much and make it awkward for people. I'm sorry, Ren."

"No," he touches my shoulder briefly. "You don't have to apologize. For anything. I'm overreacting. And I'm making this my business when I absolutely shouldn't."

I nudge his bicep. *Dang!* He's solid. "You care, and I love you for caring. You're the most consistent friend I've had in my life other than Benny. I promise it doesn't go unnoticed or unappreciated."

"I'm glad." He nudges me back. "Also—and I know you were joking around—but for what it's worth, you were right. You are *amazing*."

"Thank you." My pitch curves, making it almost a question.

"Smart *and* pretty," he reiterates.

"Yes. If only I didn't freckle like a ginger," I lament, staring off.

"I like your freckles."

I roll my eyes and shove him away as the front door slams, signaling Benny's return.

🎧

Warren's well-intended commentary on my life put my brain on overdrive. I should be sleeping, but all I can do is worry. Maybe I am too closed off.

I have no desire to open myself up more to people around me. I've got Benny and Warren. I have acquaintances at school. There's a handful of girls on my dance team I hang out with on occasion—a movie or lunch. I'm not completely void of social skills. I'm even *likable*. Not as much as Benny, but likable.

He and I are so similar in our sense of humor and interests, our personalities seem identical when we're together. But around other people, I'm more of an acquired taste. I'm slow to relax around new people, even slower to trust, and far too fluent in sarcasm. Not a fantastic combination.

But Benny? He loves people openly, without hesitation. It's why I never resent him for being adored while I'm merely a face in the crowd. He's earned it. He's brave, I'm not, and that's okay. Sure, every time I get written off as *Benny's sister*, it stings. But that's not his fault, either.

Warren called me a *hard shell*. Maybe I am. But he was right about something else, too. I *do* have my reasons.

When our mother left, I cried. Daily. Relentlessly. Benny and I watched helplessly as our father began shutting down. He managed simple tasks—getting us to the bus stop, keeping TV dinners in the freezer, occasionally asking us how our day was. Beyond that, he was lost.

He didn't disappear overnight. Initially, he still talked to us like we mattered, tucked us in at night, tried to remember important dates and events. He'd even try to console us if he found us crying.

"She won't be gone forever," he'd say. "We're going to be okay."

He wasn't convincing, but he *tried*.

With time, he drifted further away. Permission slips went unsigned. Benny and I left behind while our classmates went on adventures.

Dale gave up attending school concerts and Honor Roll ceremonies. If it happened outside of school hours, Benny and I missed it. At least until Warren's parents realized what was happening and stepped up for us. He quit coming to my dance recitals and competitions. Whenever possible, Benny found a ride and came to support me. The same way I found ways to attend his band concerts. Still, it always burned, looking around a room of proud parents, knowing our dad was too lonely and spiteful to show up.

Hope for my mother's return dwindled quickly. Within a few months, I knew what Dale couldn't accept: she was never coming back.

It hurt. Hurt turned to anger, anger to hate. Soon, I hated her so much I convinced myself we were better off. I stopped missing her, stopped thinking I saw her places. Not long after that, I stopped crying.

She left in the winter. The following summer, Benny got sick. He was sweaty with a fever, complaining of a headache.

I couldn't find Dale. I called the garage but was told he'd left hours before and should have been home long ago.

I searched every cupboard for the children's ibuprofen. Or—as I knew it at the time—the orange medicine. The stuff our mother had always given to us for fevers. I even knew which measuring spoon to use. But I couldn't find the bottle anywhere.

Benny was sobbing, hands between his knees in the fetal position on his bed. "Gigi, it hurts so bad."

I knelt over him, sniffling, wiping my tears away. "I know, Benny. I'm sorry. I can't find the medicine. I can't find Daddy."

He cried harder and turned his face to the wall, embarrassed.

I rubbed his back. Hushed him gently. "It's okay, Benny. I'm sure he'll be back soon. He'll know what to do." I wanted to believe it.

"I wish Mama was here!" he wailed. "Why did she have to go?"

That was it—the big moment. I swallowed my sobs, touched Benny's shoulder, and told him everything would be fine. I would take care of it.

And I did.

Our house wasn't far from a gas station. At night, you could see the glow of the sign from our front yard. No more waiting around for my dad to help Benny; I'd do it myself. Grabbing my piggy bank and tightening the velcro on my tennis shoes, I ran out the door.

The store clerk was tall and scrawny—an ivory face hidden behind mountainous red blemishes. My heart raced with every step, and the closer I got to the register, the less I saw of the boy behind it.

I put my piggy bank up on the counter and stood on my toes.

"Can I help you?" the clerk asked as he leaned toward me, a look of amused concern on his face.

"My brother has a fever. Does this store have medicine for a fever?"

"Kid, where are your parents?"

"Mommy's gone," I stated plainly, unashamed. "Daddy's at work," I lied, "and my brother needs some medicine."

"Is there someone I could call for you?"

"Daddy's coming home soon," I lied again, determined to fix this myself. "But Benny needs medicine *now*. He's crying."

"How do you know it's a fever?"

"His face is hot. And he hurts." I paused, swallowing. "I need the orange medicine."

He smirked, cleared his throat. "Orange medicine?"

"It's orange, and it tastes funny, but not bad. I have a lot of quarters and three dollars. Is that enough for the orange medicine?"

He came out from behind the counter and crouched in front of me. "What's your name?"

"I'm not supposed to tell my name to strangers."

"I bet you're not supposed to talk to strangers at all, are you? Or walk to the gas station by yourself?"

"Nope. But Benny needs medicine, and Daddy's not home yet."

"You're a brave kid," he said.

Stone-faced, I repeated, "Medicine." I couldn't have Benny thinking I'd abandoned him, too.

The clerk showed me their small selection. There was a heated debate since the fever reducer they carried wasn't the same color as the kind my mother had always given us. But he promised me it would do the trick. "The box says it tastes like grapes," he assured me, all seriousness.

"I guess grape is okay," I conceded. He smiled and patted my shoulder.

He showed me the dosing directions on the back, opened the box, and pulled out the measuring cup, showing me how far to fill it up.

When I asked how much it cost, he refused my money. My temper flared again, and I shouted that stealing was bad, and I wasn't bad. He relented, accepting only a quarter from my stash.

He scanned the medicine and placed my quarter in the cash drawer. Before bolting home, I paused outside the storefront to peer through the window. I watched as the clerk removed money from his wallet and added it to the register.

Benny got his medicine, and I stayed by his side, softly singing until he fell asleep. I took care of him. Me. No more tears. I don't even remember what it feels like to cry. I know it's not normal, and probably not healthy, but it's how I've survived the last decade.

Maybe I am a little too closely concerned with Benny's welfare. Maybe I'm a hard shell when it comes to my emotional well-being. Maybe my reasons are valid, maybe they aren't. But it's all I know anymore.

I lie on my back, my gaze fixed on a yellowed section of ceiling, torturing myself. Wondering whether I'm justified in my rigidity, whether I'm good enough, whether I'm kind enough or open enough. Right as I begin spiraling, my phone chirps and vibrates.

Benny: *Everyone wishes they were as amazing as you. Sleep well, seester.*

His words are a warm embrace, almost as good as the real thing. I close my eyes, releasing a contented breath, settling further into my pillow.

Chapter 6

NOVEMBER

The afternoon is teetering between sweatshirt weather and legit winter—cold enough to warrant turning on the heater in my truck. I wave to Benny, who grins and subtly gestures to his hand, intertwined with Millie's, as they walk side by side to his Corvette. I snicker, rolling my eyes, but give him an enthusiastic double thumbs up.

They had their first official date last week, and he's been driving her to school and back home every day since, leaving me to my own devices. He constantly tells me how sweet she is, how gorgeous her green eyes are, and how they haven't kissed yet, but he doesn't care because simply holding her hand is the best feeling in the world. I'm thrilled for Benny. He deserves this. And yet, a sliver of envy weaves its way into every well wish I have for them. It's unsettling.

My heater has been blasting for two full minutes, and there's no hint of warmth.

"What?" I adjust the heat and wait. The air remains cold, unchanged. "*Why?*"

The lack of heat offends me on many levels, only one of them being I *thought* my Sierra and I had a special bond, and things such as failing parts or malfunctions were against the rules. Especially without any warning.

I'm bothered on a deeper level, knowing *Dale the Mechanic* probably won't come through for me. I should be able to trust he'll save the day if I turn to him for help, but I know better. It's not like he *always* forgets I exist, but I tend to be background noise to him. He's better with Benny. Maybe it's the whole "guy" thing.

Dale isn't a *bad* dad; he's just...broken. The ghost of a man I'd called Daddy, who had called me Goose and always kissed my cheek when he came home from work and held me with his greasy, hardworking hands. He used to rub his stubbly face against mine until I giggled and squirmed away. He'd laugh, go shave, then come back and make me kiss his smooth cheek, fragrant with aftershave.

That man is a memory now. The man who laughed, joked, smiled in family pictures—mother, father, daughter, son—doesn't live in our house anymore. In his place is a pale, rough shell who pretends to be human.

Still, it's worth mentioning my heater needs servicing. Dale might listen. Might even care a little. Maybe it can give him something to focus on. A project to show him he's needed. Maybe, just maybe, it'd earn his attention and a "by the way, how's school going?"

But when I arrive at the garage, Dale is already gone for the day. Not even four o'clock, and he's left. Carlos frowns. "I'm sorry, honey," he says, and I know he's not just talking about the truck. Carlos has worked at the garage since I can remember. He knows Dale's faults as well as I do.

"It's fine, really," I lie.

"I'm almost finished up with something. Stick around a bit. I'll look at it for you."

"No, it's not that important. I've got practice to get to soon anyway." This is also a lie. I just can't be around other people right now with this anger welling inside.

"You and your fancy dancing." He wiggles his hips, slapping his oily rag side to side. "You let me know when you perform, alright? Marta and I wouldn't miss it." He smiles so sweetly I can't help but laugh.

"You bet. You could join me, if you like. You've got moves, Carlos."

"I would love that," he says, "but Marta would die of embarrassment."

I offer a gentle wave of gratitude as I retreat to my cold truck.

I fully expect to find Dale in his chair in the living room, feet kicked up, drinking beer, watching football, rambling about how so and so better kick it up a notch or it'll be a sore year.

But he's not even rambling. He's already passed out—doesn't even budge when I slam the door in frustration.

"Hey, Dad." Nothing. "I aced a test today." Not a sound. "Joined the Marines." Nada. "My truck needs some TLC. The heater isn't working." I'm invisible.

Maybe it's because he didn't bother waiting until after dinner to drink himself unconscious. Maybe it's because when Benny tried to talk to him about our college applications earlier this week, he grumbled something incoherent and promptly left the room. Maybe it's because Benny is happy with someone, and I'm here begging for attention from the one person I should never have to *beg* for attention, and I'm jealous. Whatever the reason, I see Dale lying there, unresponsive, and I can't be in this house anymore.

The studio will be empty. Friday evenings belong to solo and duet practice, and no one has the building reserved for another hour.

I unlock the door, slowly push it open, and breathe in the musk of hard work and worn leather. I pluck a pair of faded lyrical shoes from my bag and begin stretching while scrolling through my playlists. Finding the perfect mix to suit my mood—a combination of angst and disappointment—I slip on my shoes and press play.

When I teach, I'm focused solely on my students. Watching every angle and extension with a critical eye, calling out firm cues and corrections. "And one, two, three, four, five, six, seven, eight, and pas de bourrée, *double* pirouette, and land in fourth, *and watch your arms!*"

When I dance as part of a team, I bear the burden of perfection and control. It's not just about mastering choreography, but geography. One misplaced dancer can throw an entire routine down the drain, and I refuse to be a hindrance.

But when it's just me and all those obligations fall away, I crank up the volume, close my eyes, and compose combinations on the spot. My body moves instinctively, the choreography an extension of my soul. All the words I can't say, all the tears I can't shed. All my inner turmoil unraveled, surrendered to the dance floor.

I've heard the suggestion more than once when things are rough that I need to "have a good cry" about it. No. I need to dance about it.

I dance through fear and rage, love and hate, anxiety and calm. This is how I cry.

❡

I MANAGE without heat in the truck for a few days before my morning commute becomes legitimately dangerous. Frost-covered, fogged-up mirrors make it nearly impossible to navigate traffic, and I'm no longer confident I won't cause an accident.

I get up early to ensure I don't miss Benny. Ever since he started picking Millie up in the mornings, he's out the door with hardly a "Mornin'" and a bite of breakfast. I go in search of him, wiping goop from my tired eyes, and find him already lacing up his knock-off Vans. "Hey there, early bird," I croak, "what's the rush?"

"I'm taking Millie out for coffee before school," he says, straightening.

He's grinning ear to ear, wearing a new shirt, and taken extra care with the part in his hair this morning.

"You hate coffee," I observe, smiling. "You must really like this girl. And she must *really* like you to voluntarily get up even earlier on a weekday."

"She loves mornings. Amazing, right?"

"So weird," I breathe. Both of them. "Clearly you're made for each other."

"How do I look?" he asks, a hopeful half-smile on his freckled face.

"I could punch you."

"I'm sorry?"

"You're *adorable*," I assure him. "So adorable, it's annoying. So please, go before I actually punch you in the face."

"She likes the car," he says, grinning.

"Of course, she loves the 'Vette. Everyone does."

"No, she *likes* it. She's hardly impressed."

"And you're smiling about this because…?"

"She likes me more."

Benny's eyes glisten; he's so happy. All things wonderful radiate from him as he stands there, backpack slung over one shoulder, car keys in hand, his clearance rack shoes tapping subtly on the dirty doormat.

"As she should," I say. "You're a catch, Benny. I'm happy you're happy."

He takes a step closer to me, tousles my hair, mouths, "Love you," and opens the front door. Before he disappears completely, he gives me one more wide grin, accompanied by a short, boyish laugh.

Giddy. He's *giddy*.

I head for the bathroom but stop when the front door cracks back open. I turn to see Benny's head peering through the frame.

"You need something, Gus Gus? I was distracted. I'm sorry."

"Nah. Just wanted to say goodbye. See you around today, unless you're too busy…*drinking coffee*."

He rolls his eyes before making a final exit.

❦

Warren's old Ford Escort, held together by duct tape and a prayer, rolls to a stop in front of my house.

He flashes a friendly, familiar smile as I climb into the passenger seat.

"Thank you for this," I say. "I really appreciate it. I could have walked, but..."

"Don't be ridiculous," he says, waving a dismissive hand before putting the car into gear. "You can always catch a ride with me. I know it's not a Corvette, but it gets the job done."

"Hey, this baby is classy," I say, rubbing the zebra print seat covers I bought him for his birthday last year. So tacky, I couldn't resist.

"Absolutely. Thank you, again, for these. Real head turners. Wildly popular with the ladies."

"You're welcome. I knew they would be."

"Wonder how Benny's *coffee* date is going," Warren mumbles, fiddling with the turn dial on the old stereo. He settles on an alternative station with minimal static.

"Millie seems like the perfect match for him. She's really sweet." My tone betrays me.

"Tell me how you really feel," he says in a deep murmur.

I huff a weak laugh. "Really, I think she's great. But I don't know her well. I'm just a little...hesitant."

"Overbearing," he teases.

"Cautious," I correct.

"Jealous," he says, then winces. "Sorry, too far."

"No. Not really. You and Benny make up almost my entire social circle, and I've had you both to myself for so long. Sharing isn't my superpower."

Turns out the only thing I can't unreservedly give to Benny is space. It hurts to let go, even a little, which is my problem, not his.

"What's wrong with your truck, anyway?" Warren asks.

"No heat."

"Have you told Ben?"

"When? He's gone like, *all* the time now." I shrink into my seat, annoyed with my possessiveness.

He halts the car at an all-way stop and shoots me a dubious, sideways glance.

"Alright," I relent. "I hate it a little—a lot, actually. I know it's stupid, because he absolutely *should* be out with a sweet, pretty girl who adores him. But I miss him."

"Change is hard."

"And it's rarely good," I mutter through my teeth.

We ride the rest of the way to school in silence.

"I hate to ask, but can you drop me at the studio after school? I'll hang out there until my classes tonight and hitch a ride home with Kali. Or walk. Whatever."

"Of course. But don't walk home. If you need a ride, call me."

"Sure," I lie.

"*Gus*," he says, slow and deep.

"I promise," I revise. "I'll call."

And I do. I rely on Warren all week long. It's annoying, having the freedom of my vehicle stripped away. I keep thinking I'll ask Benny for his help—he's always better at talking with Dale—but whenever I see him, he's got this lovestruck glimmer in his mahogany eyes, and I can't bring myself to drag him into my mess.

I want to, though. I want to be selfish and let Benny know how his frequent absence has revved up Dale's irrationality. When Benny's around, Dale's grounded. He's not always nice, thoughtful, or even conscious, but he's grounded in a reality of sorts. So long as I tread lightly and maintain a delicate balance, all is well. But without a buffer, Dale sees too much of my mother in me. Gets pulled back to the past. Gets hurt. Then he gets angry at me for it.

I gather my courage and mention the truck to Dale again. Gently, cautiously. I do it first thing in the morning before he's had a chance to work too hard, drink too much, or become too agitated.

"I'll buy the parts," I say. "I'll help you fix it." I'm useful with a toolbox and more than willing to dedicate my time and energy to the task. He should know this. "I can't do it by myself, though. Maybe there's a time I could bring it in, and we could work on it together? Or maybe Carlos could help me if you've got too much on your plate already?"

I know I'm taking a risk by mentioning Carlos. But I'm hoping my careful phrasing prevents Dale from registering any insult.

"You don't think I can fix it?" he snaps. "I'm the best damn mechanic there, I'll have you know."

This used to be true. The only reason he still has a job is he owns half the business. He bought the old partner out years ago when things were still good. When we were still a family.

"I know, Dad. I also know you're busy. And I want to have it fixed before winter *really* hits."

His features soften. "I'll drive it to work myself," he says. "I'll do it today."

"Really?" I try to hide my shock, but it seeps through.

"Yeah, I'll see what I can figure out."

"I'll stop by after school, before dance. See if I can help."

"Sure," he grumbles. "That's fine. See you then."

I hear Warren's brakes whining as he parks in front of the house. Grabbing my backpack, I rush for the door, but stop and backtrack toward my father.

"Thank you, Dad," I say. "This means a lot."

His stubbly face contorts into something resembling tenderness. "Of course, Goose," he says. "Of course."

After school, Warren drives me to the garage. No Sierra in sight. No Dale, either. Carlos approaches, wiping his hands on a soiled rag.

"Good to see you, August. Can I help?"

"My dad's not here? My truck?"

"He didn't come in today, honey," he sighs, shaking his head. "I'm sorry. We called several times. No answer. I figured, maybe he's sick." He shrugs.

I curse under my breath, then apologize. Carlos reaches to touch my shoulder but stops himself, eyeing his greasy hands.

"It's fine," I say, forcing a close-lipped smile. "It'll be fine. Carlos, I think it's a leak. I'm getting air, but not heat."

"Well, depending on *where* the leak is, it could be a simple fix or a massive pain in the rear. Won't take long to diagnose it, though.

Figure out how invasive of a surgery it'll be." He winks, and I humor him with a quiet laugh. "I can tow it here for you tomorrow morning on my way in."

"No, that's too much," I rush. "I'll bring it by in a bit and leave it." It's warm and sunny. Windows should stay clear enough to make it a couple miles.

I ask Warren for this one last favor of the day. Drop me home, follow the truck to the garage, and drop me by the dance studio. He obliges. Happily.

I don't deserve Warren.

I find my keys dangling on the hook where I left them for Dale this morning. I find *Dale* asleep in his chair. No beer cans near him. Not even a pack of cigs in his shirt pocket. So maybe he really is unwell. Or maybe he's trying *really* hard to piss me off, in which case, it's working. I leave with a slam of the door, not caring if I wake him, start up the truck, and peel out of the driveway.

I leave the keys with Carlos at the garage, touch his shoulder as a silent, *thank you*, and shuffle to Warren's car, a deep, aching sense of dread swimming through me.

By taking matters into my own hands, I've poked the bear. I've thrown off our delicate balance, and there *will* be hell to pay when I get home tonight.

Chapter 7

I postpone going home as long as possible. I stick around for every single class. I do homework in the office or observe in the corner. I pitch in during a cheer class, helping spot as the students learn a new stunt. I even convince Kali to stay after the last class of the night, begging her input on some tricky choreography in my solo. When I'm out of excuses, she drives me home.

I can always smell it when he's angry. The moment I open the door, it hits me—musky, un-showered man odor mixed with alcohol and a hint of cigarette smoke.

"August Elizabeth!" he hollers, turning in his recliner. The TV displays the nightly news. "The hell you been?"

I stare at the meteorologist on-screen, wishing she were predicting a dangerous storm, the end of the world, anything important or distracting.

"Teaching," I answer. "Homework. More teaching." *You know: responsibility.* I don't say it out loud, but I *really* want to.

"It was your turn to make dinner tonight," he scolds, annoyed.

Since when is this a thing? We take turns now? Isn't it perpetually "fend for yourself" night around here?

I settle on, "I didn't realize. Do you need a sandwich or something?"

"I can make my own damn sandwich."

Then what is the point of this conversation?! I hold my lips in a tight line, swallowing my contempt.

"You took your truck to the garage," he says. "You ask Carlos for help? Bet he loved that."

"I need heat, Dad. It's getting colder, and once the snow falls, Benny and I always ride together. In the truck. It's safer."

"You think I don't know that?" He stands, stepping toward me, the alcohol and cigarettes on his breath releasing into the room with every word.

"It's one less thing you have to worry about now, Dad," I say, trying to ease the tension. "It's there, and Carlos said he'll diagnose the issue tomorrow and order parts. I should be able to cover the cost myself."

"You think I can't provide for my family?"

There is no winning with Dale, especially not for me.

"You're just like your mother," he shouts, "always trying to make everything *my* fault." He's at full volume by the end of his rant. Spit from his mouth lands on my nose. Slowly, careful to keep my expression flat and unwavering, I bring the collar of my shirt up to wipe away the saliva.

"Well, say something, selfish brat!"

The front door closes behind me. I flinch, and my heart sinks.

"August," Benny says cautiously. "Dad. Everything okay here?"

Dale huffs, slowly shrinking from his hulk-like appearance back to an average Joe.

"Everything is fine," I say, locking eyes with Dale.

"Fine and dandy," he says with disdain. His stocking feet trudge across the creaky hardwood floors to his room, and he slams the door behind him. I doubt we'll see him until morning.

"Gus," Benny whispers, his hand touching my shoulder. "Gus, look at me."

I plaster a smile on my face and whip around. "Hey," I say. "You eat? I'm about to make a glamorous PB&J. Want one?"

He frowns. "August, what happened?"

"Nothing. Dale being Dale," I say, coolly. "You want a sandwich or not?" I turn toward the kitchen before he responds.

"I ate, thanks."

"Ooh, with *Millie*?" I turn back, fluttering my lashes at him. "Am I ever going to meet this girl properly, or are you too ashamed of me?"

"Gus, please."

"It's *fine*, Benny," I snap, harsher than I'd meant to. "I'm fine. Everything's fine."

"Clearly not," he says. His hand latches onto my shoulder, stopping me in my tracks, only two steps from the fridge. "Warren texted me a bit ago. Wanted to make sure you'd found a ride home because he couldn't get a hold of you."

"I always turn my phone off at the studio," I deflect.

"Why did you need a ride, August? And where is your truck?"

"Can I please make myself a sandwich?" I ask, eyeing his hand on my shoulder.

"Only if you talk to me."

I almost lose it. I almost scream at him. *What? You suddenly want to talk* now? But I don't. I release an agitated sigh, flexing and releasing my hands. Benny recognizes the gesture and backs away, taking a seat at the wobbly kitchen table.

I find the good bread in the cupboard, the kind I buy with my own money every week and hide so Dale doesn't eat it all. Brand name buttermilk—thick, rich, and delicious. I coat each slice with a generous helping of creamy peanut butter, so the jelly ends up encased between it. I pour a glass of ice water, take a bite of my creation, and sit opposite Benny.

"Okay, go," I offer, my mouth full, my voice sticky with peanut butter.

"Warren has been giving you rides?"

I chew, swallow, and drink before answering. "For about a week. I couldn't keep driving the truck without heat. The windows fogged up in the mornings. It wasn't safe."

"How did I not notice this? Why didn't you tell me?"

I answer both questions at once. "You've been gone before me every morning and home after me every night since—" I cut myself off.

"Since I started seeing Millie," he finishes, letting his shoulders slump. "You're right. I've been oblivious to everything else." His head falls into his arms, and he takes several slow breaths before making eye contact again. "You should have told me, Gus Gus. I'm still here for you. You're still the most important—"

"Benny, I love you, but you deserve to have a world beyond me. And I'm glad you do now. Millie is super sweet. And happy. Her world must be so pleasant and colorful, and..." *Completely lacking in drunken, angry dads with irrational thought processes.* "I wanted you to be happy. I've made it work so far, and I thought if I chipped away at him subtly, over time, he'd help me get the truck fixed, and it would be fine. But after promising me he'd take it in today, he didn't. So, I dropped it off with Carlos. Hence the yelling. I knew it would piss him off, but I did it anyway. So, really, it's on me."

Benny cradles his head in his hands, his fingers rubbing his forehead. He takes a minute before meeting my gaze again with glossy eyes.

"Don't be upset, Benny. Please. It's okay, now. You're home. I've missed you." I should have tucked those final words back, deep inside, rather than unleashing them. Benny's first tear falls.

"I let you down, Gus."

"No, Benny. *No*. You didn't. You've never let me down."

"Except I did." His voice cracks.

"*Benjamin.*"

"I did, August. And it won't happen again. You ride with me. You borrow my car when you need it. And I'll get the truck fixed myself."

"You've got enough on your plate—"

"I can't promise it'll be fast. But I'll get it done. Things slow down after the Thanksgiving Day Parade with band. And my physics project is almost done."

"Benny, listen to yourself."

"I'll *fix* it, Gus," he nearly shouts, his fist pounding the tabletop.

Then, softer, "I'll talk to Dad. And I'll fix it. And I won't leave you alone with him anymore. I promise. Okay?"

"Okay, Benny," I say gently, nodding. "It's okay."

"Okay."

"Would you like half of my sandwich?" I ask, hopeful.

He twists his lips, then reluctantly accepts half my dinner. "You do make a wicked PB&J," he says.

"Put that on my headstone, will you?"

⚜

BENNY, Warren, and I fill our lungs with the crisp, chilly air—still sweatshirt weather. No snowfall yet. Birds chirp, and students file into the building. The first bell of the day will ring in minutes.

The frosted ground vibrates under my sneakers as a compact, silver Audi comes into view. Thick, obnoxious bass resounding from its speakers.

"Are there no noise ordinances in this town anymore?" I grumble. Who *is* this, and why are they blasting *trap* music? So annoying. The fancy box screeches into a parking spot and a tall blonde stranger emerges from the driver's seat. Without meeting him, without even speaking to him, I know he is completely unoriginal.

Warren takes a deep breath, observing New Kid. Appraising the shiny coupe. Keeping a straight face, he says, "He must keep a lot of after-school jobs to afford that."

Benny and I laugh—me, louder than necessary. New Kid is well-dressed and overly groomed. The air of confidence about his walk is gag-worthy.

"An Audi?" Warren asks when New Kid is safely in the building, out of earshot.

"Yes," Benny answers sharply.

"A new one," I add.

"So ridiculous." Benny shakes his head, his disdain etched in his features. The origin of Dale's American-Made Car worship is unknown, but it's a sort of religion he passed on to Benny.

"It's pretty," Warren says through tight lips.

"Oh sure, it's shiny," Benny concurs. "But I wouldn't trust it as far as I could throw it. I mean, we all know I'm biased, but it doesn't mean I'm wrong." He is absolutely biased, but neither Warren nor I argue with him.

"It's so tiny," I say, cringing. "My Sierra could quite literally crush that thing. So easily. I would hardly need a running start."

"Let me know beforehand." Warren nudges my arm. "I'd like to watch."

"Well, my truck has to be drivable first," I mumble.

"Soon, Gus." Benny pats my head with a little too much force, and I smack him. "Once the Thanksgiving Parade is out of the way, I'll have far more free time. Dad and I have already ordered the parts. Besides, if you'd have told me sooner—"

"You sure you're even allowed to be here right now?" I ask, detouring the conversation. "Millie must be missing you."

"I told you, she's doing a make-up test for government."

"Mr. Bannerman never comes in earlier than necessary. Either she has mad persuasive skills, or you're lying."

"He's lying," Warren says blandly. "She's scared of you, Gus. Isn't ready to hang with the *group* yet."

A sound bubbles up in my throat and releases loudly into the air. Like a snort, but deeper. From my soul. Scared of me? Wow. I hadn't seen that coming, but now it's in front of me, it's hilarious. And also, somehow I'm proud? Maybe?

"Millie's not *scared*," Benny argues. "She just thought I should spend some time with you guys—like it used to be—so it seems less like she's trying to cut me off from my family and friends. Which she's *not*, and I think it's ridiculous she's worried about it. But she really wants you to like her. She respects you, Gus."

"I'm flattered," I say, mostly meaning it. "She seems entirely wonderful, and I appreciate her...concern. We've definitely missed you." I include Warren to seem less desperate. Less needy. But I can't help but add, "I've missed you." Just once, I'd love to play it cool.

Benny's eyes hold mine, and I read his guilt. *Dammit.* I hate he's anything other than happy right now. I send him a silent message. *It's okay. You haven't done anything wrong. This is normal. We're fine.* But he stabs the toe of his shoe against the ground several times, a gesture typically signaling internal conflict.

"I should have known something was wrong. It shouldn't have had to be spelled out for me."

"Let it go, Benjamin," I sigh. "Besides, it's not a huge deal. Warren has been more than generous with his chauffer skills."

"Warren's car is a death trap. Neither of you should be riding anywhere in it."

"Hey," Warren says, "my car might not be shiny or smooth. Or reliable. Or even drivable some of the time... I forget where I'm going with this."

"It's gotten us where we need to go," I say, half-smiling up at him. "And I really appreciate it."

"Don't mention it." He grins, his eyes lingering on mine.

Benny coughs loudly, throwing a stern glare in Warren's direction.

First bell rings, and we begin walking toward the building. "Alright," Warren exhales, "let's get this BS over with."

᎗

NEW KID IS in government with me. He takes the seat in front of mine. His blonde hair bugs me. It's supposed to give off the appearance of carefree disarray, but each strand is strategically placed. Whatever product he'd used proved effective without being heavy, though. There are worse traits in a person than grooming. He even smells good, which I also find annoying. All of him *bugs* me. And I have no logical reason.

Maybe it's the expensive car out in the parking lot. I hate rich kids who flaunt Mommy and Daddy's money. I mean, I don't know him. Maybe his family is rich but *not* obnoxious. I don't know. I don't care. Well, clearly I do because it's irritating me so much I have a hard time focusing on anything other than the back of his head.

I imagine New Kid finds Mr. Bannerman's monotone voice about as engaging as the rest of us do. His head bobs midway through class. I'm not one-hundred percent sure he's dozing off until Mr. Bannerman directs a question at him in a stern and sour tenor. This happens to a student at least once a week. Mr. Bannerman is smart, and sometimes our classroom discussions are engaging and—rarely—even fascinating. Yet, his voice can lull anyone to sleep, if they let their guard down.

Poor New Kid fell victim on his first day. I gently nudge him with my pen and whisper, "*Judicial.*" He repeats the answer, giving a convincing performance for having woken abruptly from slumber, and the class moves on.

At the bell, the blonde boy turns around. "Thanks," he whispers through a grimace. "Not the best first impression I've ever left on a teacher."

"Yeah," I nod, "falling asleep on the first day more than likely put you on his radar for a while." He hangs his head, chuckling. I like his laugh more than I expected to. "Don't worry too much, though. We take turns dozing off every few days." I make my way toward the door; he follows close behind.

"If I closed my eyes, I could have sworn he was the teacher from that really old movie with the low, dull voice. You know what I mean?"

"Um," I stop in my tracks. "His name is Ben Stein, and I'm pretty sure that's just his voice. More importantly, *Ferris Bueller's Day Off* is not an 'old movie.' It's a cult *classic.*"

"Struck a sore spot, did I?" he asks. I shrug and keep moving.

"Actually, no. I'm mildly impressed you even knew what it was."

I don't look back as he laughs proudly. "Mildly impressed, huh?

I'll take it." He's walking in stride with me now. "I'm Seth, by the way. Seth Davidson."

I offer a glance, a flinching smile. "August."

"Do you have a last name?"

"It's entirely possible." I stop at my locker, shift textbooks and notebooks around. "Well, I'm sure you'd like to get to lunch, so…"

"Is it an open campus? You want to go somewhere with me?"

"You mean, do I want to go somewhere with you in your shiny Audi? An A5, right?" He nods, baffled. "Trying to impress me again, Seth?"

"Would it work?" He smirks, confident.

"Not even a little." When he realizes I'm not being coy, he struggles to maintain his cocky grin.

"Okay," he says. "What kind of car would do it for you?"

"Not car," I correct, failing to tame a smile. "Truck. Maybe a mid-50s F-100. Or a mid-60s 250 Highboy. Maybe even a Power Wagon. You know, something classy." I'm daydreaming.

"Okay," he snarls, "Miss High and Mighty. What do *you* drive?"

I twist my lips, inhaling a defensive breath. "Well, technically, nothing at the moment." He erupts into a haughty laugh, and my smile spreads. "Hey, someone put a curse on my Sierra, alright? It's beautiful—late-nineties, solid; I put a lot of work into it with my dad and brother. It *should* be flawless. I swear, it's sabotage." He's still chuckling at me, and I find myself pausing to admire his smile. His good humor. His cherry lips. His blue-gray eyes. His tall, solid frame. How did he fit in an Audi? I clear my throat, closing my locker. "I *will* be driving it again," I say. "Soon. You'll see. It's beautiful. At least to me."

Benny's shuffling books around in his locker behind me. I should introduce them; despite first impressions, this Seth guy might not be so bad. I'm contemplating inviting Seth to lunch with us when I catch him appraising me with a look of reluctant acceptance, like I'm not exactly his type, but close enough. I saw this look often. I'm average, not striking. I'm strong, not tiny.

"Well, maybe I'll take you out in it some time," he says. "Try to convert you." The overconfidence creeps back into his voice. He'd let his guard down for a bit, but it came wafting back in full force. "I've never had any complaints before." He winks—actually *winks*—at me. *Gross*. Now he's gloating about taking other girls out in his car? "It's got a killer sound system in it." And now I remember the trap he had blaring as he drove up this morning, which is one of my most hated genres of music.

"Look, Seth, I'm not sure what this is. If you think you're doing me a favor or something? I don't know. But you're standing in front of the wrong locker, wasting your words on the wrong girl. I'm not interested." His mouth gapes, his head tilts. "Bye." I turn and walk away, not once glancing back.

Benny catches up to me in seconds. He puts his hand on the top of my head, tousling my hair gently. "Gus, was it necessary to be rude to the new guy on his first day?"

"It was justified," I snap. Benny stops walking, frowns. "He gave me the *look*, Benjamin." I shudder as I say it. "It set me off."

"Wait? What look?" I stare back, eyes wide, my hands up. "Oh, the 'she'll do' look?"

"Yes!"

"Well, now I'm pissed. Maybe I should tell him off, too."

"Maybe you should," I intone.

"I mean, we all know you're the ugly twin, but I'm the only one allowed to mention it."

I smack the back of his head and walk away, rolling my eyes. "Jerk."

Chapter 8

"What's got you in a sour mood?"

I don't even startle as Benny enters the studio. I turn off the music and pack up my media player.

"Who says I'm in a sour mood?" I ask, though I'm clearly fuming. My private lesson was a nightmare; I'm not sure it's worth the money to choreograph for this girl. She doesn't like the music I picked for her. How does a person *not* like Brandi Carlile? There's got to be a special place in Hell for that, right?

I pull on faded, cut-off sweats over my tight lycra dance pants. "Thanks for picking me up," I offer, trying to sound as grateful as I feel.

"No problem," he says lightly. Then, cocking his head, he asks, "What in the name of Rammstein is going on next door?" Heavy electronica pumps through the walls. A loud voice calls out encouraging yet terrifying cues. "Is that a new teacher? Odd way to lead a dance class."

I scoff, slipping on my shoes. "Oh, it's not a dance class. Kali rents out the room for some sort of strength training class once a week."

"When did that happen?"

"Back in September. She's always had some sort of Pilates or yoga class here on the weekends. But this..." I sigh, throwing my hands up.

"It's different," he says. "Doesn't really vibe with this place." I let out a humorless laugh. "So, why so angry?"

"Nothing. Everything. Leslie put me in a mood. People are stupid."

"Particularly?"

I stop putting my gear away and wrap my hands around an invisible neck. "She's a nightmare student," I yell, strangling the air. "I should never have taken the job. When she hired me, she gave me control over the music, but she's refused to dance to everything I've chosen. Now she says she wants to use K-Pop because she apparently '*just* discovered' it and is in love."

"There are worse offenses…"

"Look, love the music you love. Fine. But don't tell me I can choose whatever and then throw a fit when I give you *amazing* options. There isn't enough money in the world to keep this going; she refutes everything I say."

After forcing myself to take a calming breath, I notice Benny's slumped shoulders, his pursed lips. "What happened?" I ask, and he sighs. "What did Dale do now?"

"Oh, nothing too serious. Sam texted me today." Our cousin on Liliana's side. Our only cousin, period.

"Oh? How is he? How's Uncle Ryan?"

"Disappointed. They invited us all for Thanksgiving, as always. Apparently, we turned them down this year. News to me."

Irritation instantly shifts to rage. "And me!" I shriek. "Why would he refuse? It's not like she's *ever* there. They see as much of her as we do."

"I know."

"I've been looking forward to going. I miss them so much."

"I know."

I rub my temples. Benny clenches, then unclenches his fists. I hate this day.

"So," Benny sighs, "we have a dilemma."

"Right. Be miserable all together or go by ourselves and have a good time. Not much of a dilemma, really."

"We'd feel guilty."

I scrunch my nose. "Would we, though?"

"August," he says, a hint of a smile on his face.

"Why did he say no? Why now? What is going on with him?"

Since we were tiny, we've spent almost every Thanksgiving with the Fosters—Uncle Ryan, Aunt Hannah, and Sam. It's the single social gathering Dale doesn't outright refuse to attend. Until now, apparently. Ryan, Hannah, and Sam are the only real familial relations we've kept in contact with. Dale's side of the family is sparse and hardly communicates. If for no other reason than he didn't want to see us lose a friendship with the only cousin we knew, Dale continued to let Benny and me have an open relationship with the Fosters (even though they're *her* family, as he often reminded us).

"Benny, something is wrong. More wrong than usual." He stares at me sadly, unable to argue. "He's drifting."

"Maybe we should rethink colleges. Eastern Oregon's a great school." He shrugs, tilts his head. "Who says we need to venture off?"

"Benny, Newport is *hardly* a great trek across the globe. And we don't even know if George Fox will take us, or if we'll win enough scholarships to afford it. As for choices two and three, neither Salem or Pullman are outrageously far away."

"You're right. I know. I'm just…"

"Me too. Of course, I'm worried. But are we supposed to live our lives solely for him now? Is that what we've come to? We can't even move a few hours away? Be normal college freshmen?" I close my eyes, taking another calming breath. "Benny, you're a good son. I know you love him despite all the history. I do, too. He's *Dad*. I'll always love him. But that house is suffocating me. I don't know how much longer I can bear it."

Benny chews on his bottom lip. Wrings his hands. "I'm not saying we have to live with him. I *know* how he can be with you; it makes me sick to my stomach. I'm only wondering if maybe we should be close enough to visit on weekends. Or at least a couple times a month. Give him a reason to tune in once in a while. He's our dad, August."

I touch his arm, gently shaking my head. "You don't have to save him. Or any of us. You don't have to save the *world*, Benjamin." His eyes glisten. "Com'ere." He accepts my hug without hesitation, letting a few tears fall—but only a few—as he tries to reconcile what he wants with what he thinks Dale needs.

"We don't have to decide about college right now," I say after a long silence. He gently breaks the hug and wipes his eyes. I tuck the last of my gear into my bag and hoist it over my shoulder. "We'll keep our options open," I finish. He nods, twisting his lips and wiping his face once more.

"Right."

The class next door ends and the music stops vibrating through the walls. The hallway fills with echoey voices.

"The only thing we really need to decide," I say, "is what to do about Thursday."

"I know. You're right." He pauses. "I don't want to miss it. I really don't."

"Then let's go. And for once, let's stay the night. Spend a couple days. Enjoy ourselves. On Saturday or Sunday, we can do a fancy sit-down dinner at home with Dale if it matters so much to him. I'll make it myself."

"It's not the worst idea. It *might* work. But—"

"Benny, he's going to find something else to hold a grudge about if it's not this. You know he will. If he's not mad about us spending Thanksgiving in Hermiston, then he'll be mad you worked on my truck without him, or I spend too much time dancing. Or because we didn't park in the exact right spot. Something will always be wrong in his world, and it will always be someone else's fault." He frowns, knowing I'm right. "Look at it this way. It's a trial run. How will he do if we're both gone for two or three days?"

He huffs, releasing the tension in his shoulders, and I know he's with me on this. Cue the hallelujah chorus.

"I made a road trip playlist," Benny informs me with boyish glee.

"But is it better than *my* road trip playlist?" I shoot back, glaring.

"Psh! Heck yes."

"Fine," I relent, putting my phone away. "You're in charge of tunes." Benny's shoulders dance as he connects his phone to the stereo. I point a finger. "Do *not* make me regret it."

"Oh, you'll likely regret it. I, on the other hand, regret *nothing*."

I turn the key over, Benny presses play, and "Call Me, Maybe" blares over the speakers.

"Really?" I ask, pounding my head against the steering wheel.

"Really, really," he answers, eyes alight.

"Okay, then." I shift my truck into gear, head shaking. "Let's go."

Unable to persuade Dale to accompany us to Hermiston for Thanksgiving, we're making the trip solo, and it's the most excited I've ever been to make this drive. Carlos spent the last week helping Benny get my Sierra winter road ready. Snow tires, a working heater, and an oil change give us the confidence to embrace our minivacation from Dale.

Leaving town feels like escaping the cover of an ominous cloud. As we approach the interstate, it's as though I'm breathing again after unknowingly holding my breath for months.

I've never had a typical relationship with my father, but this year has been different. Strained. The more distance I gain from him, the more I realize how much this strain has weighed on me, and the more I want to keep driving. Maybe Newport isn't far enough away. Maybe Hawaii, or Alaska. Put an ocean between us and the old man. Is it too late to apply to more colleges? I should check the deadlines.

"Gus? You alive?"

Benny's voice pulls me back to the present, where CCR's "Bad Moon Rising" is playing.

"I'm here," I sigh. "Looks like we're about to hit snow."

"I can drive," he offers.

"No, it's fine. You did good with the playlist," I say, smiling. "Solid song."

"Enjoy it while it lasts," he says mischievously. "Enjoy it while it lasts."

※

My heart quickens as we turn onto the Fosters' dirt road. We've never been here alone. With Dale, we've always felt pressured to mute our enjoyment. Without him? What epic shenanigans might ensue?

Their once white-washed, split-level farmhouse is faded and could use a fresh coat of paint. The barn, assembled from mismatched, reclaimed wood, has a sagging roof. The timeworn log fence on the west side of the property needs mending. And it's the most beautiful place on earth.

Before I've even parked, Sam is in the front yard, his arms waving wildly, a goofy grin on his bronze face. I let Benny say hello first. They exchange the typical "bro hug," a handshake mixed with two firm pats on the back.

"You shot up, young man!" Benny observes.

"Almost as tall as you now, *old* man." Sam beams.

As Benny steps out of the way, I swoop in for my hug. "My favorite cousin!" I squeal, giddy. Last year, Sam reached my ears. This year, he's got a solid inch over me. "Dang, sixteen was nice to you. All I got was acne."

"Gross," he says through laughter. Then, squeezing me, he adds, "You're my favorite too. Just don't tell *that* guy."

"Ha-ha." Benny retorts blandly. "Sam, help me with the bags?"

"Sure. Go on inside, Gus. Mom's practically peeing herself to see you."

Smacking his shoulder and running for the door, I call out, "I'm telling her you said that."

I kick my boots against the front step to rid them of wet and heavy snow—the perfect consistency for snowman or igloo building. It's a juvenile idea, but I'll ask the boys to "play" in the snow with me later. I could use a good snowball fight.

Warm, thick aromas breeze over me as I open the front door. Buttermilk rolls, honey ham, and— "I am *not* smelling your delicious pecan pie right now." Aunt Hannah and I are the only ones who even like pecan pie, so she hasn't made it in years, opting for crowd-pleasers instead like apple, pumpkin, or chocolate cream.

Her gleeful squeal grows louder as her feet pad toward the entry. "August, my sweet girl!" Making no attempt to stop herself from plowing into me, she enfolds me in a massive hug, trapping my arms against my sides. "You made it! I'm so glad you made it."

I cough a laugh. "Me too. The place looks great."

She squeezes tighter, swaying me side to side. There is only one person alive who gives better hugs than Benny, and it's Aunt Hannah. It doesn't hurt she always smells like lilacs. I could follow her around all day, sniffing at her shoulder like some needy family pet, and never tire of her scent.

"Thank you for coming," she whispers, then kisses my cheek. "Thank you, thank you."

When we finally peel away from each other, I catch her sniffling and wiping at her glossy hazel eyes. She's lovely in a floral print blouse and long, gray maxi skirt. Her brunette hair falls all around in loose waves. She's easily the most naturally beautiful woman I know. Not stunning. Simply beautiful.

"Thank you for having us," I say. "We came prepared to stay. That's okay, right?"

"Yes! I hope you're alright with the pullout in the den. I figured the stinky teenage boys belong in the stinky teenage boy's bedroom." Perfectly timed, Sam and Benny enter the house, stomping their boots on the rug.

"Gee, Mom. Love you, too." Sam feigns offense.

"Thanks so much for having us, Aunt Hannah," Benny says. "Brace yourself because this stinky teenager is gonna hug you."

She closes her eyes, embracing Benny tightly. "I've missed you both so much." She sniffles again. "You stay here as long as you want, any time you want."

"Where's Uncle Ryan?" I ask.

Hannah wipes her face again, then smooths her blouse. "He's out grabbing more firewood. He'll be in soon, then he can take you out to meet the mare."

"*What?*" Benny and I gasp in unison.

"Sam didn't tell you?" she asks, wide-eyed.

I smack Sam's shoulder. "He did *not*. Is she gorgeous? I bet she's gorgeous." Hannah's giggle answers my question. "Can I move in? I've always wanted a horse."

"Don't tease me," she warns. "Now, you kids set your bags down and make yourselves at home. There's enough food to feed an army."

"Or a few teenagers," Benny corrects, playful.

"Or that," she laughs. "Or that."

The mare's name is Sadie. I hold an apple in the palm of my unwavering hand. After a couple sniffs, Sadie's wet, slobbery mouth brushes against my skin as she accepts my bribe. My free hand strokes the chestnut hair between her eyes.

"Admit it," I whisper to her. "I'm your favorite."

"Aren't you everyone's favorite?"

Uncle Ryan sidles up next to me and strokes Sadie with his tan, calloused hands.

"I'm glad you two came, kiddo," he tells me, gently nudging my shoulder. "I know it couldn't have been easy, defying your dad."

"I don't know why he refused to come this year," I say, holding eye contact with Sadie. "I don't understand anything he does or doesn't do, really. But we love you guys. We couldn't *not* come."

"It means a lot to us. Hannah cried when your dad refused the invitation. Sam would never admit it, but he was pretty red-eyed himself there for a bit."

"And clearly, you were a mess," I tease, "unable to function on a basic human level."

"Damn right. Tore my heart out thinking I wouldn't see my favorite twins."

I rest my arms against the stall door, let my chin settle on top of them.

"She needs a friend. Sadie," I say. "She's lonely." She nickers, jerking her head. "See?"

Ryan laughs. "We're working on it. She was a rescue. Opportunity just knocked last month—bit of a now-or-never situation. We chose now. We'll find her a companion soon. In the meantime, the dog loves her, and she seems to tolerate him alright. It's a start."

"Poor Remy," I sigh, referring to their Newfoundland, curled up at my feet. He twitches at the sound of his name, then settles. *I know how you feel, buddy*, I think. How many years after Liliana left had I spent chasing after Dale's approval? Too many. And he'd only ever tolerated me. He seems to do so less and less with every passing minute. Without even realizing words are surfacing, I release them.

"I'm sorry about my dad. That he didn't come this year, and he's simply shown up in previous years without even bothering to be pleasant. You deserve better."

"August, don't go apologizing to me—or anyone else—for anything your daddy does. You are not responsible for him—his anger, his shortcomings, or any of it. You just be you. Be a kid."

"I'm eighteen," I start.

"Which only sounds old to you, honey. Be a kid."

Uncle Ryan means well, but he seems to be forgetting something. Girls whose mothers leave them and fathers resent them don't have the luxury of remaining *kids*.

"Now come inside," he urges. "Hannah plans to take about three hundred pictures before she'll let us cut into the pie."

"Pecan," I whisper, already tasting it on my tongue.

We stay two nights, because one isn't enough. Two isn't enough either, but Benny insists we leave Saturday afternoon in case Dale wants to do some sort of family dinner on Sunday.

Leaving Hermiston is the hardest thing I've done to this point in my life, and I don't even think I'm exaggerating. Everything about Ryan and Hannah's drafty farmhouse is comforting and wonderful. The food is warm and delicious. The constant background ambiance of fireplaces crackling in the living room and den is calming. The snow-caked property encased in rolling hills and nearby mountains is another world. One I've been dreaming was my own since we arrived.

Sam's jokes make me full-belly laugh. Aunt Hannah's hugs are healing. The way Uncle Ryan talks to me as though I'm anything but a disappointment—unlike how my father views me—makes me feel young. Innocent. Untainted by my broken parents.

This house, this family, is *everything*.

The drive back to La Grande is an unwelcomed alarm, pulling me from my blissful dream. For a moment, it had been tangible. I had held joy in my hands, absorbed it into my heart. Now it leaks over the faded seat covers, down through the floorboards, leaving a trail of depression along the highway.

"Promise me," Benny starts, then takes a slow breath.

"What?"

"Promise me, no matter where we go next year, let's do this again."

"Oh, absolutely."

"I mean it, Gus. Maybe we can't make it for Thanksgiving, specifically. But let's do this every year. No matter how crazy things get, we have our little reunion for a couple days. You and me and them."

Just us. Benny doesn't include Dale in this promise. The significance of this isn't lost on me.

"Every year," I agree, smiling more sincerely. "I promise."

Chapter 9

December

"How was your Thanksgiving?"

I glance up from my desk, peering around the room. *Is someone speaking to me?*

"August?" It takes a moment to recognize the voice. I turn around. Seth sits behind me. "Hey," he offers through a smile. "How was your Thanksgiving?"

"Fine," I answer cautiously.

"What did you do?" he prods.

"Visited some family in Hermiston. How was yours?"

"Not terrible. Big crowd. Minimal family drama." I wonder if he truly *knows* the meaning of family drama.

"Nice."

"I saw you last week. At that Bailey's place."

"Bailey's School of Dance?" I ask, tilting my head. He nods. "Well, I work there. And I dance there. I basically live there. What were *you* doing there? Looking into a class? Didn't peg you for a dancer." Though that would kind of be amazing. A male dancer at the school? A strange hope builds inside me.

He laughs, sounding mildly insulted. "I'm most definitely *not* a dancer."

Aaand, there it goes. "Don't judge what you don't understand. Male dancers are amazing athletes. Haven't you ever seen one in action? There's at least ten reality shows you could watch."

He rolls his eyes, smirking. "Whatever. It was a strength class."

"Oh." Makes far more sense, but I can't help but be disappointed. He's tall. Strong but not bulky. He would probably make a great partner.

"Yeah, coach requires everyone to take some sort of weight or strength training outside of practice. The class works with my schedule."

"Hm," is my only answer, my mind still busy. Seth probably lacks grace and flexibility, but we could work on it. There's a serious shortage of male dancers at the studio, and I *love* partner work. *Oh gosh, I'm eyeing him up and down like an idiot.* Why am I fantasizing about dancing with this guy?

The fantasy abruptly ends as he suggests, "Maybe you should come tomorrow, instead of to your dance lesson. Show me what an *athlete* you are."

Mr. Bannerman stands at the front of the classroom, ready to begin. I have no time for the full, passionate, rather vulgar rebuttal which comes to mind. I settle for, "Eat glass," and watch his cocky smirk give way to shame.

🎧

On the first Saturday in December, despite incoherent grumbling, Dale gets in the truck with Benny and me to venture to the Christmas tree lot. He doesn't even make any snide remarks about my driving or tell me how to properly navigate the neighborhood I've lived in for eighteen years—a rarity.

He rubs at his temples when Benny and I find a radio station playing Christmas music and begin singing along, though I hear him offer a coarse, muffled laugh now and again.

He's quiet as Benny and I choose the tree, as he pays for it, as we load it in the truck, as we drive home. Not a word.

We find the perfect spot in the living room. The tree stands tall and proud in the corner, next to the inoperable fireplace.

"Well, Dad, it's an excellent tree," Benny offers. "Really great. Thank you."

"Hm," Dale mumbles.

"I already found the decorations, Dad," I offer. "Pulled the boxes out. You can spare yourself the frustration this year."

Again, he mumbles.

Benny and I lock eyes, silently mulling over how much more effort we should put into trying to revive old traditions. We always decorate the tree together. No matter how awkward or difficult things are. But do we force him now, when he so clearly wants to be anywhere other than here, with us? Do we give him an out?

Benny tries again. "Next year, you won't have to put up the tree so early. You won't have us nagging you until we're home for Winter Break."

Dale ponders, looking either angry or sad. Maybe both. Then, he sighs, "I knew I couldn't keep you kids from growing up and moving on. I just wish it hadn't happened so fast."

Benny and I exchange wide eyes. *It speaks!* In full sentences!

"I s'pose it was inevitable," he finishes.

Benny puts a hand on Dale's shoulder. "You're still stuck with us a while. Don't mourn the loss yet."

Again, Dale stands in silent contemplation.

Benny and I remain still, calm. We stand amid a mine field; one wrong move could be deadly.

I've already made my first batch of the traditional triple chocolate Christmas cookies. Right now seems like the perfect opportunity to offer him one—a gesture of goodwill. Before I can get the words out, Dale speaks again.

"Washington State, was it?"

"George Fox is our first choice," Benny corrects. "In Newport."

Dale whistles. "Fancy. And expensive."

"We're applying for every scholarship in the state, Dad," Benny says.

"We might be overreaching," I admit, shrugging. "But we've got backups. We also applied to Washington State and Willamette."

"And University of Washington in Tacoma and U of O," Benny adds.

"Casting a wide net," Dale says, thoughtful. "That's smart, I s'pose."

I offer a weak, close-lipped grin.

"Well, it won't be the same. Without you two, I mean."

"We'll visit, Dad," Benny assures him. "We can even video chat if you miss our faces." Benny's one-sided smile gets the better of Dale. He lets out a small chuckle.

"Do you want a cookie, Dad?" I try. "I made about a hundred of 'em."

"There's something I haven't told you kids." Dale's gruff voice is low, hesitant. "Your mom called back in October. Right around your birthday."

This news affects me more than I want it to. My heart beats in my throat, and Benny shoots panicked eyes at me. We both watch Dale, awaiting further information.

"She's living in Eugene now," he finishes.

"Wait, she's back in Oregon?" I mean for it to be an internal thought, but it slips. Last we'd heard, she was in Atlantic City. That was years ago.

"When?" Benny asks. "When did she move back?"

"When she called..." Dale clears his throat. "When she called, she'd been living there about a year, she said."

She's been in the same state for over a year and hasn't bothered to communicate with us? Not that I really *wanted* to talk with her, let alone *see* her. But wouldn't any other mother have at least *tried* to reach out to us?

"I think we should decorate tomorrow," I say, knowing this all won't be any less awful come morning.

"Do you think he tried convincing her to visit?"

Benny ponders a moment. "It would explain a lot of his behavior. If he asked and she turned him down."

We lie on the basement floor atop beanbags and pillows, sharing a plate of cookies as we attempt to digest the news.

"I knew something was going on," I say. "I've had that stupid dream about that stupid night at least four times since school started. And he's been harder—" *on me than usual.* I don't finish. Benny doesn't need another weight on his shoulder.

He hears the words I don't say. "I'm so sorry, Gus," he whispers.

"Why call him if she had no intention of visiting or trying to? Why call at all? Unless the *goal* was to make him miserable."

"I wouldn't put it past her. She torments him."

"She's a plague on this family."

"I'd like to say you're being melodramatic, but..."

"Well, U of O is out," I say spitefully.

"Definitely. Not moving to Eugene if she's there," he agrees, "even if she doesn't stay long."

"Not worth risking it."

We each grab a cookie and eat in silent contemplation.

"I don't know if I've ever said this." Benny looks at me, serious, then averts his eyes to the ceiling. "I'm really sorry if it's been harder for you than for me—wait. That came out wrong!" he hurries. "I'm an idiot." His hand grips my shoulder a moment. "I didn't mean that in an 'I'm better than you' way. I only meant..."

"You mean it's easier for people to approach the boy who still has a dad than the girl whose mother left. A boy who has his father must be alright, but a girl without her mother must be lost. It's fine. The pity stares suck, but you get over it."

"This goes far beyond pity stares, Gus. You took on so much after she left."

"It's fine, Benny. I'd do it all over again if I had to."

"August—" he starts.

"Hey, nerds!" Warren's voice trickles down the stairs. "Where've you been?"

Before Warren comes into view, I touch Benny's arm. "Don't worry about me."

He tries smiling, but it looks more like a frown.

"I've been trying to reach you both," Warren says, standing over us. "There's a bonfire at Josh Harvey's tonight."

"Janey's brother?" Benny asks with an audible smirk.

"Why yes," I say slowly. "Yes, it is."

"What? What's the joke?" Warren asks, sitting between Benny and me, stealing a cookie from the plate. "Delicious, August. As always."

"Thank you."

"So, what's this about Janey?"

"Oh, Warren..." I sigh, sitting up. "How do you miss these things?"

"What?"

Benny stretches, yawns. "She likes you. A lot, apparently."

Warren squints. "Really?"

"She's had a crush on you since last year," I say. "Keeps asking me to set you two up."

"I had no idea." He ponders this news a moment, then glares at me. "So why *haven't* you set us up yet?"

"You kidding me? I barely have my own social life. You can't expect me to be in charge of anyone else's."

"Huh." Warren snags another cookie, thinking about it. "Funny. I had a similar conversation with someone this week. But about you."

I snort. "Yeah, right."

Benny sits up, intrigued. "Who?" he asks.

Warren sneers, "Seth Davidson."

Benny laughs as I draw my lips into a twisted frown.

"No way." I wave my hand dismissively. "Never."

"I swear," Warren assures me. "He came up to me after calculus the other day and started talking to me."

"And said *what*, exactly?"

"First, he asked if *we* were dating. Which, of course, was a fun conversation."

I throw my head back, groaning. "I'm so sorry, Ren."

He waves me off. "Please. It's fine. Anyway, he wasn't sure if he'd pissed you off, which seems likely, since he's a primitive moron. He asked if I'd help smooth things over. I think he wants to ask you to the Winter Ball."

"Gross," I say instinctively, not sure I mean it. "His latest offense, of many, is making some snide remark about dancing and athleticism. Every time I think he's a decent person, he says something judgmental or cocky or sexist, and I resolve to never speak to him again."

"Well, I made zero promises. Basically, I said you're capable of making your own decisions, and you don't need me to guide you."

"Thank you." I scrunch up my nose, half smiling. "Really. You're the best."

"I know," he says, shrugging. "I don't like the guy. He's a jerk who thinks way too highly of himself. And I saw him walking around with a bulky camera the other day? Who does that?"

"I'm sure it was part of a pick-up line or something," I say, rolling my eyes.

"But...a camera, Gus. A legit camera. Dude's weird. What do you think, Ben?"

"I think he just needs good friends," Benny says, because he represents the best in all of us.

"Are you volunteering?" I ask.

"Maybe we should find him a better fit."

Warren and I let out sharp laughs.

"Look," Benny continues over us, "I'm not saying no. I think he could be a decent person underneath the facade, but I don't need any more friends who are trying to date my sister."

Warren punches Benny's arm. "I don't *try* anything," he protests. "Now, call your girlfriend, Ben, and let's bail." Then, to me,

"Are there more cookies? Also, completely unrelated, will you marry me?"

"Ohmaword, Ren," I mumble, tossing another cookie at him. Then, more seriously, "Go ahead. Eat it. It's not poisoned at all."

Deadpan, he shoves the cookie in his mouth all at once.

Benny pulls out his phone and texts Millie.

A bonfire in December means couples huddled under blankets. No thanks.

"You guys go. Have fun. Say hi to Millie and Janey for me," I tease with raised, flirtatious eyebrows.

"You *have* to come," Warren whines.

"I'm not in a bonfire mood. But you guys should go have a great time."

Benny's eyes hold mine. "You shouldn't stay home alone," he whispers. "Not tonight."

"I don't plan to," I assure him.

Chapter 10

The comforting scent of leather and sweat greets me as I unlock the studio door and slip inside. It's all mine, and I intend to have a good therapy session tonight.

Hard work. Practice. Loud music. They always heal my wounds. By the time I go through my solo once, I'll barely remember how it felt learning my mother had been back in the state for over a year. After a second run-through, I'll hardly remember the conversation at all. After I dance freestyle for a song or two, I'll be out of breath, blissfully unaware that for any part of this day, I felt irrevocably crushed.

I start with last year's solo to "The Sky is a Neighborhood" for my warm-up because Foo Fighters make everything better. I improvise a few places where I've forgotten choreography, but I don't withhold my intensity. I'm winded by the time it's over—fully in the zone. As I scroll through my music, stretching out my warmed-up muscles, something comes over me. I go right past my solo music, selecting a song Kali introduced me to some time ago. She clings to what she calls her *emo days*, and she's always trying to convert me.

It's a little darker than I usually go, but right now, in this moment, I turn it full volume, breathing in time with the sad guitar intro as I walk to the center of the room.

I experiment with the flow between broken, contemporary movements and slow, gliding turns and extensions. Near the end, the vocals give me the perfect opportunity for continuous fouettés as heartbreaking screams of "On my *own*" echo off the studio walls.

The song over, I crumble to the floor, struggling to catch my breath. My limbs are loose, tingly, almost numb. Why is my chest so heavy? My plan to overcome anger has backfired, allowing grief to build in its place. Abandoned by a mother, ignored by a father, desperately shadowing my brother who deserves independence. I'm an obstacle for everyone in my life.

A chain of memories and regret weaves itself inside of me, tangles around my heart, and tightens. I clutch at my chest, gasping, desperate for the damp air of the empty room to bring me relief.

The sound of the front door takes a few moments to register. *Crap*, I forgot to lock it.

"We're...closed..." I screech. "Need...to leave."

"August?"

Footsteps pad closer until he appears at the door. *Seth?*

"You can't be here," I say, panting.

"Are you okay?" he asks.

"Fine," I lie. "*Why* are you here?"

"I think I left my phone here after my class. Drove by in hopes someone might be around. Then I saw your truck. Are you sure you're okay?"

"Lost and found is in the office," I say, ignoring the question. A few slow breaths in through my nose, out through my mouth, and I'm regaining control. "I'll get my keys."

"It's just that...you don't look okay."

I meet his eyes for the first time. Even from the doorway, they shine—gray-blue, like the ocean. His lips curve down in concern...or judgment. I can't quite tell. A slouchy gray beanie covers his blonde hair.

"It's nothing," I say, eyes on the floor. "Overdid a jump, landed wrong. I'll be fine." I rub my ankle to sell the lie.

"Could have fooled me," he mumbles. "Your dancing was flawless. Looked more like a mild heart attack than a rolled ankle."

"What?" My head snaps up, horror no doubt etched in my features.

"You see that giant wall of windows behind you?" he asks, smirking. "You're not invisible, you know."

"So you stood outside in the cold, watching me through the window?"

"And you didn't notice, I might add. Very focused."

"That's terrifying," I whisper. "And mildly creepy."

"Aw," he says, his hand to his chest. "What every guy hopes to hear." I stare, my lips in a hard line. "August, I'm sorry. Really. If I scared you or creeped you out, it wasn't intentional. It was this lightbulb moment of 'I think my phone might be there,' and I didn't think. I just came by."

"Then you walked from the parking lot to the other side of the building and *watched* me through the window," I point out.

"How could I *not* watch you? That was literally the most amazing thing I've ever seen. It gave me...*feelings*."

"Feelings?" I sputter, raising an eyebrow.

"Not like...inappropriate feelings. I didn't mean..." His cheeks redden as he fumbles for words. "Like, I thought I might cry. Or something. It was...*beautiful*. You're..." He throws up his hands, then pulls his hat down over his face.

"Let me grab the keys for the office," I say, simultaneously flattered and mortified.

Seth pulls the cap off his face and crumples it in his hands. His hair sticks up in disarray, his forehead sweaty and pink.

"Thanks," he says, backing away from the door frame.

Seth's phone is easy to spot in the box Kali keeps in her office.

"I'm surprised no one let you know," I say. "We usually call or text a frequented contact."

"Well, you wouldn't have been able to. It's locked. Thumbprint recognition."

I let out a low whistle, wide-eyed. "Well, look at you," I say, not kindly.

"I know, I know. First-world problems. I can't believe it took me so long to realize I'd left it here."

I stifle a laugh. "Me either. A teenager not glued to their phone? Sounds sketchy."

He shrugs. "I used to be. Glued to my phone, I mean. Not sketchy." We exchange a quick grin. "Not as much these days."

I brace myself against Kali's desk, crossing my arms. "Oh?"

He steps back, his shoulder resting against the door frame. "The longer I'm away from my old friends in Portland, the less they reach out. Seems I'm rather forgettable. And I haven't really made any *real* friends here yet."

"I thought I saw you hanging around with Mike and Maribel. You know, the *cool* kids."

"They're alright." He stares beyond me, as though I might not be in the room with him.

"Must be hard," I say softly. "I've never moved, left old friends behind. Never had to be the *new kid*. But I *do* know what it's like to feel forgotten. I'm sorry."

"Who'd forget you?" he asks, a playful grin on his cherry lips—flecks of green dance in his ocean eyes.

Without answering, I turn off the lights and close the office door behind me.

As Seth follows me back into the room, something builds in my chest, but it's not unease. I can't pinpoint it, but it puts me on alert. Makes me acutely aware of my appearance. I pull a sweater from my bag and slip it over my skin-tight tank. My feet slide apart until I'm on the floor in a wide V, stretching out my still-warm muscles. Small beads of sweat gather at my hairline and trickle down my forehead.

"Throw me a towel, would you?" I ask, pointing to a shelf in the corner. Seth obliges, and I thank him as I clean my face and neck.

"How long have you danced?" he asks, slowly making his way toward me.

"Shoes," I say, pointing.

"I'm sorry?"

"No street shoes on the dance floor," I inform him.

He slips off his sneakers, then steps onto the Marley flooring.

I fold forward into my v-sit, my arms in front of me, my forehead touching the ground.

"*Ouch*," Seth says, his cringe audible.

"My whole life," I say through a small laugh. "Since diapers, anyway. I don't remember a time I *wasn't* in dance classes." I tuck and roll my body upward, reaching my arms above my head in fifth position, then over to one side. "My mom enrolled me the moment I could walk."

"Was she a dancer?" he asks, joining me on the floor.

"Maybe. Probably. Who knows?" My dad. My dad knows. But he won't tell me because it hurts. And I look like her, which makes it hurt more. I can't say any of this to Seth, of course, but my mind races with all the tension and secrets of my broken family. My body reaches up center, then to the other side.

"What about you?" I ask, deflecting.

"What about me?"

"You play...*basketball*?" I'm not sure I'm right until he nods, a smirk on his face. "Because you love it or because you're good at it?"

He shrugs.

I sit up, shake out my legs, then bring them into a butterfly stretch.

"Is there anything you're passionate about?" I ask, holding his gaze.

"Maybe. Haven't quite figured that out yet."

I stare in silence, unable to discern what's happening in my chest. Am I nervous? Is that what this is? He smells like spearmint gum and woodsmoke, and I strain against the urge to bury my face in his chest and inhale.

"I like photography," he says, almost in a whisper. Like maybe he's a little ashamed of it.

I tilt my head. "Really?"

"Really."

He smiles, and I find myself staring stupidly again.

"You go to the bonfire tonight?" I ask.

"For about a minute. It wasn't really for me. Then I remembered about my phone…"

"Ah, I see."

"Little surprised you weren't there. Seems like you and Ben do everything and go everywhere together. Well, you and Ben *and* Warren."

"Usually, yeah. But I needed some therapy tonight," I say, then regret it.

Maybe he reads my regret, because he doesn't pry further.

"What's it like? Having a twin brother?"

I sigh, shrugging. "Mostly, it's people asking me questions about what it's like to have a twin," I tease. Seth laughs, then tries to mimic my butterfly stretch. His legs bunch awkwardly in front of his chest. "You're a natural," I say. Then, "It's amazing, actually, having a twin. It's weird and wonderful, and I can't imagine my life any other way. Benny's my best friend. There's nothing we wouldn't do for each other, which is why it's so important for me to give him space from time to time. Skip out on a bonfire so he can spend guilt-free time with his—with Millie."

"His girlfriend?" he asks, grinning. "Is that the word you're afraid to say?"

"Not afraid," I protest. "Not even jealous. I'm happy for him, but it's new. It's hard. I'm trying, though."

"It's hard to share someone you're used to having all to yourself. When my dad remarried, I was thrilled for him; he'd been lonely for so long. And my stepmom is great, really. Super sweet. She doesn't try any of the *best friend* stuff. She's cool. But I still hate it a bit sometimes. Even five years later."

I don't ask him where his mom is. I don't ask his stepmom's name. I simply stare at him in his limberlessness while a grin spreads slowly across my face.

After a moment, he abandons the stretch, shaking out his legs and cringing.

"Not bad for your first time," I say. "Stretching is a huge part of being a *well-rounded* athlete. You should work on it. If you play your cards right, I *might* even help you."

"Oh yeah?" he asks, raising an adorable eyebrow. Something foreign beats inside my chest, and I can't help but think this is what longing feels like. "You think you could handle me as a student?" he asks, and I clear my throat. Shake out my shoulders.

"Hey, if I can teach a bunch of toddlers with the attention span of a goldfish, I could probably teach you a thing or two. I taught Benny once," I blurt before realizing my mind has gone there.

"Oh?" He perks up, raising a curious brow.

"Uh, yeah. There was this competition when I was twelve. I entered to do the waltz with this boy named Marco. Great dance partner. I adored him. But his family moved away about a month before the competition. I was heartbroken. I loved having a male partner. And I *knew* we were going to crush our category."

"How horribly sad. Poor baby August."

"Yeah," I laugh. "I know it seems silly now, but it was devastating."

"It's absolutely tragic!" he says, frowning, a hint of playfulness in his tone.

"Benny, being the pure soul he is, couldn't stand my heartbreak. So, he learned the routine."

"Wow. That's love."

"I mean, he was no Patrick Swayze. But bless him, he tried."

"Wait. Which one's Patrick Swayze?" he asks, squinting.

I almost snort. "Never mind. Anyway, we came in fifth."

"Well, hey—"

"Out of five," I finish.

Seth's full-belly laugh fills me with an unnerving warmth. I'm crushing on this guy. *Hard.*

It's snowing when we step outside into the frozen air. I love this part of winter. How the snow quiets the world around and reflects the moon's brightness.

"Careful," Seth says, gently taking my elbow and walking me to my truck.

"Thank you," I whisper. I can't hear my voice over the thumping of my heart at Seth's thoughtful touch. His exposed neck so close to my face. Spearmint and woodsmoke still rising from his skin.

"I know I didn't make a great first impression on you," he starts as I hop into the cab, sticking my key into the ignition. I twist my lips, blink at him. "Okay, I made a bad second and third impression, too."

"Could have been worse," I admit, turning the key over. My engine disturbs the tranquility of the snowy night.

"I think we should keep talking, though," he says. "Keep trying. You might find you like me."

"Maybe," I holler over the engine. "Time will tell."

"I mean, I'm at *least* as cool as Warren, and you seem to like him a *lot*, so…"

"What?" I snap. "What are you implying?"

"Nothing," he rushes. I glower at him, and he fidgets. "It's just I see you guys together. How he looks at you."

"You know nothing about Warren. Or what he means to me. And taking cheap shots at him as though this is some lame teen-movie competition for my heart—or whatever—will get you nowhere with me."

"August, I didn't mean…" he tries to string a sentence together, stunned by my outburst. "I'm sorry if… I thought…"

"I need to get home, Seth," I say, calmer. "Honestly, I *was* enjoying this." I gesture between us. "Maybe someday, you can drop this desperation to be the coolest guy in the room, and we can talk again. I like down-to-earth, no-frills Seth. He's actually pretty great." His shoulders slump momentarily, then he nods. "Goodnight," I say, pulling the cab door closed.

"Goodnight," he says. I don't hear it, but I see his lips moving through the glass.

Chapter 11

Christmas Break can't come fast enough. Ten more days and I'm free; I can almost taste it. While everyone else at school is singularly obsessed with next Saturday's formal dance—who is taking who, who is wearing what—I'm knee-deep in choreography for the studio's Winter Recital next Friday. Between staying caught up on schoolwork and spending every spare moment at the studio, I'm running on fumes and in desperate need of a time-out.

It's impossible to keep my days and commitments straight. Maybe that's why I left the lights on in my truck last night. I've never done it before, and it's completely unlike me to do such a thing. But my battery is dead, and it's the only reasonable explanation.

"I swear I didn't leave them on, Benny."

"It could be a crummy connection," he offers.

"It's this *truck*. It's cursed. One thing after another this year. I'm losing my deep and enduring love for it."

He laughs through a frown. "I'm so sorry, Gus. Let me grab the cables and pull my car around."

"Dale has the cables. In his pickup. At least that's the last place I saw them."

"Don't we have two sets?"

I shrug. "Not that I know of."

"Well, change of plans. I guess I'm driving today."

I hang my head. "I'm sorry, Benny."

"Aw, Gus. It's not your fault. It's not a huge deal, anyway. It's only to school and back. Worse things have happened." He nudges me, and I force a smile.

He tries to lift my spirits with a mini snowball fight while his car warms up. He even lets me choose the radio station as we head down the road. He serenades me in an obnoxious voice to provoke a laugh. It works. I join in. We bob around, singing as we travel cautiously down the snow-packed roads.

The speed of travel doesn't match our rhythm, but we keep at it anyway. We're still singing at top volume as the school comes into view. Then it happens. *It* happens. Everything, all at once, yet somehow in horrid, slow motion.

A cacophony of metal-on-metal steals the air from my lungs. I can't breathe. Why can't I breathe? I'm signaling my brain to draw in air, but nothing is happening. *Inhale, dammit! Why can't I breathe?* My mind races as the car spins out of control. My head hits something. The window? It burns, and my eyelids droop.

Finally, I'm able to gasp a heavy, anxious breath. I scream for Benny, expecting him to reassure me. To say, "Hold on, August." But he doesn't. I try again.

"Benny! Where are you? Talk to me!" Benny's not answering, and my mind is a foggy mess. I'm not entirely sure this isn't a dream. A terrifying, vivid dream. That tracks for me, right? After another gut-wrenching screech, something warm trickles down my face. My entire body goes limp, control draining out of me as though I've sprung a leak. Everything goes black.

I wake up screaming to a hazy world. There are too many voices, and they're all shouting over me.

Calm down, miss.
Need a C-Collar over here!
You'll be out soon.
She needs fluids!

My screams fall silent as adrenaline fades. I wait for anything to make sense. The blurs around me, or the foreign noises fading in and out. Nothing.

"Ben...?" My voice is weak, hoarse. "Benny?" I try to move my arm to feel for him. My fingertips twitch. It's all I can manage.

"Hold still, honey," a stranger demands. "Don't move. Just hang on a little longer."

I don't *want* to hang on; I need to be free of this prison. I need to know where my brother is, what's happened, and why the hell I can't move a muscle. Noises escalate—wailing and gnashing—becoming more insufferable and confusing with every passing moment. My eyelids are heavy. Maybe if I just go back to sleep...

"Miss! Stay with me."

"August! Her name is August!" That voice *is* familiar.

"Ren?" I attempt.

"Miss," I hear again.

"Dammit, her name is August! August!"

It smells awful, like a first aid kit and gun powder. I'm aware of the leather seat under me, and I reach for the other one—the seat should be...right... It's empty. Why is it empty?

"Benny!" Adrenaline returns, and my eyes fly open in search of him. "*Benny!*"

"Easy, easy. You can't turn your head." A man stands outside the car, his hands holding my arm through the broken window. He's pressing a needle to my skin. A neck brace restricts my movement. None of it makes any sense, and I don't have the patience to sort it out.

"Benjamin! Answer me, *now! Please!*" I try again to find him.

"Mi—August, you can't turn your head, do you understand? Try to hold still." The needle breaks through the skin. The nameless paramedic tapes it down, then attaches a tube. "It's only a precaution," he continues. "You hit your head, and there's some strong bruising at the shoulder, and we need to make sure your neck is okay before that C-Collar can come off. Do you understand me, August?"

I try to nod, then remember the brace. Right. Verbal cues only. I finally croak out a "Yes."

He nods. "Good girl."

"My legs are so heavy."

"You're stuck. We'll get you out soon, okay? Any minute now."

"What happened? Where's my brother? I need my brother."

"You were in an accident. A semi rammed into you, sent you into the path of an oncoming car. The boy driving the other car—your brother, too—we got them out first. They've been life-flighted..."

And I don't hear another word. If Benny's already en route to a hospital and they've merely stuck a C-Collar on my neck and offered me fluids, it's serious. He could be *dying*—no. He can't be. I can't think like that. I close my eyes, despite all instructions to the contrary. My world descends into darkness, my mind shielding itself from the unfamiliar, the unsafe.

🎧

WHEN I BECOME aware of sounds again, of voices, I'm in bed. I think. The brace is gone, along with the unwanted pressure. No longer restricted, imprisoned in my own body. Now I just feel limp. Useless.

Unfamiliar voices hum quietly, like white noise, followed by an uproar of laughter—a sitcom?

There's another voice I don't recognize—a real one. Solemn, hushed.

"It went well, Mr. Haiz. As well as we could have hoped for, considering."

What went well? What is happening? Why isn't anyone talking to me? I try to join the conversation. *Hello! I'm here. What's going on?* But when I move my lips, nothing comes out.

"I can't say we're out of the woods. I know that's what you want to hear, and I *wish* I could say it confidently. But he's stable for now, and we have every reason to believe he'll make it through the night. Why don't you get a little sleep now? You've had a long wait, and you must be exhausted. Go up and visit with him in the morning."

"Thank you," someone answers. Dale.

Dad? Dad, I'm awake. Please talk to me. Tell me it's alright.

I can't find my voice. The words remain trapped inside my loose, foreign body.

Perhaps a smaller task—like opening my eyes—is a better place to start. It takes all my energy and focus. Maybe it's a full minute, maybe it's a lifetime. But I blink. Once, then twice. The light is too bright, but I hold on to it because even blinding light is better than this darkness where I'm invisible and no one is talking to me.

"August?" A blurry face whispers my name. I know his voice.

"Warren?" I try. It comes out a single-syllable groan.

Another face rushes into view. "August? August? Baby, it's Dad. Open your eyes, honey. I'm here." Someone takes my hand. I strain to keep my eyes open.

Slowly, the blurs come into focus—Warren and my father. Beyond them, a white room. A small television mounted in the corner airs a commercial for Burger King. Am I hungry? I don't think so. That's not what this sensation is.

The TV, a dim lamp, and a screen displaying my vitals are the only sources of light, yet it still seems too bright. I strain to read the bulky clock on the wall—one o'clock. One o'clock when? And where?

Every breath is a painful, heavy struggle. Cracked ribs, maybe. My left leg is on fire. Broken? But none of these uncertainties hit as hard as not knowing where *he* is. I want to scream his name, to see if he comes running, but everything is foggy, and my chest hurts.

"Wha—" is all I manage, trying to lift my head. I'm too tired. It hurts too much. I sink back into the rough, bleach-washed pillowcase.

"August. Rest. Take it easy." My father's voice is wary. His breath is heavy with cigarettes—he's been stress smoking.

I tuck my chin and cautiously begin sliding my hands around my body. I search for casts, for bandages. I'm scraped up and tender to the touch, especially where the seatbelt dug into my chest and shoulder, but I find no casts, no wraps, no broken bones. Straining, I bring my hands to my face. My lip is all wrong—swollen and torn.

My head is bandaged on the right side, near the hairline. But no extraordinary damage I can discern. So why does my leg feel ready to detach from my body and run away in protest of the pain? Why does my chest no longer house my heart, but knives and broken glass?

"Whe...s'Benny?" My voice is low, throaty.

"Shh, honey. Shh." Dale puts a hand on my forehead.

Warren steps back. "I'll go tell them she's awake," he says.

"Who...?" He leaves anyway. I turn back to Dale. "Where's Benny?" I say, clearer now.

"He's been out of surgery for about an hour now. He's...he's fine." Dale tries to smile, but I sense the lie.

"I know it's bad. I can feel him."

"Goose, there was an accident. Do you remember?"

"I woke up, and they told me Benny was g-gone." With a strange beep, something tightens around my arm. "What the...?"

"Blood pressure cuff," he answers. "You're fine. It's fine."

The band fills with air, constricting my blood flow until it beeps again, then empties.

"See. All good," he says, smiling.

"Dad, I need Benny. He's hurt. I can feel...I can feel how...b-broken he is." There's a boulder on my chest. I can't get in enough air. No, *Benny* can't get in enough air. "He needs me, Dad." My voice grows stronger as fear and rage surface. What Hell is this where I can't move, and Benny isn't here?

Dale hushes me again and kisses my forehead. "There was a semi. It skidded through the stop and sent you right into the way of another car. Benny couldn't do a thing. It was awful. Honey, it's honestly a miracle you're all still alive."

Warren comes back into view. "They're paging a doctor," he says quietly.

I search his features, tired and pale. His eyes are red-rimmed.

"Where is he, Ren? Where's Benny?"

Warren opens his mouth to speak, but Dale cuts him off, stroking my hair with his rough, grease-stained hands.

"The ICU. He took the worst of it, and he's in rough shape, honey. But he made it out of surgery. He's a fighter. You're both going to be *fine*." But his voice betrays him; he doesn't believe these promises. "You hit your head, and you have some nasty bruises. The doctor couldn't tell us why you wouldn't wake up. They said there were no serious injuries; you just wouldn't wake up. You had me so worried, sweetheart. But now, you're awake, and it's alright."

My head? I reach back up to the bandage at my hairline, wincing.

"Ten stitches," my father says, answering my silent question.

"Who's 'all'? You said, 'you're all alive.' Who else?"

"A boy from your school." His tone harshens. "He was going way too fast for these conditions. Couldn't stop in time." The words emerge from him angrily, then fall flat. I know this tone of Dale's well. Too well. "He messed up his jaw a bit. Broke a leg, too, I think. But nothing life-threatening." He sounds almost disappointed about it. Letting go of my hand, Dale begins pacing the room.

Slowly, I adjust my heavy head to get a clearer view of Warren.

"Hey, Ren." It comes out a croak. I clear my throat, then try again. "Couldn't stay away, huh?"

He shrugs. "The second I knew where they were taking the two of you, I just drove. I didn't really think."

"Wait...*where* are we, exactly?"

"St. Al's."

"Boise?" I ask. He nods. "What about school?"

He rubs his forehead, then rakes his fingers through his hair. "I can't... August, I can't leave." I look beyond him, where a chair and a roll-away bed line the wall of the room, both full of pillows and crumpled sheets. Slept in.

"Oh, Ren..."

"But if you want me to leave—"

"No, I don't." I smile weakly, and he returns the gesture. "Dad?"

"Hm?" He stops pacing.

"How long is Benny in the ICU for?"

"Honey, are you in any pain?"

"*Dad!*"

The monitor next to me beeps, alerting the world to my quickening pulse.

"Ah, just in time," a sweet alto voice breaks the tension in the room. "Hello, August. I'm Dr. Morris. I'm on call tonight."

She points to the nurse who follows in behind her. "Jenny and I are going to check you out if that's alright."

"Don't bother. I'm fine. Just take me to my brother."

"Right. I heard we had twins staying with us." Like it's the Ramada Inn and not a hospital. I stare, annoyed.

"Honey, I can't even imagine your anxiety right now, but you were unconscious for a *while*. Not typically a good sign in my experience." She cocks her brow to drive the message home.

Nurse Jenny, a pale, broad woman, comes at me. I instinctively recoil until I realize she's removing the blood pressure cuff.

"You'll sleep more comfortably now," the doctor says, smiling. My eyes narrow to slits. "Look, I get it. This sucks. But we'll get through it as quickly and as painlessly as possible. Your cooperation isn't necessary, but it makes our jobs a lot easier. 'Kay?"

Warren and Dale leave the room while Dr. Morris and Nurse Jenny interrogate me, poking and prodding as they go. I stare at the ceiling, counting the seconds until it's over.

"Well," Dr. Morris says with a sigh, touching my shoulder. "If you'd have come in awake after the accident, you'd have been discharged by now. Everything looks fine. You'll be sore for weeks, honey, no sugar coating it. Seatbelts save lives, but they also make your insides mushy for a while." She pauses, waiting for me to nod in agreement or maybe laugh humorlessly. Anything. I stare, unfazed. She finishes, "Okay then. Sleep. Please. It's the best thing for you. We'll get you discharged first thing in the morning."

"So, this is done?" I ask, not caring how ungrateful I sound. "We're finished?"

"We're finished. Jenny will get you some pain meds here in a bit, help you get some sleep."

"They won't—" I start, but stop, because they won't understand this pain isn't mine. It's Benny's. "Thank you," I revise. "But I *need* to see my brother. I need to know how he is."

"August, even here, there are rules. He's in the ICU, and he's resting."

"Resting? You mean unconscious?" She frowns. "You don't understand; he *needs* me." People never understand. We're two halves of the same person, and without the other, we fall apart.

"August—"

"*I* need it. I can't sleep. I can't be calm. I can't *breathe* right until I've seen him. Let me hold his hand for a few minutes, then you can give me all the drugs you want. I promise to shut up and sleep."

The two women exchange glances. Jenny wears a subtle grin.

"Assertive girl," Dr. Morris murmurs.

❦

A COMA. The doctor tells me before Jenny gets the wheelchair—another condition of visiting Benny—and takes me to the ICU.

My Benny. A coma. What circle of Hell is this? And why does it smell like urine, latex, and hopelessness?

They tell me to prepare myself for the visit, so it won't be too jarring.

Internal bleeding.

Major surgery.

Broken leg.

Possible brain damage.

Know more when he wakes up.

"It won't be easy," they'd said. "He doesn't look like the Benny you know." But that's garbage because he's *my* Benny, and I'd know him anywhere, under any circumstances.

Outside Benny's room, Jenny pauses. "Are you ready for this?" she asks again. I nod. "Ok, then." She wheels me to his side. "I'll give you a few minutes." She turns on a low-watt lamp and leaves the room.

She's brought me to the wrong room. The boy in this bulky hospital bed isn't Benny. It can't be. This boy is so pale he's almost gray. His leg is in a restrictive cast. There's a patch over his left eye, a bandage across his nose. Purple patches in random places on his face and arms. He looks lifeless. My Benny is vibrant.

The boy's cheekbones are familiar, despite the bruising. And I recognize that nose, identical to the one staring back at me every time I look in the mirror. If this boy opened his eyes, I'm sure they'd be Benny's, too. But this can't be *my* Benny.

My Benny would give me his signature smirk and say something cheesy like, "You should see the other guy."

I would ask, "So, you're fine to drive me home, right?"

He would play along. "Sure, in about six to eight weeks."

"Oh, come on. It's only a few broken ribs; you're perfectly fine to operate heavy machinery."

"Operate heavy machinery, run a marathon. Yup, count me in. Let's go."

This boy is silent, motionless. Tubes obstruct his face; a machine helps him breathe. He's broken.

I reach out for his lifeless hand, covered in minor scrapes, bits of dried blood. My free hand ghosts gently over his face, his arms, his chest, barely brushing his injuries. My fingers sense the bandages wrapped tightly around his chest. As I relax my hand there, I swear my own ribs absorb the pressure. Gasping, I withdraw my touch.

"Benny?" I whisper, swallow loudly, then try again. "Benny, if you can hear me... Look, I *know* you can hear me, so listen up. Come back, alright? Don't even think about leaving me." I stroke his hand as I ramble.

"Do you think... Do you think you could open your eyes for me, Benny?" I brush his forehead, push back his jet-black hair. "I know you wouldn't open your eyes for the clowns with the stethoscopes and the needles and the...and all the other crap doctors carry around with them." A weak laugh escapes my cracked, swollen lips. "I know you wouldn't open your eyes for them. They told me you couldn't; you're in a *coma*." I roll my eyes, waving a dismissive hand. "But that was for them, not me. Maybe you were scared. But I'm here now. It's me, Benny. It's August. And you can wake up, now."

The machines hiss, the screens beep, his chest moves, but his eyes don't open. No sounds rise from his throat. His hand remains warm and limp in mine. No signals, no hope he's in there, fighting his way back to me or listening at all.

"Please, Benny. Please. Do me a solid and open your eyes." For a moment, I imagine tears welling. I don't *feel* them welling, but this seems like the right moment for a meltdown. Dry eyes are a betrayal under these circumstances—I'm certain. My voice cracks, my breaths grow rugged and labored, but no tears surface.

"Benjamin," I yell, "come on! Wake up and tell me *I* look like hell. Make a crack about how you thought *I* was a terrible driver. Where's your morbid sarcasm when I need it?" Nothing.

"I don't know where you went, but wherever it is, it can't be better than what we've got going on here. So, come *back*. I miss you, Benny. And I need you. Desperately." I swallow hard. "I love you, Ben. More than I love myself. More than I love my life. Dancing. All of it. It's all garbage compared to you, and it's literally *nothing* to me if you're gone. You're the best part of my life. You've got to come back. I can't do any of it by myself. School, dance, college, Dale... I can't handle any of it without my best brother." I take a deep breath. A mistake. *Ow!* I rack my brain for anything else to say. Anything to bring him back.

"Don't just do this for me. Do it for Warren. You should see him, Benny. Poor boy is a wreck. He loves you so much. He needs you almost as much as I do." I offer a hopeful, lopsided grin, as though I'm waiting for these revelations to pull him back from the dark, distant ledge.

Beep. Pump. Hiss. The rise and fall of his chest. Repeat.

"Benjamin Xavier Haiz!" I scold through clenched teeth. He

hates his middle name. "You come back to me, dammit. I *know* you're in there." I pause for a few slow, shallow breaths. "Okay. Fine. I'll let you sleep for now. But I'll be back soon. I promised nurse *Jenny* she could knock me out with the good drugs. But I'll be back, young man, and we're going to go over this until you wake up. Okay?" I wait for a twitch of his hand, movement under his eyelids. There's nothing—only emptiness.

"You won't leave me, Benjamin. You wouldn't dare. And I'd never leave you. Ever. That's why we sing that stupid song with each other all the time—we *mean* it. I wouldn't leave you dying. I won't. You're waking up, you hear?" Nothing.

I strain my neck, blinking heavenward. "Bring him back to me," I whisper. "Don't take him. Don't you dare take him from me."

In the hall, navigating our way out of the ICU, a sliver of an image causes me to plant my feet.

"*Stop*," I say firmly.

"What's wrong?" Jenny panics.

"Stop." Though my voice is quiet and controlled, fury radiates from every pore. I wheel myself closer to the door of a dimly lit room, where his face is visible under the glow of a monitor. *Him*. With those big, ocean eyes I've found equally intriguing and annoying. Now I detest them.

When Dale said a boy from my school, I never imagined. But he'd also mentioned *driving too fast*, so I guess I should have. Sounds like Seth in his stupid little car.

Seth is blinking rapidly, his body shaking. Wires and braces surround his face, preventing him from excessive movement. He appears otherwise normal.

Facial damage? Benny's in a coma, fighting for his *life*. Meanwhile, Seth Davidson messed up his face and broke a leg, and he's in there *crying*?

Jenny notices my fixed glare.

"His airbags didn't deploy," she whispers. "I'll be right back."

She enters his room and tugs at the privacy curtain, but it only half-closes. I watch as she leans down, cooing over him.

"What are you doing awake again, sweetie? Too much pain?" Her voice is delicate, butter-soft. Like she's afraid anything else might hurt him.

She puts something to his face. Tissue? Is she wiping away his tears? *What the hell?* I can't stop myself. I wheel through the open door as she adjusts something in his IV drip.

"August, this isn't your room," she says. "Out. Now. I've done you enough favors tonight." She pushes my chair back toward the door.

"*You.*" It's all I can think to say. His eyes move around the room, unable to find me. More tears glide down his cheeks. "*You* did this."

"August, *no*," Jenny scolds.

"He can't wake up. He can't *breathe* on his own."

A deep, mournful cry rises from the back of his throat. Something stings in my chest, like shame. But I don't apologize, because nothing in life is fair, so why should I be?

Chapter 12

Whatever Jenny gives me for the pain messes with my head; I have drawn-out, murky nightmares and awake feeling completely detached from my body. Unable to move, I moan.

"August?"

"Dad?" It's barely a whisper.

"G'mornin', Goose." The cigarette on his breath is fresh. He must have just come back from a "break."

I scan the room with narrowed eyes. Warren's holed up in the recliner, a pillow shoved between his shoulder and head, a blanket awkwardly draped around his arms. His dark, exhausted eyes answer my gaze, his lips twitching into a weak smile. Dale looms over my bed, tired and tortured.

"What time?"

"Barely seven. Benny's doc will be back on duty soon, and we'll know more. You're up just in time." He offers a hopeful grin. Like he really believes we're about to hear the best possible news. "I sat with him most the night; I think he looks good. More color this morning."

I attempt a smile, but my lips hurt. This *is* good news. Isn't it?

"They'll discharge you this morning, I think."

Even better news. Let me out of this bed; let me be with Benny.

Jenny enters the room, followed by another nurse. "Good morning, August," Jenny says.

"You're still here, huh?" I ask hoarsely.

"Just for you." She winks. "But my turn is up. Time for day shift. This is Sharon." Jenny points to the other woman in scrubs. "She'll take amazing care of you, and Dr. Hall will be in around eight. Someone from the lab will be up to do a little blood work soon."

"You are full of good news," I deadpan.

"No one loves needles, but sometimes they're necessary. Your vitals are great, and you show no cause for concern. If your blood work looks good, I see no reason Dr. Hall won't release you by lunch. In the meantime, order some breakfast and eat what you can. Then, Sharon can help you get set up with clean towels and shampoo. Wash some of that grit away."

"I can shower?" She nods. "Well, you do have your merits, don't you?"

¶

AFTER BLOOD DRAWS and a tasteless breakfast, I'm given the okay for a shower. Warren knocks on the door before I can process my disappointment of having nothing but disposable underwear and a clean hospital gown from Sharon to wear.

"Hey, you," I say. I hold out the gown in my hand like an offering. "Hospital chic. All the rage these days."

He smirks. "I've heard. *But*, if you wait like, thirty seconds, you'll be glad you did."

"What?" I ask, squinting.

"I called reinforcements," he says.

A familiar, airy coo travels down the hallway.

"Kali?"

He grins, stepping aside as Kali sashays through the door. "Hey, baby cakes," she sings, her sparkling white teeth a contrast against dark red lipstick. Her offset rainbow bob sways as she hurries to engulf me in a hug.

My arms dangle uselessly at my sides.

"Mom has a closing today," Warren says. "She wanted to be here for you but couldn't."

"So she called the next best thing," Kali says, still holding me.

"Okay?" I say, not grasping why either Mrs. M or Kali would show up for me right now.

"Here," Kali says, pulling away. She digs inside the gym bag slung over her shoulder and pulls out a stack of neatly folded clothes.

"You," I stutter, "drove all this way to bring me clothes?"

She nods, wide-eyed. A subtle, *duh!* Then, jerking her head back, "That sweet thing called his mama from the middle of the mall last night, asking what size to buy you."

"You went shopping for me?" I ask. Warren shrugs, braces himself against the wall.

"I know you're not going anywhere until Benny's better. You needed clothes."

"Ren..." For the first time since the crash yesterday, something other than pain wells inside.

"So, nothing against sugar snap back there," Kali says, winking, "but Mrs. Mitchell thought maybe you'd benefit from a...*woman's* touch." She eyes the pile of clothes and lifts the shirt, revealing a soft, cotton lounge bra and a new pair of underwear.

Ah.

"This was..." I swallow. "Thank you." My eyes shift between them. "Both of you. You're amazing."

"Do you need anything else?" Kali asks, her voice low. "Any other *essentials*?" I shake my head, still processing this gesture. "Did they give you soap? Shampoo? Do you need a razor?"

"I've got all I need now," I say, accepting the clothes, trying on a smile. "Really. Thank you."

"Of course, my love," she breathes, pushing my hair back. "Of course." Her eyes glisten, and she blinks, chuckling. "I swore I wouldn't cry. I wore makeup on purpose." She fans her face, and I swoop in for another hug—a proper one.

"You're the best, Kali," I whisper.

She kisses my cheek, then pulls back. "Okay. You," she points, "shower. Get dressed. I'll be back with contraband. Coffee?"

When I shake my head, she looks at Warren. "Coffee?"

He nods, wide-eyed. "All of it. Bring all the coffee."

"You got it, honey. Are you a breakfast burrito guy? Pancakes?" She turns back to me. "You still love those awful, greasy breakfast sandwich things? Whatever the two of you want. It's on me. And I will not accept 'I'm fine, thanks' as an answer."

I let Kali make a list of food to bring me, even though I know I won't eat any of it. A shower helps me feel almost human, but still not quite. I can't be right until Benny is.

Warren and I await the doctor to approve my discharge, fidgeting. Knees bouncing. Hands wringing. At least I'm doing it in clean clothes.

"I hate this," I say through clenched teeth. "Why is it taking so long?"

"I don't know." He begins pacing. Again. "How are we supposed to just...*wait*? He's just *lying* there, and we're supposed to accept that? Not *do* anything?"

I stand from where I'd sat perched on the edge of the hospital bed and hobble toward him.

"Com'ere." I reach my arms out for a hug. His body answers mine, and we weave ourselves together, relaxing with a shared sigh. "Thank you for being here," I mumble.

"I couldn't be anywhere else right now, Gus. You two are..." his voice breaks, and he clutches me tighter.

We linger, and he cries into my hair. I can't help thinking he's crying for both of us.

Last night, I scolded God in anger. Now, Warren's gentle sobs begin to smooth out my jagged edges, and I make a gentler plea inside my mind. To God, the universe, and anyone else who might be listening. *Heal Benny. Please don't let him leave me. I'll do anything—be anything—if you just let Benny stay.*

Dr. Hall arrives around nine, my father trailing behind him after another visit to Benny's room.

"August, good morning," Dr. Hall says. "How are we feeling today?"

I blink emptily at him.

"Okay, I see we're cutting to the chase."

He fusses over me for ten minutes, asking questions, moving limbs, examining scars.

"I'd like you to follow up with your regular physician in about a week. Okay?" When I say nothing, he asks, "You *do* have a regular physician, right?"

"I don't know," I say, staring at my father.

"She hasn't needed a doctor in a while," is Dale's non-answer.

"Well, how about I recommend someone?" I shrug. The doctor nods and continues, "I'm also writing you a referral for physical therapy."

"Physical therapy?"

"For your neck and back. Your father says you're a dancer." He grins, eyeing Dale. "We can't have you going right back into the swing of things without getting your strength back."

"Oh. Is that all?"

"Yes. You'll need P.T. for two or three months, I expect. Afterward, you'll be better than new. Stronger." I stare blankly at him again, hardly registering a word he says. None of this matters. Nothing about me is important right now. "Now, I'm going to have a quick talk with your father, and someone will be in with your discharge papers soon."

"You're releasing me? You promise?"

"Yes," he says, laughing.

"Finally," I huff. "Can they bring the paperwork to Benny's room? Can I sit with him now? Dad, please? Let's go."

The doctor nods. "Shouldn't be a problem."

The men move into the hallway, sharing a private conversation. Warren offers me his arm as I limp toward the door, but I only make it two steps. There's a crushing weight on my chest, and I buckle to the floor, straining for air.

"August!" Warren fumbles over me.

"August, what's wrong?" Dad rushes to my side, followed closely by the doctor.

"Can you tell me where it hurts?" he asks, reaching for my wrist, checking my pulse.

But this isn't my pain. "It's Benny," I squeak. "Help him."

"August?" Dr. Hall asks, skeptical.

I grab at my chest, gasping. "Benny can't breathe." No one's moving. No one's listening. "He can't breathe!" I scream, shoving fumbling hands away from me. "Help him!"

"No. Please, God, no," Dale says, running out of the room. His shrill, steady cries of "No!" trail down the hallway. He understands. He believes me.

While strangers drag me back to the bed, Benny fades. The part of my heart beating solely because he exists—the part that senses his pain and reads his thoughts—is breaking away from me. My soul cracks wide open, and the bond severs, then drifts away.

"*No*," I shriek. "Save him! Please." But they're still not listening, and Benny slips farther away. "Benny, don't leave me. You can't leave me."

Benny and I have been so connected in life, I always expected when he died, he would pull me right along with him. I pray for it to be true. It *needs* to be true. My breathing slows, and my eyelids droop.

"Wait for me, Benny," I whisper. "I'm coming."

"August."

A thick, unwelcomed voice intrudes the blankness of my mind.

"August. Wake up." It's deep. Slow. A draining battery.

I try opening my eyes. Everything is blotchy, blurry.

"Come on, hon," the voice says, a little clearer now. A face comes into focus. Sharon?

"Come on," she says, "wake up."

I jolt up, too quickly. My hand rushes to my head as the room spins around me.

There's something new inside—an emptiness. "Benny. I can't feel him anymore. Something's wrong."

Panicked, I search the room. No Dale. No doctors. Two lumps on the floor. No, not lumps. People. Warren, hunched over, hiding his face and shaking, and Kali next to him, holding him, rubbing his back. Spilled coffees and a greasy fast-food bag leak onto the floor near the door. An orderly with a mop works to clean it up.

I slide off the bed and crawl toward Warren and Kali. There's a blankness about Kali's face I've never seen before. Her vibrance—her relentless, sparkling joy—is missing.

"Oh, sweetheart." Sharon comes up behind me and grabs my shoulders. She puts herself in my path and leans down.

"Where's my dad? Where's Benny? What happened? *Dad!*" But he doesn't come running. No one is coming. Because Sharon has said *sweetheart* in that tragic way. I can't feel Benny because he's gone.

"No." I shake my head. "No."

"August, I'm so sorry," she says.

"*No!*" As if arguing will change her reply. I push her away, scooting closer to Warren. He won't meet my eyes, and his face is red and wet with tears and snot. I touch his knee.

Kali reaches an arm toward me, inviting me into the huddle. I smack her gesture of comfort away. I don't need her hugs because this can't be true.

"It's not true, Ren. Tell me it's not true."

"His body had endured so much," Sharon says behind me. "His poor heart couldn't take it."

"You're wrong. He can take it. He can survive anything. He's strong."

"I'm so sorry," she whispers.

I glare up at her. "Benny has to be alive!" I scream. "If I'm still here, so is he. He couldn't *possibly*..." I fumble for the words while Sharon kneels in front of me again. "If he had died, I would have died too." I say it as gospel truth because all my life, I've believed it. She takes my shoulders again, but I break from her grasp, climbing clumsily to my feet. I touch my ribs. No pressure. No pain. Same with my leg. Nothing. Just that horrid emptiness inside—a hollow, rotted shell where he should be.

"*No!*" I hug myself, doubling over. Kali maneuvers toward me. Sharon puts another hand on my arm. Even Warren shifts to stand, but I ignore them all and run away.

They stop me at the entrance to the ICU, refusing to let me through the doors. I tell them I need to see my brother. I *must*. But no one lets me in. Sharon arrives, tugging at my arms, attempting to lure me away.

"You're wrong!" I scream, fighting to escape the grasps of faceless hospital personnel. I unintentionally ram my head into the wall when I break free. It shuts me up momentarily—long enough for Kali to come into view and hold my shoulders.

"He's gone, August," she says hoarsely, her bloodshot eyes burrowing into me. I shake my head. "I'm *so* sorry. But he's gone, now."

I look past her, toward Warren standing in the background. He's holding his hands over his face, shielding himself from my meltdown, shaking as he sobs.

"Tell them!" I shout. "Tell them, Warren! He wouldn't leave me here."

Warren crumples to the ground, turning away.

"He'd never leave me!" I say again.

Kali puts her hands on my face, strokes my cheeks. "It's not what he chose, baby. It's just what happened."

What *happened*? It's just what *happened*? How? How has this happened? Because I let the battery die in my truck? Because Benny felt guilty spending time with Millie, and he was with me instead? Because a trucker rammed us from behind? Because Seth was speeding through an intersection? The only person not at fault in all these scenarios is Benny. So why is he gone?

Something warm trickles down my face, and the thumping in my head rivals Benny's full-volume drumming. *Benny*, I think. Or maybe I say it out loud.

"I hurt my head," I say. Kali nods. "I think it's bleeding." She nods again. "I might throw up."

"It's ok," she says.

"I hurt my head," I say again, collapsing against her.

Chapter 13

Dale and I drive back to La Grande in stunned silence. He detours from the route when we're minutes from home, taking us to the junkyard.

He pulls around back, where *it* sits in pieces on the frozen ground. Dale parks, kills the engine, and gets out. I stay buckled in my seat, staring at the metal wreckage formerly known as a beautiful red Corvette.

Without a moment to spare, I open my door and lean out, vomiting what little food I've eaten today onto the cold, hard ground. A few feet away, Dale falls to his knees. His rage boils over, spilling out his mouth and into the sky. Incoherent wails echo across the lifeless scrapyard. I wipe my mouth with my sleeve, close my door, and wait for the storm to settle.

He curses my mother, and God, and Seth, and himself. That calm, collected, mature father he'd been when I awoke in a hospital bed is gone now. I'll never again see the dad who'd told me everything would be alright. The dad who'd called me "Goose" and held my hand.

When the accident happened, he'd come back. *Dad* had come back, grateful his children were alive, resolved never to take another moment for granted. He'd praised God for giving him a second chance to do things right. But when second chances disintegrated into dust, Dale resurfaced, cursing the same God he praised only yesterday.

I understand his resentment at being cheated, and I honestly don't blame him. How else should someone feel, trapped in this nightmare where we remain, and Benny doesn't. It's an insult.

Red-faced and still whimpering, Dale climbs back into the driver's seat. He clutches the steering wheel, his knuckles whitening under the strain.

"Dad..." I start, not knowing how I expect to finish the thought. What even *is* the thought? But before I can string together any useless words for the explosive moment, Dale holds up a hand to silence me.

"Don't say a word. You shut your mouth."

THE DAY of the funeral arrives much like fluoride day in elementary school. It creeps up out of nowhere, slapping me in the face. Everyone hates fluoride day, but it's inevitable. I have to get up, live it, tolerate it, rinse around its awful taste in my mouth until the timer buzzes, and I can spit it out again. I'll go through the motions because I have to, but I'll hate every nauseating moment.

I select a black dress from my closet, hold it up to the light, examining it. It's never looked more hideous. My hand jerks and I drop the hanger; it thuds against the carpet. I stumble to my bed, still in my underwear, staring at the crumpled black mass on the floor.

Does it matter what I wear? Will lightning strike me dead if I walk through the doors of a church for a funeral not dressed in black? Would I care? Doubtful. After pointless deliberation, maybe five minutes, maybe an hour, I pick the ugly dress off the floor and slip it on, put shoes on my feet, run a brush through my hair, and knot it at my neck. I don't bother looking in the mirror.

It's too bright outside. Sunny and delightful to the untrained eye. To everyone *not* on their way to their twin's funeral.

Dale's wearing a suit—another rarity. Were this any other occasion, I'd make an effort to tell him how nice he looks. How his tie matches his shirt. Something. Instead, my lips hold a tight line, and my eyes focus solely on my lap as I take my seat, and he shifts into gear.

The chaplain has a quiet waiting room for us while everyone takes their seats. Uncle Ryan, Aunt Hannah, and Sam peek tentatively at the doorway. I stand, smiling to see them, then my face falls because I remember why they're here. They enfold me in a group hug, and I stand still, breathing them in as though I might draw strength from theirs. Ryan goes to Dale and puts a hand on his shoulder, which Dale rebuffs with a grunt.

"It's time," a voice informs us.

Time? Time for what?

"August," Ryan says softly. I realize Dale is already walking out the door toward the chapel, where the congregation waits.

I follow Dale to the front pew, horribly exposed and on display for the world to judge.

They'll be wondering, *how is she handling it? Will she cry? Will she faint?*

I stagger toward the front of the chapel and take my seat, my knees buckling under me.

Colors fade. I'm watching a fuzzy TV, not my life. This can't be my life. Everything is wrong, and this world will never feel safe again. Never be right again. I know this for certain because ahead of me is a closed casket, surrounded by exaggerated bouquets of roses and lilies.

I avert my gaze from the casket as quickly as it's drawn there, focusing again on my lap. Dale is next to me on the bench, but for the gap between us, and his inability to look at me, I may as well be alone. Well, until Sam takes a seat next to me. I almost jump when he does, but then he takes my hand and releases a slow, painful breath, and I know I'm not in this alone. I glance beyond him, where Hannah sits huddled against Uncle Ryan. Both of them silent but steadily crying. Why aren't *I* crying? Half of my soul dying should have trumped the *no tears* rule. Yet here I sit, weak limbs and an empty chest, but dry eyes.

I hear my name mentioned solemnly through the speaker. I

glance forward, realizing the impossible moment has arrived. I have to speak—damn Dale for this. I will never forgive him.

I walk mechanically to the podium, once again naked and exposed. I mutter a few syllables, then a few more. I'm not sure what I'm saying. Nothing is enough, so why does it matter? I can hardly hear myself over my rage for my father. He forced this asinine task upon me.

"No one should have to speak at their child's funeral," he'd said. "No one!" He'd thrown his hand up.

"I'm no more capable of speaking at my brother's funeral than you are your son's. I can't do it, Dad."

He'd shaken his head, reinforcing his demands. I suggested asking Benny's band instructor to do it; they'd been close. Maybe Warren's parents would do it; they knew Benny almost like he was theirs. They'd been there with me—along with Warren and the Fosters—to help write the obituary and make the arrangements.

"A family member should do it," Dale said, his voice cracking, intensity rising, "and you and I are the *only* options!"

"No," I'd snapped. "Don't you dare dump on them. They're *here*. They're *helping*. And I'm sure Uncle Ryan would—"

"*No*," he'd shouted.

"Just because Ryan is *her* brother doesn't mean he is in any way responsible for her vanishing act. She left me too, Dad. And I hate it. And it sucks. But Ryan had *nothing* to do with it."

"Don't talk about her!" He'd yelled, raising a hand above his head, all the fury in his eyes of a charging bull. Then he froze, gasped, and cried. "Deliver the eulogy, August," he'd whispered. "Do this for me." He'd hung his head, retreated into his bedroom, and remained there until this morning.

Despite all my arguing, all my pleading, here I stand before a chapel full of mostly strangers, eulogizing my better half. My reason for breathing. How is it even possible I'm still standing when he's lying in a casket? It makes no sense.

People sniffle, raise tissues to their noses. My brain struggles to process this information. All these people are here crying because Benny is gone.

I glimpse Warren out of the corner of my eye and immediately focus on the podium to avoid him. No. Can't look at Warren. I'm barely standing. If I see his sweet freckled face misshapen with heartbreak, I'll collapse.

I wish I were speaking gracefully, honoring Benny's memory with stories of his constant compassion and desire to make the world a better place. I should be talking about how his natural musical talent is the stuff of envy. How he loved music. How he loved Warren. How he loved *fiercely*. I should be sprinkling in a little black humor; Benny would have loved that.

There should be someone here ready to sing "Two Little Boys" or another of Benny's favorite songs. But I couldn't arrange anything the way I should have because nothing makes sense without him here to guide me through it.

A string of inadequate thoughts brings my remarks to a pathetic end.

"I always assumed I'd have Benny with me 'til the end," I whisper. "I'm not sure how I'll manage without him. But I'm thankful for every precious minute I had *with* him." Because that's what you're supposed to say. None of it rings sincere—all the *grateful* crap. What am I supposed to be grateful for?

Zombie-like, I shuffle toward the pew amidst sniffles and muffled cries. My leg thuds against something hard—the edge of the pew—and I hug my elbows as I crumble awkwardly, taking a seat right there and not between Sam and Dale as I'd been previously. Dale appears to be a mile away. Am I even in the right pew? I don't know, and it doesn't matter.

A hand grips my shoulder, and I nearly cry out. I relax when I recognize Warren's familiar breath and the strong scent of Tide on his clothes.

"He loved you so much," Warren whispers behind me, nearly choking on the words. My hand reaches up to squeeze his. Tightly, fiercely, I clutch him, fusing his skin to mine, desperate to banish the loneliness consuming me. His muffled sobs echo in my broken mind. I'd be crying right along with him, was I anyone else. Tears would be preferable over this boulder on my chest, this inability to breathe. The room fades around me.

I'm lurched to my side as Warren forces himself between my limp body and the end of the pew.

"Breathe, Gus," he whispers, his voice breaking. "Don't stop breathing. He needs you to breathe." Warren folds his arms around me, his hand pressing my face into his chest, his thumb stroking my cheek. His warm tears fall into my hair.

Warren's pain only intensifies mine, and I can't help but think, *it would kill Benny to see Warren hurting like this*. Then I go numb, because Benny's already dead.

Warren begins exaggerating his breaths, encouraging me to breathe in time with him. To stay strong, keep going. I reach my weak arms around his waist and squeeze, letting his body meld with mine. Maybe Warren will absorb me completely, and I can disappear.

I hear a mild growl from Dale, and I imagine it's a response to the sight of Warren holding me. He can growl all he wants; I'm not moving. I've tried to comfort him in the wake of our shared tragedy, and he's ignored me at every turn. No doubt he wishes it were Benny left here with him and not me. He probably forced me to speak today as punishment. I see it in his eyes every time we share a glance. They seem to scream, "Why wasn't it you?" Not that I blame him. It's a valid question, and frankly, I'm furious with God for taking Benny and leaving me here. Benny was better. *Benny was better.* The thought revolves around me constantly, every breath I take.

The service ends, and I don't even know it until Warren whispers, "It's time," in my ear.

Dale stands and leads the way down the center of the chapel, the rest of the congregation seated, waiting, staring, judging. I'm frozen at the front of the room, Benny's casket to my right. I don't think I can leave him.

"He'll be alone if I go," I say. Or at least, I think I'm speaking. Maybe it's in my head. "We can't leave him here."

"We're not leaving him. He's coming with us."

Oh, right. Warren, Mr. Mitchell, Sam, Ryan, Dale—the Pallbearers. They'll take him to the cemetery. *Internment,* they call it.

I haven't moved yet, and everyone is staring at me. A flush of embarrassment rises in me, and I turn toward Warren. "I'm sorry," I breathe, "I can't. My feet..."

Warren waves his hand, and Sam appears on my other side. They hide me from the crowd, hold me steady, and walk me out of the chapel.

They transfer Benny into a hearse parked outside the church, all of them wearing sunglasses to hide their red-rimmed eyes from the sharp glare of the sun. The irony of the sunny December day is a cruel joke Benny would have laughed at.

"Beautiful day for a funeral," he would have said.

But I find no humor in the sardonic sun.

Six covered chairs sit near the burial site. Maybe I hoped setting a place for Liliana would act as a summons. Like the old movie—"*if you build it, they will come.*" She doesn't come. I silently curse her. Maybe for the hundredth time today. Maybe the millionth. If there were ever a day for her to pretend she's not a heartless shrew, it's today. It's *now*. I didn't expect her to weep openly over his coffin or anything, but she could have at least *shown up*, especially after calling Dale and admitting to being back in Oregon.

Warren takes the seat Liliana has chosen not to fill, and holds my hand in both of his, rested in his lap. Seated on the other side of me, Dale props his elbows on his thighs, supporting his head in his hands. I think to reach out and touch his shoulder but find it impossible. How can I offer him any solace when I'm in pieces?

The service is blurry, dreamlike. This isn't real—it can't be—and my brain checks out, leaving my body a mere ornament.

I'm vaguely aware of someone offering a prayer and reading a scripture. An explanation for the eighteen roses resting on his coffin. Some nonsense about how he's in a *better* place.

Why do they always spout *better place* garbage at funerals? Is it a rule? *Sorry, grieving family, but you weren't good enough. They've moved on to* better *things.*

More lies float around in the air.

It was his time.

Called to serve above.

In time, we will all find peace.

Peace.

Is that what this is? This broken glass inside of me—was it born out of peace? The tears Warren continues to cry, which mix with the snot running down his chin and fall into his lap—are these his *peace* tears?

Before it's over, someone says another prayer. They pray we find comfort. Hope. They pray we celebrate life and not mourn death. What life do we celebrate? Eighteen years? A joke. Yet, they pray, pray, pray.

I haven't prayed or even thought about God since the day he refused to answer my pleas. Since the day he'd said, "NO." I've tried getting on my knees once, maybe twice. My legs won't abide. They say no, as God said no. *No.* Not this time, August. Not now.

The church hosts a potluck after the services "for the close friends and family." But all these people can't be his close friends and family. Too many. Everyone from school, even those who never knew him. All the teachers. Is there school today? What day is it? Are we already on Christmas break? Christmas? Are we even supposed to have Christmas this year? Clearly not.

With Warren still by my side, holding my hand, I enter the building, unsure why the hell I'm even here. I should go home. What was I thinking coming here? That it would be rude not to come, probably. Since I'm one of the few members of his family, and family should be here. I scan the room for familiar faces. Dale sits in a corner, Carlos standing next to him, a hand on his shoulder. Marta brings Dale a plate of food, and he nods but doesn't accept it.

Hannah and Mrs. M thank people for coming, intermittently wiping their eyes with wadded tissues.

Sam stands next to the picture display, a conflicting joy and sadness in his features as he picks up a frame to examine it closer. A picture of the three of us last Christmas, when Sam came for a surprise visit and stayed an entire week.

Ryan and Mr. M bring more rolls and casserole dishes from the kitchen to the common room, where people line up with paper plates and plastic forks.

Who are these people? What am I doing here? For a moment, I even think, *Where's Benny?* Then I throw up down the front of my dress.

"Oh gosh," I whisper, a hand over my rancid mouth.

Hannah materializes in front of me in a blink, wiping me with a wet rag.

"Take her home, Warren," she says softly, a hand to my chin. The washcloth moves across my lips. "You go home, baby. We'll take care of this."

"I'm sorry," I say. The bile lingers, burning my throat and nose.

"No, honey. Don't apologize. Warren will take you home, and you'll get cleaned up and take a nap. Can you do that for me?"

I nod. Warren gently turns me around and leads me out the door. I hear Hannah asking Sam to find her a bucket of water. They're cleaning up my puke and sending me home for a nap. I wonder if I deserve them, then immediately push the thought aside because I always wondered if I deserved Benny, and look what happened.

We're almost to Warren's car when Millie appears in our path, arm in arm with a woman who must be her mother. They have identical pointed noses and thick, smooth, auburn hair.

"Oh," she says quietly. Her green eyes are glossy, her cheeks splotchy. Millie's face, normally contoured with makeup, is all-natural today. "August, I—" her voice breaks. She covers her face with a hand, breathes slowly through her tight lips.

He should have been with you, I think. *Then it wouldn't have happened. You could have saved him. This is my fault.* But I stare, mouth slightly agape, my knees growing weaker by the moment.

"You were good for him," I croak. "Thank you for being good for him." I might throw up again; I have to get out of here.

My body lunges forward, my feet barely catching up in time to save me from falling on my face in my puke-stained dress.

Warren drives me home, one hand on the steering wheel, one hand rubbing my back. "I've got you," he keeps saying. "I've got you."

People stroll along the sidewalk in their winter boots and jackets, enjoying the fickle sun, walking their dogs, visiting with friends. Traffic is steady with people shopping, going out to eat, living their lives on this beautiful day.

Meanwhile, Benny is in the ground.

Cars are parked in front of the house. When I open the unlocked door, strange women bustling about greet me—folding laundry, washing dishes, rearranging the fridge and freezer. Disposable containers topped with foil line the countertops.

They stare as Warren and I enter cautiously.

"We wanted to help," one woman says. "Please don't be insulted. We arranged it with your aunt. And with Meg—Mrs. Mitchell."

I look to Warren, then back to the strangers scattered throughout my house.

"We wanted to relieve some burdens. There are casseroles in—"

"Sure," I say, pushing past them to the bathroom, where I lose what's left in my stomach into the toilet.

"This was so kind of you all," Warren says, his voice muffled through the bathroom door. "But August needs some privacy now. And some rest. Please."

I turn on the shower, slip out of my dress, and throw it into the small wastebasket.

The water is volcanically hot, melting away the stench of misery and bile. The sting of each scalding drop is preferable to the aching in my hollow chest every time I remember Benny is gone.

There's a moment when I first wake up where I delusionally think the nightmare is over and all is well. Then it washes over me—a monsoon of grief and loneliness.

When the shower runs cold, I step out, unsure if I remembered to use soap or wash my hair.

Emerging from the bathroom, wrapped in a bleach-stained bath towel, I almost trip over Warren. He's sitting on the hallway floor, his arms crossed, his head drooping, snoring softly. I step around him into my room, get dressed, and take an unhealthy dose of migraine medicine before I wake him with a gentle hand on his shoulder.

"Hey you," I whisper.

He startles, eyes darting side to side. "Gus, I'm sorry. I didn't mean to..." He struggles to his feet, hands dragging across his face.

"S'okay," I mumble. "Long day." Cold water trickles from my wet hair down my spine, and I shiver.

"Here," Warren says. His arm wraps around my shoulder, and he guides me into my room. He pulls back the corners of the fresh bedding—courtesy of the hoard of church ladies—and I crawl between the sheets. He disappears a minute, then reappears with a glass full of orange juice. "Hydrate," he orders gently, and I accept the glass with shaky hands.

The juice burns my raw throat, but I drink it all, then settle under the covers and burrow my head into my pillow.

Warren pulls the desk chair up next to my bed. "Sleep. I'll stay and make sure no one else tries to sneak in and retile the kitchen or paint your bedroom or anything." He winks.

A quiet, numb laugh escapes my chapped lips. "Thanks. Really. You've been so... I can't imagine..." I trail off for a minute. He waits. Silently. Patiently. "I'm grateful you're here," I manage, extending a hand toward his.

He accepts my hand, then leans in and kisses my forehead. A

warm tear falls from his face onto mine. "Anything for you, August," he says, his lips brushing my skin. "Always." He sits back. "You're my family. You know?" His voice cracks, and he closes his eyes, wincing as more tears fall.

"You're mine, Ren," I breathe.

After a few slow, deep breaths, he tries on a smile, but his eyes betray him. "I promise, Gus. You can count on me. For *anything*."

He reaches to nudge my unbrushed hair out of my eyes, and I snatch his hand. "I know," I say, adjusting his hand between my face and pillow, his palm perfectly cupping my cheek. "Thank you," I whisper, letting the heaviness and exhaustion of the day settle over me.

I awake to pitch-black emptiness. My hand fumbles for my phone, then I remember it didn't survive the crash, and I have no phone. The *crash*. Benny. All of it washes over me again—the funeral, the church, the vomit-stained dress in the garbage.

"Warren," I whisper to the darkness, not sure why I would expect him to be there still. I'm alone again, now and forever.

So, this is Hell. I understand the concept now. Hell is any place I'm forced to live without my better half.

I always told Benny I would do anything for him; walk through Hell if I had to...

Damn cruel irony.

Chapter 14

Warren stays away. Maybe because he hates the idea of coming over and having only me here to greet him. Maybe because he blames me for the accident. I know *I* do. And Seth. And the trucker. And my truck. And Dale, for having the jumper cables. And the weather. And God, for not listening.

Ryan, Hannah, and Sam stay in town for a few days after the funeral. They help Dale and me sort through the legal garbage. It's not enough someone died; we're forced to fill out a bunch of paperwork because of it. We can't sit numbly, wallowing in our grief. We have to talk with strangers about Benny like he's a case number. It's disgusting.

As if *that* isn't enough, I'm forced to return to the police station to talk about the accident *again*, this time with a detective. Hannah drives me there, sits with me, holds my hand. Translates when my words are too quiet to travel the small width of the desk.

An insurance adjuster keeps calling the house, asking to talk to me. Ryan does all the talking unless it's necessary for me to speak. They ask how I'm *feeling*, how I'm *recovering*. As though I might one day wake up and not be missing a brother.

Sam sits with me on the couch, passing the hours with mindless TV or video games. His silent company seems to help more than all the hand-holding, back rubbing, and sandwich making. All those things are kind and thoughtful, but zoning out in front of the TV, thinking of nothing, is the closest I get to *not* hating myself.

Their help can't last forever, though. They have lives to return to.

Hannah offers to bring me home with them, and I almost say yes. I cling to her hand as it's time for them to leave, and her eyes ask me again if I'm sure I won't stay with them.

"I can't leave him," I whisper. Benny would never leave Dale behind like I'm desperate to. My lips shape the words, "I can't," but internally, I'm crying, *TAKE ME WITH YOU!*

Someone has to stay for Dale, though, and I want to be good like Benny was. To do the *right* thing as he would have. So, I let go of her hand and watch them drive away. Snow crunches under the weight of their tires, and once they turn the corner, there's nothing left for me but the falling snow. All the world is quiet and calm. Inside, I'm screaming, straining against the newness of this waking nightmare.

Dale sleeps in his stuffy bedroom, rank with booze and body odor. He sleeps fourteen hours a day, at least. I worry about the garage, whether he'll lose our income, and how we'll keep the house. But what would it matter? This house is all wrong without my beautiful Benny, and maybe it wouldn't be the worst thing if we let it burn to the ground.

My life will now and forever be separated by *before* and *after*. Before the crash—before everything fell apart—and after. After it went to hell and Dale quit showering and started smoking a pack a day. I've stopped showering, too, which requires an effort and concentration I can no longer muster because I'm defective now.

In the before, Christmas was colorful. Benny and I wore Christmas pajamas every year, plucked from the racks of the thrift shop each spring when everyone else discarded theirs. We opened our scarce array of presents while listening to holiday tunes on the radio. We worked together to cook dinner—turkey, homemade rolls, stuffing, potatoes, *all* the carbs—and Benny always forced us to sing one carol together before we ate.

This year, the only evidence of the season is the tree we

decorated in the *before*. It's hideous to me now; I should tear it down. I will when my energy returns. It *will* return at some point. Won't it?

I unplug the phone, because who cares? All that's left is Dale, me, and nothing but the television as a link between us. He acknowledges me only in grunts of disapproval, and I don't mind. If he doesn't expect anything of me, at least I can skate by as a barely functioning human, and no one will call me out on it.

Sometimes I manage to sleep, and I drift into an empty blackness, trapped, unable to move. Unable to speak. I awake in a panicked sweat, calling for him. *Benny*.

Restless, I trade my bed for the couch and flip through TV channels sitting in my grimy pajamas. *It's a Wonderful Life* plays on almost every channel. Clearly, they haven't received the memo it is *not*, in fact, a wonderful life after all.

Merry Christmas, Benny. For a second, I think I hear him whispering back, and my heart leaps. When I look over, there's nothing but a vacant seat next to me.

🎧

I PULL myself out of another nightmare, screaming, "I'm not supposed to be here!" as I awake. Sweat drips from my hairline as I push myself off the couch and gaze around the empty living room.

Dale is gone, and so is his pickup. He's probably at a bar or a liquor store. Maybe he found an open pharmacy and is getting a refill. The medication is supposedly a *mild* sedative, but when he sleeps, he sleeps like the dead. I can't tell if I'm judging him or jealous.

I meander to the kitchen and peruse the fridge. People keep leaving deli trays and disposable dishes full of lasagna and tater-tot casseroles on the front steps. None of it sounds appetizing, but my stomach is growling, and I know I should eat. Reaching for a container of questionable leftovers, I catch a whiff of myself and prioritize showering instead.

The doorbell rings before I make it to the bathroom. My first thought is, *Warren!* Something resembling excitement rises in my chest. But Warren never uses the doorbell, so I continue toward the promise of personal hygiene, ignoring whoever stands on the other side of the door.

The bell rings again, followed by the faint hum of voices. It takes a moment, but I recognize the melody, even if the words are muffled. Who the hell thought it was a good idea to show up to this house signing "Silent Night"? Is this a cruel joke? Or do these strangers not *know* we're the haunted house on the block, and they shouldn't be here? The only people who've ever gone caroling in this neighborhood are...*us*: Benny, Warren, and me.

Benny always passed out antler headbands or Santa hats and led us caroling around town with Shirley strapped to his back. Our neighborhood, Warren's, retirement homes, daycares. This year he'd been so excited to take Millie.

I stomp to the door, throat on fire, stomach turning. I'm ready to swing it open and shout profanities at these morons. Their song transitions into "We Wish You a Merry Christmas". I stop as my hand grips the knob. What good would it do? I could scream and swear. I could tell them just what a bloody merry Christmas it *isn't*. Throw them off my front steps. Tell them to get lost or go to Hell or shove some mistletoe down their vile throats. And maybe it would be cathartic. But that would fade, and I would still be here, alone. *Twinless.* I'm *twinless.* Where once I was part of something so special—something far beyond singing together or looking alike. Something rooted so deeply in my DNA I believed it to be unbreakable—now I'm nothing. Now, it's just *gone.* And screaming at these idiots with questionable intentions won't change that.

The voices grow distant as the group moves down the block to some other unsuspecting neighbor, and my hand falls from the knob.

"If this was you, Benjamin," I croak quietly, "it wasn't funny."

Chapter 15

I stare at the tree until the ornaments all blur together. With a deep breath, I take them down, one by one, placing them carefully in a box. I go overkill bubble wrapping anything Benny made or favored. Elementary school pictures, framed with popsicle sticks and glitter. His handprint captured in clay. A miniature keepsake drum kit. I seal everything safely inside an unmarked box and stash it in my closet.

When I step outside to toss the tree, I stumble over something camouflaged in the snow. Closer inspection reveals crushed cookies and a soggy, faded card with a smeared message.

Hoping to sweeten your Christmas. You're in our prayers.

I throw the cookies and the card in the garbage bin and abandon the prickly tree to the ground beside it. Dale can do the rest; I got it this far.

As I shuffle through the snow back to the house, a pair of headlights illuminate the whitewashed ground, zeroing in on our front steps. I stop walking but don't turn to see who it is. It's not Warren; I'd have heard his car coming a mile away. Doesn't sound like Dale's pickup either.

The engine quiets and a door clicks closed.

"Hey, sweetie."

Kali. My body tenses—inside and out.

"I don't want to intrude. I just needed to check in on you. I've been tryin'a call you. And I know you don't wanna talk to anyone."

She sighs. Snow crunches under her feet as she inches closer. "I was worried, honey."

My eyes still fixed on the front door, I manage a slight shrug.

"Are you eating? Drinking? Do y'all need groceries? Can I take some laundry or anything?"

I jerk my head.

"You sure?" She waits, I hold still. "Okay, sugar. Listen, there's no rush. No rush at all. The other instructors and I—we'll cover your classes for January. February, too. If you need it. Don't worry about a thing. You take the time you need, and when you're ready, we'll all be there for you. All of us. We love you."

"I can't," I mumble. I thought it would hurt to say aloud, but I'm not sure I feel anything. "I'm not coming back."

"You don't have to decide anything—"

"I can't," I say again, then climb the stairs. With my hand on the doorknob, I manage a hushed, "I'm sorry," and step inside.

How could I ever dance again? Dancing was something I loved in the *before*; it has no place in the *after*.

Dance is about free expression. It's about heart and soul—luxuries I no longer possess. I'm powerless, numb, and I don't belong on the dance floor—just another hole in the fabric of my life. Or, what *was* my life.

Kali's car whines back to life, and she drives away.

I don't set out to do it on purpose; it just happens. As Kali's headlights disappear and the hum of her engine fades, I stagger toward the stairway.

Anxiety steadily builds as I descend the steps, afraid the emptiness below will consume me.

It hits me all at once as I open his bedroom door. *Benny.* His entire aura greets me there, ghosting over me as I stand frozen in the doorway. Everything looks as it should and entirely wrong at the same time.

Aside from the dark gray suit missing from his closet—now buried in the earth—everything is exactly as he left it. Bed half-made, dirty clothes in the hamper, shards of wood on the floor around the drum set, and his guitar case propped against the wall. Lived in, as though he'll be home any minute.

I can see it—Benny walking in, throwing his backpack onto the bed, grabbing his guitar, and sitting down to play. Or maybe he's putting his earplugs in and grabbing a beaten pair of drumsticks from the five-gallon bucket in the corner. I see it all, down to the way his eyes close and his lips curl into a lopsided grin as he loses himself in the music. But no matter how long I stand there, *waiting*, Benny doesn't come. There's only the bittersweet illusion of him.

I start walking, something pulling me here, then there. *Go this way. Grab these things.* I don't realize what I'm doing until I hear the clicking of knobs and a rush of water. I look down—a pile of his dirty clothes in my arms and the old washing machine filling in preparation.

I won't let the dirty clothes rot in his hamper, ruining the scent of him. Maybe it's wrong. Maybe I shouldn't be touching anything. But I can't think of another way to do it.

I shower while I wait for his clothes to dry. *Finally.* I battle with myself as I shampoo my hair. *Twice.*

You should take better care of yourself, August. He would want you to.

Why does it matter what I do? Who cares if I give up?

But he would want you to care.

But I can't care without him here. I can't do any of it without *him*. *Twinless.* I'm twinless. The word mocks me.

I put on fresh clothes, brush my teeth for the first time in who knows how many days, then put his clean things away.

Sitting on the edge of his bed, I lean over to smell the sheets, so full of the memory of him. I let out a sharp, mangled cry and burrow into his blankets, placing my head on the precious pillow he'd slept on. I breathe it all in once more, then turn my face into the fabric and scream until my voice gives out, my eyelids droop, and the world falls away.

When I open my eyes, I'm seven years old again. Crying on my bed. Covering my ears to drown out my parents' ugly voices. I wait for Benny. I know he'll be here any moment—that's how it always is. When I think I can't handle this anymore, Benny shows up, places a hand on my shoulder, and I know I can do anything because he's with me. I'm not alone.

But this time, he doesn't come. I call his name, but he doesn't answer. The fighting gets louder. I sob and shriek, but Benny never comes. I wake up panicking, sweating through my clothes, my heart newly shattered.

I stay in Benny's bed for days. I sleep and dream, or don't. I always wake up confused, gasping for air. But I get a drink, go back to sleep, and do it all over again.

Sometimes Benny appears in my dreams, but he won't speak to me. It's infuriating. I scream at him, but he won't answer. "Talk to me!" I plead. But he just smiles. "Say something!"

I startle awake a sweaty mess, breathless. I force myself to sit up, turn on the bedside lamp, and wipe my forehead. I fumble for the plastic cup of water on the nightstand. It's warm and stagnant, having sat there for hours, maybe days. I've lost all sense of time.

A dim light shines through the window. There are three small taps, then someone calls my name. "August!" The voice is muffled but audible. I startle, dropping the cup. "Sorry!" the voice says, easily traveling through the thin pane of glass. I glance upward and find Warren's face illuminated by his phone.

"Warren?" My muscles weak and stiff, I slowly stand from the bed and walk toward the small window.

"August, it's me," he calls. "Open up!"

"What are you *doing*?" I flip the bedroom light on and slide the windowpane over. He's already removed the old, bent screen from its frame.

"Move over, let me slide down." Somehow, he fits himself

through the small, "dungeon" window, as he's always called it, and lands lightly—almost gracefully—on the carpet. He closes the window, then meets me with a dark, worried gaze.

"What...? How...?" I wipe both hands across my greasy face and back through my matted hair. Oh, gross. Time for another shower. Grateful for my PJ top of choice—a hoodie—I tuck away my tangled, black strands and begin tugging at my sleeves. I swallow a lump in my throat before I'm finally able to ask, "What are you doing here?"

"I've wanted to see you," he says, and I hear what he doesn't say. He's wanted to, but couldn't. "I figured Christmas was probably horrible, and New Year's Eve would be pretty empty, too." He pauses for a slow, tortured breath. "It's all been empty for me if I'm being honest. Sorry if I scared you." He grins sheepishly down at me, shrugging his shoulders.

"But the window? How did you know I was down here?"

"I honestly didn't know if Dale would let me in or not. So, I snuck around to knock on your window. Your lights were all off, and you didn't answer. I had a feeling you might be down here."

"Scared of Dale, huh?" I ask, frowning.

"He seemed pretty pissed at the—" He stops himself, swallows. "I don't think I'm his favorite person right now, and I didn't want to get you into any trouble by showing up or anything." He pauses to gather his thoughts or wait for me to respond. My lips are dry, my throat hurts, and I have no idea what to say. I stare, empty. "I'm sorry if I scared you," he says again.

"S'okay," I say, shrugging. I stumble backward until I bump into the bedframe. I mean to sit at the edge of the bed but awkwardly thump onto the floor.

"Geez, Gus. You okay?" He sits next to me, touching my shoulder.

Am I okay? Such a loaded question. I stare at my knees.

"It was like I *had* to stay here," I say after a lull. "Almost to recharge or something. That's weird, right?" Not just weird. Stupid.

"Not to me." We're silent for several minutes before he clears his throat. "How are you...*doing?*"

My shoulders slump as I release a sharp, humorless laugh.

"Sorry," Warren says, rubbing my back. "Stupid question."

"It's not, really," I assure him, finally tilting my head up, meeting his rich chocolate eyes. I've missed them. I've missed *him*. "Anyone else asks, and I'll break their legs. But it's you. I'll allow it."

His arm reaches around my shoulders, and I collapse against him. "Good to know," he says, pressing his lips into my hood.

I sniff the fabric. *Gross.* "I'm sorry you're seeing me—smelling me—like this. I'm disgusting."

He laughs. "You're not disgusting."

"You're a lousy liar, but I don't have the energy to argue with you."

"That's fair."

"Is it really New Year's Eve already?" I ask.

"Yup." His lips smack on the *p*.

"Guess I've been here longer than I thought."

"You lose track of a day? It's okay. No one would blame you."

"Try *days*. Plural. I don't know how many. I think I came down a couple of days after Christmas. Maybe?"

"Gus," he sighs. "Have you been eating?"

My hand instinctively rubs against my stomach. "Sort of," I mumble. "I mean, I went upstairs to grab snacks once or twice, but I never checked the time. And until you spilled my water, I'd been hydrating," I tease gently.

"Gus, you need to eat something. And you need some fresh air."

"Don't tell me what—" I stop, taking a deep breath. Anything Warren says to me comes from a place of love and genuine concern. "I know, Ren. I know. But I also needed to sleep. I couldn't sleep for days after the...you know." I meet his gaze. "I was so tired, Warren."

He sighs, leaning in. "Of course, you were." He kisses my hairline, then wraps both arms around me. I settle against him eagerly; I hadn't realized how lonely I was until now.

"Some carolers showed up on Christmas," I spit out, my words muffled against his sweater.

"Crap," he breathes.

"I almost unloaded on them. Kind of wish I had. Might have felt good to yell at someone, you know?" He huffs a quiet laugh. "Then, Kali stopped by. And Ren...I couldn't..." I chew on my cheeks. "I couldn't even look at her, and I know I should have been ashamed of that, but I wasn't. I was just...*empty*. And it was like his gravity pulled me down here. Like, I hoped maybe if I was here, I'd *feel* again." All of this sounds even dumber out loud than it did in my head. "What a freakin' train wreck, huh?"

"Not even close."

"Liar."

"No, Gus. Really. And seriously, no one would have blamed you for yelling when those idiots showed up. I *told* them not to come here."

I adjust against his grip, squinting up at him.

"Those same church ladies who came over that day? They asked my mom and me to come caroling, and I explicitly told them *not* to come here. Said it was the worst possible idea."

His lashes flutter as he stares at the ceiling, his lips twitching. I study the freckles on his face, always lightened in the winter months. Come spring and sunshine, they'll turn a dark red-brown.

"Hey," I say, "it's okay, Ren. Thanks for trying."

He frowns. "I'm sorry I failed. Caroling was always..."

"Benny's thing."

"Yeah."

I fall back against his chest, and his head rests atop mine.

"I hadn't been down here since before..." my words trail off. "But after the carolers and Kali, it felt like I needed to be here. Closer to him. Like I was...safer? Safe enough to sleep. *None* of this makes sense. I'm such an idiot."

"It doesn't have to make sense, Gus."

"Which part?" I ask, almost laughing.

"Any of it. Grief is grief. It takes new forms daily. You can't shove it in a box or expect it to be logical."

"How are *you* doing?" I ask, nudging my head against his chest.

"I miss him," he says. But his words, sticky and low in his throat, say so much more.

"Oh, Ren." I reach both arms around his middle, squeezing. He cries then, shaking as he whimpers into my sweater.

"I'm sorry, Gus," he says, sniffling and digging his palms into his eyes.

I sit back, grabbing his shoulders in my weak hands, my eyes holding his. "Don't apologize to me, Ren. Please, cry with me when you need to. Sneak in through the window when you're lonely. Keep talking to me about him, whether you want to reminisce about the good times or tell me how miserably you miss him. You're all...You're all I h-have—" My heartbeat rises into my throat, and my head weighs a hundred pounds. My hands grab my hollow chest, and I start tugging and scratching.

"Gus, *breathe!*" he says. "You're okay. You're okay. Just breathe." He inhales dramatically through his mouth, urging me with his eyes to follow along. "You've got this. I'm right here."

I grab at his arm, my nails digging into the fabric of his sweater, clumping it up in my hands. Finally, I manage a long, painful gasp.

"Good job," he says, pulling me close again. My head falls into his lap. He pushes my hood back, brushes my knotty hair with his fingers. "Good job. You're okay."

"Does he come to you in your dreams?" I ask after a long silence. "Does he say anything to you?"

"Not yet. I mean, I dream about him. But he's never said anything to me. I wish he would, you know?"

"I was dreaming of him before you showed up. But he wouldn't say anything to me either. Why won't he talk to me, Ren? I miss him s-so—"

Warren shushes me, continuing to smooth down my hair with his hands.

"Maybe he's not ready to talk to us yet," Warren says, as though this is a perfectly normal conversation we're having. "Give him time."

I look around the room, Benny's phantom presence everywhere. I've tainted this holy place.

"I can't stay down here anymore," I whisper. "I'm ruining it. It's starting to smell like me."

"Gus, there's no right or wrong—"

"I'm ruining it," I say with finality. "I ruin everything."

"August," he breathes. "Please, don't—"

"Happy New Year, I guess," I say weakly.

"Yeah," he mumbles. "Happy New Year."

Chapter 16

JANUARY

School is back in session, and I have no idea how I'm going to do this. How do I get up, get dressed, and spend seven straight hours acting like a normal, functioning person? How do I even *exist* around people anymore? All these people who *haven't* been living in a cage for the last month.

What if they *talk* to me? How do I talk to people anymore?

Warren offers to drive me, and while I hate the idea of him being responsible for me, I doubt I'd actually get myself there if left to my own devices.

I managed a shower this morning. I even put on clean clothes—not pajamas—and brushed my thick hair into a low ponytail. But when Warren pulls up outside, and I step through the front door, I realize I've forgotten shoes. I take slow, deep breaths as I change out of my wet socks and try again.

You can do this, August. You have to. It's time.

But can I do this? Should I even try? I honestly have no clue. But Warren is waiting so patiently for me, and I owe it to him to try. He smiles as I take my seat in his Escort.

"I have a surprise for you," he says.

"We're graduating early and I never have to go back there?" I hold a grimace as I await his response.

"If only," he sighs.

"Bummer."

"I called Mrs. Higgins last week."

"Mrs. Higgins, the *guidance* counselor?" My pulse quickens.

"About our schedules," he rushes, touching my shoulder.

"Oh," I breathe.

"We have identical schedules now."

"Identical?"

"One hundred percent."

Thank you isn't a big enough word, but I say it anyway, squeezing his arm.

Warren doesn't rush me when we get to school. We sit in his car, watching from the parking lot as students file through the front doors. Just as I clutch my backpack and reach for the door handle, resolved to get it over with, a head of blonde hair emerges from a white sedan, and I freeze.

A woman helps him get his crutches from the car, touches him lovingly on the back, then drives away. He stares at the building a moment, adjusting his crutches under his arms. Then he, his cast, and subtle headgear are off to first period.

"He's coming back," I whisper.

"August, I'm sorry. I couldn't bring myself to tell you. I tried."

My jaw clenches as I watch Seth limp inside.

"I didn't think he'd come back," Warren says. "I figured he'd switch to online school, or maybe test out. I never imagined he'd brave the rest of the senior year *here*. I still can't believe he's off scot-free."

I flinch, my heart sinking into my stomach. "What?"

"You don't know?"

I turn to Warren, searching his face for signals. "They said any trial would be months away. That I'd get a letter if I had to appear."

"Hasn't anyone called you? I thought they would have let you know."

"I unplugged the phone," I say blandly.

He nods, wearing a sympathetic smile. "I don't blame you."

"So what happened? What did I miss?"

"It's all on the truck driver, Gus. All of it. The state charged him with second-degree manslaughter, though there's talk he might plead down to criminally negligent homicide."

What does it say about me that Warren knows these things and I don't? I've purposefully avoided the news. Made it impossible for anyone to call and update me.

"There was no evidence suggesting Seth was 'driving recklessly.'" He makes air quotes with his fingers. "He had the right of way. Both impacts, all the injuries, they all came down to the semi."

"Oh," is all I can say, casting my eyes down at the backpack in my lap.

"It's not right, Gus. You have every reason to be angry."

"I think I'm just numb, Ren." I twist my lips, shrug my shoulders. "What does it matter who gets charged with what? Whoever takes the blame, he'll still be gone."

He sighs. "I know. You're right."

"This does explain some things, though."

"Dale?" He asks. I nod. "Has he gotten worse?"

"He's so furious all the time. And he blames Seth as much as the semi driver. The first impact was bad; the second was fatal. That's all Dale sees. I'm sure it's killing him that Seth's a 'free man' or whatever."

"We don't have to go today," he says. "We can ditch."

"Nah." I pout my lips, lower my voice. "Might as well get this BS over with." He laughs at my weak imitation of him, and we head inside.

I instinctively head straight for my locker, my backpack slung over one shoulder, at the ready. I'm reaching for my Chemistry textbook when I sense someone next to me, in front of *his* locker. My heart flutters as I turn to greet him, but I don't recognize this new boy. He's short, quiet. An imposter. They've given away Benny's locker already. I stare at the open metal box before me, unable to do anything productive.

Voices dance around me; I'm today's hot topic.

Didn't even cry at his funeral.
Not a single tear during the eulogy.
So unnatural.
Don't be so judgmental. We can't even imagine.
But she should have cried.
The moment one group moves along, another emerges.
Poor thing.
Can't believe she came back.
So heartbreaking.
She should have cried.

I'm still staring at my mess of textbooks and notebooks when familiar voices breeze my way.

"No," says Maribel, "he's not in jail. I think the trucker is, though."

"Oh," Mike says, "I heard they charged him with vehicular manslaughter. Or vehicular homicide. Something like that."

"No," Maribel says. "I think maybe they took his license away."

More people join the conversation. Everyone has a different story about Seth and whether the truck driver will plead guilty and spare the state a trial.

Maribel speaks again. "Did you see the headgear? Poor guy. I feel so terrible for him."

"You feel terrible for *him?*" someone asks.

"He looks so beat up," she replies. "He's eating through a straw, still. I wish I could do something. This must be so hard for him."

"I feel bad for *her*," someone says. "I can't imagine."

"Yeah, but I mean, she's not even hurt—"

"Hey, morons!" I jump at Warren's voice behind me. "She's not deaf. Shut it."

"Hey, man, I'm sorry."

"Save it, Mike. Just shut up and keep that crazy away from us. Leash laws, man."

"Hey!" Maribel squeals.

Warren sidles up to me, offering a playful hip bump. When I chew on my lips, unable to respond or smile, he leans down.

"I'm so sorry, Gus. They're idiots. Do you want me to take you home?"

"Nah," I say. "The day hasn't even started yet. I'm sure it will get *much* worse."

"Solid attitude," he teases. Then seriously, "Will you let me take you home when it does?"

I stare at my open locker, unchanged since I first opened it five minutes ago.

"Could I keep my books in your locker?" I ask. "I can't be here. It's wrong. You know?"

Warren snatches up my things and carries them toward his. For the first time this morning, I notice my surroundings. My throat burns as I scan the "We miss you!" and "We love you!" posters. Benny's face surrounded by signatures and notes from students and teachers. My knees wobble, and I reach to brace myself against a wall. My hand lands on a bulletin reminding students grief counseling is available. A sign-up sheet hangs next to it. I read a handful of names, a few decent kids who knew Benny through band. The rest, I can't even put faces to. Who are these people? And where do they get off needing *grief* counseling?

Not fully understanding what I'm doing or the hurt I'm potentially causing, I tear the page in half, ripping it from the wall. The paper crumples in my hand, and Warren gently touches my shoulder, removes the paper from my grasp, and places it in the garbage can. He puts all my books away, except my chemistry textbook, and takes my shaky hand in his.

"Sorry," I whisper. "I didn't mean to."

Still holding my hand, he walks me to chemistry, not saying another word about it.

Somehow...*somehow*, with Warren at my side, holding my hand from class to class, I survive my first day back. It's over. It's finished.

And I can go home and hide in my room until morning if I want to, which I do.

As we approach the exit, I glance at the walls and notice the banners have all been taken down. Unable to convey my relief and gratitude, I squeeze Warren's hand.

"You're welcome," he whispers, weaving his fingers through mine.

※

Here's the thing about living half a life: it doesn't get easier. You get used to it. There's a difference.

When people say, "It gets easier," what they mean is, "Eventually, you become numb to the fact that your life has lost all meaning. You learn to go through the motions day in, day out, until you die."

At least, that's what I'm gleaning from the experience.

I keep a few of Benny's shirts and his band jacket tucked away in one of my drawers. When I feel utterly alone, I pull them out and breathe him in a while. I'm not sure if it helps or simply gives me the illusion I'm strong enough to make it without him.

Though I've started driving myself to school, I still follow Warren around like a sad puppy all day. Speak *only* to him. I don't even look at anyone else if I can help it, and not only to avoid accidental eye contact with Seth, who has two classes with me. We share an unspoken agreement to pretend the other doesn't exist. It's better this way. What would I say to him anyway? *Sorry about your fancy car. Wish you'd have died in place of my brother.* Truly unconscionable things to say, for sure. But this is who I am now—a horrible person with horrible thoughts swimming around in my head. All because the one person I always tried to be my best self for is six feet under the frozen ground.

I enter my house in stealth mode, holding my breath as I slip through the door and close it behind me. I take slow, calculated steps, desperate to get to my room without alerting Dale to my arrival. Nerves swarm when I realize he's not reclining in his chair, eyes closed, as he is most afternoons.

"What are you doing home?" He shouts from the kitchen. I cower at the fullness of his voice. The last time he went on a tirade, it ended with his fist through the drywall, inches from my face.

I clear my throat, looking around the kitchen for a safe place to stand. "It's four o'clock, Dad; school's been out a while." No place is safe; he can reach me wherever I am.

"Then what took you so long?" His too-loud voice reverberates through the too-small kitchen, and I shudder.

"I went to the library for a bit," I lie, "to work on a few assignments." The truth is, I've sat outside in my car for the last thirty minutes, freezing, too scared to come inside.

"I thought you taught dance until late on Wednesday."

Today is Thursday, but I bury that thought, not willing to die on this hill.

"I don't teach anymore," I say, avoiding eye contact.

"What?" Dale stammers. "You don't teach?"

"No." I shrug, my eyes focused on a chipped bit of hardwood.

"Gave it up, did you?"

"I guess so, sir."

"Figures," he spits.

I flinch as the fridge door thuds closed. His beer can hisses open, the carbonation fizzing over the top.

"You were never much of a winner," he says after a sloppy gulp. "You never could hold on to anything good, could you?" I'm a convenient target for these words, clearly meant for the woman I resemble. "I guess this was long overdue," he mutters, walking past me.

I relax as he settles back in his recliner with a heavy *thunk*.

This is routine now. My mere existence triggers Dale, and yelling is his release. The hole in the drywall was a one-time escalation, and it was my fault. For a moment, I stupidly forgot I no longer had a

Benny Buffer, and I sassed Dale when I should have shut up. A mistake I won't make again.

Whenever possible, I make myself invisible, skulking through the house when he's at his most oblivious. I leave early every morning and don't come in until I've exhausted my options: library, chatting with Warren, driving around. The library had been too busy today—too peopley. Coming home too soon was my second mistake, and while I've escaped relatively unharmed today, a third mistake could be fatal.

What have I called Dale for so many years? The ghost of a father? Now I guess I'm the ghost of his daughter, and together we are the ghost of a family. A family who doesn't live here anymore.

Chapter 17

FEBRUARY

My Amazing August,

I call your house every week in hopes you might have reconnected the phone again. Uncle Ryan and I (Sam, too) miss you dearly. The farm keeps us busy, and Sam is constantly involved with some club or another, but we hope to visit you soon. Maybe in the Spring? We miss you, sweet girl. We love you.

Ryan and I are here to help you however we can. However you'll let us. And our door is always open to you. Always.

Love,
Aunt Hannah

Hey You-

Mom says I need to make a note on here for you, or whatever. You know I don't do pretty words, Gus. I just miss you, and I wish you'd get a new phone so we could text, because you know I hate actual phone conversations (not like we can even do THAT right now), and apparently you don't check your e-mail anymore because we've sent you about a million of those, too. All unanswered.

Sorry, I'm being harsh. Mom is going to smack me when she reads this. Consider it my penance. I don't blame you for hiding. I'm not exactly holding it together, myself. I joined like, six clubs this semester to keep my mind busy. Wish I could say it helped.

Write back. Or call. Or e-mail. Carrier Pigeon. Something.
Miss you.
Sam

🎧

Hey Darlin – Ryan here. You say the word, Pumpkin. You say the word, and I'll come get you. You'll always have a home with me.

The letter from Hermiston pulls *all* my emotions to the surface. I have to bury them back down, down, down to a tiny corner of my broken soul. I know it's human to feel things. To hurt. To cry. To fall apart. But I'm sick of falling apart; it's better to accept numbness.

E-mails. They've been sending me e-mails. I'm not sure why the thought hasn't occurred to me before. But now it's *all* I can think about—the computer in the basement, full of who knows what. I've never once thought to get on and see what he might have left behind. Log onto his e-mail. Check his files for...*anything*. I know he used the software I bought him to record at least one song, aside from the one with both of us singing, which I begged him to delete. There could be evidence of him. His music. His words.

Wouldn't anyone else have checked for such treasures within days? A few weeks at most. Here I am, nearly two months later, and I haven't once considered it. Guess there are consequences to accepting my half-life for what it is, rather than trying to process my grief or *cope*. That's the word Warren and his parents use. Once in a while, someone kindly touches my shoulder or holds my hand.

How are you coping?
We all cope differently.
Do you need help? A counselor? We can find someone. It might help you cope.

I don't want to *cope*. I'm not entirely sure I want to survive.

I pull out a notebook from my backpack and flip to a blank page.

Dear Family,

I'm sorry I haven't checked my e-mail or called. Neither of those things should be interpreted as a slight against any of you. I'm just not all here anymore. You know? I'm okay. I think. Mostly. I'm skating by, anyway. I'm even driving again, which I never thought I would. Warren—you remember him?—was taking me. But he's like Sam—he has clubs and baseball and commitments, and I don't. As Ryan would say, I cowboy'd up and got behind the wheel. I hate every minute of it, but I do it.

I love you all. Thank you for your generosity and your incredibly kind offer. But I'll stay where I'm at for now. I want to finish school here. With Warren. In a familiar place. I'm not really up for being the "new girl" at this point in my senior year. You know? Again, nothing against you guys. I love you. I know I said that already. But it seems relevant. So I'll say it again.

Love you all. Miss you. Give Sadie an apple for me and rub Remy's belly.

Gus Gus

⁂

I USED to live for four-day weekends, back in the *before*. Back then, my weekends in February were reserved for dance competitions. If a winter or spring extended weekend *wasn't* dedicated to competitions, I'd sleep in. I'd slip away to the studio for extra practice, spend hours hanging out with Benny and Warren in the basement, or meet up with Kali for a coffee date to strategize for the *next* competition.

In the *after*, I have nothing. I have nowhere. I have no one—just Dale and a house full of ghosts.

Dale stays at the garage an entire shift on Friday, which gives me eight blessed hours of freedom. Freedom to breathe without worrying I might do it wrong. Once he comes home, I hide in my room. I pass the time by rereading my last letter from the Fosters and writing back to them. When that's done, I force myself to keep reading *The Great Gatsby*—even though it's depressing as hell, and I hate it—until my stomach growls so loudly I can't ignore it anymore. How could I forget snacks? So unprepared. *Didn't we have this conversation, August?* I scold myself internally—*no more mistakes.*

My first thought is I might sneak something from the fridge without him hearing me. But outright leaving the house is safer, and I could kill for a massive burrito right now. I carry my shoes in one hand and my keys tightly in the other, so they won't jingle.

I'm almost to the door when an empty whisky bottle shatters against the wall in front of me, which should probably shock me more than it does.

"Get more!" he slurs.

"I can't, Dad. Eighteen, remember?"

"Aren't you supposed to be smart? Figure it out."

"How about I go get us some dinner instead? Takeout? Pizza? A big ol' supreme pizza, just for you?" Something to absorb the booze.

He stands from his chair, stumbling toward me. "I don't want a damn pizza," he says, his saliva splattering across my cheek. I want to cringe, flinch, maybe vomit, but I hold strong. If I stand tall and hold my ground, maybe he'll back off. But he doesn't. He grabs my hair and tugs. Hard. "I said get me more. *Now.*" The words fall around me slowly, dangerously. Then, as if he's two different people, he lets go of my hair and straightens his shirt. "Cigs, too, while you're at it," he finishes, turning away.

"Dad, I *can't.*" I try not to show fear, but my voice shakes. "It's getting late. We should eat something. Please, Dad. I'm hungry."

He groans as he grabs his keys, staggering out the door. *"Fine.* I guess I have to do everything around here, don't I?"

I want to tell him he can't drive; it's too dangerous. But I let him go. Maybe I'm selfish, but I want to flee, and having him out of the way makes it possible. If he gets arrested for drunk driving, I'll deal with it later. If something worse happens... Well, I've already got one death on my conscience, and a morbid voice inside asks, "How much worse could it get?"

I'm knocking on Warren's front door before I've even processed where I am. He draws me inside.

"I was about to come to you," he says. "I've been worried. I would have come sooner but—"

"I'm fine, Warren," I say, cutting him off. "It's fine. I'm just..."

I pull off my coat, take off my shoes.

"You're what?" he asks, frowning.

"You got any food?"

᎑

WITH WARREN's parents out of town for the weekend, he's ordered enough Chinese takeout to feed a family of ten—or one teenage boy. I help myself to more than half of it, realizing how hungry I am after the first few bites.

With full bellies, we lounge in Warren's bedroom, listening to music. I prop myself up on his mattress, leaning against the wall and tracing the lines of his comforter with my finger. He sits across the room on his ancient beanbag he refuses to throw away, even though every time you sit on it, more of its insides spill out.

A melody plays through Warren's speakers—one of his favorite songs. But it was also one of *his* favorite songs.

"Can you change it?" I ask, hardly aware I'm speaking. He does. "Thanks."

"I get it," he says. "There are a lot of songs I can't listen to anymore. If I do, they make me cry."

"I hear crying is healthy."

"To an extent," he says, a distant look in his eyes.

"It occurred to me a week or so ago..." I trail off.

"What did?"

"Hannah and Sam wrote to me. Well, Ryan, too. Just a short note." I'm rambling. I readjust on the bed, wriggle my shoulders.

"Sam said they've tried e-mailing since they can't reach the house when they call."

"You still haven't plugged it in, huh?" he asks.

"Nope," I say, over-enunciating. "And it occurred to me what a terrible person I am. Because not only have I ignored all my e-mails and social media—not that I was active before—but up until Sam mentioned it, I hadn't even thought to check Benny's. I haven't gotten on the computer. There could be pieces of him."

He nods. "There have to be."

"How can I look?" My chest tightens. I tug at a phantom cord around my neck. "I'm barely functioning now. And that house is…" I bite my cheeks, shaking my head. "I'm not sure I could handle whatever I'd find on there. What if it's like losing him all over…" I sense Warren about to rush to my side, but I'm not ready for comfort yet. I hold my hands up, taking slow, controlled breaths.

"I could look for you," he offers quietly. "If you want. When you're ready."

"Maybe. But not yet."

"August?" he asks, almost in a whisper.

I take another breath in through my nose, out slowly through tight lips. "Yeah," I say, wiping my face.

"Your house. Your dad. Are you okay there?" He's frowning, and I realize it might be a response to my expression. How much am I giving away? "How is your dad?" he asks, still staring. "The truth."

"Well," I start, my hand instinctively rubbing at the tender spot behind my ear where he'd tugged my hair earlier. "When he's not blatantly telling me how much of a disappointment I am, he's implying it. And when he's not doing either of those things, he's passed out. He rarely works a full eight-hour day anymore and spends all his money at bars or the liquor store. I have no idea whether the mortgage is secure or if the power might get shut off without warning." I reign myself in, embarrassed at having divulged so much. I scrunch up my nose and huff. "I never thought I'd wish for the days when my father was a functioning alcoholic. Now he's just a shadow."

"*Gus.*" Warren's next to me in seconds, holding me close.

Hesitantly, I reach my arms around his waist. Realizing how wonderful—how *human*—it feels to hold someone, I tighten my grasp and bury my face in his chest. He rubs my back.

"I'm here," he says. "It's okay now."

Nothing is okay, but I won't argue with Warren. Not when he's the only person in the world grounding me, giving me any semblance of safety in the *after*. My fingers clutch the fabric of his shirt, and I draw a sharp breath inward. He smells the same as always—heavenly. A mixture of powerful, name-brand laundry detergent and body wash.

Warren's posture changes and his breaths grow labored. I worry I've crossed lines and made him uncomfortable.

Desperate to cut the tension, I mumble, "Um, do you know you smell really good?" I laugh nervously against his chest—his solid, warm chest. *Whoa, August. Down, girl.*

He coughs, and we simultaneously break from the embrace. I hold his gaze in mine, watching his lips curl into a goofy grin.

"Um, thanks," he says. "I didn't know."

"Well, you do." I bite at my bottom lip, tug restlessly at my shirtsleeves. "You're lucky your mom buys the good laundry soap," I ramble. "We get the generic stuff that *says* it smells like sunshine, but actually, it smells like sadness." His head bobs as he laughs. Why am I such a dork? I'm making this so much more awkward than it needs to be.

"You smell perfect, Gus," he says, his laughter fading.

I've always known Warren is attractive, but something about these last several weeks—all the hand-holding, the way he places a protective arm around my shoulder whenever I'm overwhelmed or excessively down—has brought new feelings to the surface. They're not to be trusted, but sometimes they're *strong*. Right now, for instance, they're begging me to throw years of friendship down the drain and lunge at him. *Kiss him. Kiss him hard.*

As if reading my mind, his hands slide up my arms, his fingers gently folding around my neck. We hold each other in a silent, cautious stare.

The pulse in Warren's wrist quickens against my flushed skin. *Is this happening?* He breathes a charming sigh, leaving me a melted mess.

"August," he whispers.

"Hm?" *Kiss him. Do this, August. Just grab his gorgeous face and—*

"It's late. I should probably walk you out."

Well, crap.

This is smart, though. This is reasonable. This is right. Yet, his hands don't leave my cheeks, and I don't move. I'm about two seconds from saying *to hell with it* when he leans in, softly kisses my forehead, then stands.

Before I have time to think it over and change my mind, I grab his wrist. "Wait. Please."

He stops, turns back to me.

"I wanna ask you something," I whisper, my heart racing. "I don't want to make you uncomfortable or take advantage. You can tell me no, and I swear I'll understand."

"August," he says, taking my hand in both of his. After a moment's hesitation, he slides his fingers through mine. "Ask me anything. Always."

My mouth goes dry. I swallow and lick my lips before I'm able to speak. "Can I stay? Here? With you?"

He stiffens, his eyes glancing down at our woven hands. *Here it comes*, I think. *I'm sorry, August*, or *I don't think it's such a good idea*. But he says nothing.

The silence becoming unbearable, my heart humming in my chest, I look away. I start pulling my hand back, but he doesn't drop it. Instead, he steps closer. My head snaps up, desperate to read him, but he reveals nothing.

Without a word, he guides me under the covers and tucks me in. He pulls a spare blanket from his closet and wraps himself up before lying next to me, his arm reaching around my stomach, his nose nuzzling my hair.

We don't acknowledge this shift in our dynamic. We don't say anything, actually. Warren simply holds me until I fall asleep. Which, with him there—keeping me warm, keeping me safe—doesn't take long at all.

Chapter 18

MARCH

Time passes, whether we will it or not. There's no stopping the world—no escape. There are simply things—people—who make it less excruciating. It's smoother sailing when you have someone around to help drown out the noise. Nights aren't so threatening when there's someone there to hold you close every time you wake up from a nightmare. Life isn't such a constant danger zone when someone's around to help you navigate the darkness. The holes in your heart don't heal, but they fade into a constant, dull ache. They get bigger—sharper—whenever you hear an acoustic guitar or see a red Corvette driving down the street, but you survive. You *survive*. Even when you're so broken, it seems only logical you won't. That you'll actually fall down and die because it hurts so damn much.

You don't. I don't. I live. And time marches on. With Warren.

Warren. The reason I force myself from bed every morning to shower, and eat, and show up to school to do mediocre work. Somehow, I'm still getting all As—probably because teachers pity the poor girl with *extenuating circumstances*.

"Gus, can you hand me my folder?"

Warren points to a navy pocket folder half-tucked under my thigh. I pull myself off his bedroom floor and walk to where he sits at his desk, diligently revising his book report for *The Great Gatsby*.

"Thank you," he says, offering his charming smile I've grown to love in new ways these last several weeks. I spend every possible moment with him; I'm at his house more than mine. I love his home, and I love his parents. They're always around without ever hovering, they care without being overly emotional, and the pantry is *always* full.

"You hungry?" I ask, my hand resting on his shoulder. "I think I need snacks."

He laughs lightly, "I *always* need snacks."

"Kay, I'll go scavenge."

"My pioneer woman," he quips, his hand grazing the small of my back.

I bite at my bottom lip, blushing, and a laugh surfaces from somewhere deep inside my hollow shell. As soon as my cheeks flush, they pale, the blood draining to my feet until I'm not sure I can stand anymore.

"Hey," Warren whispers, gently pulling me onto his lap. "It's okay."

No, it's not! I want to scream. But there are no words for my shame.

"August, you're allowed to smile." He brushes my hair behind my ear, holds my face with gentle hands. "You're allowed to feel whatever you want, whenever you want. Your laugh is amazing. You should never be ashamed of it."

"Ren..." I can't finish the thought. My words have leaked all over his carpet, and I'm hollow again.

"Hey, come back," he says, cautiously manipulating my face so our eyes meet. "Come back to me."

My forehead rests against his. "I'm trying," I say. "I'm trying to...*be*." But I'm not even sure it's the truth. "I don't know what I'm doing, Ren."

"Me either," he murmurs. His breath has a sweet richness to it, like vanilla. His hands slide from my face to either side of my neck, my pulse reverberating against his fingertips.

Hesitantly, I bring my hands to his shoulders, then his face. I sit back enough so I can see him, watching my fingers trace his features. Baseball practice has started, and his skin is tan, his freckles a dark red-brown. I brush his fluffy strawberry blonde hair out of his face.

"Without you, Warren," I start, then swallow. "Without you..." My thumb brushes over his lip, and he tenses. I've crossed the line we've never discussed.

"Gus, what are we doing here?"

My heart beats in my throat.

"You sneak over," he whispers, not wanting his parents to hear—wherever they might be. "You sleep in my bed. Or invite me into yours. Almost every night for a month now."

Nothing ever happens. He just holds me. But even blinded by grief, I know how selfish I'm being and how unhealthy this is for us.

"I-I... I know, Ren. I've been so needy. I'm sorry."

"No, that's not..." He sighs. "That's not what I'm saying. And I don't want you to be sorry. But I think I've reached the point where I need a little clarity. Am I a warm blanket for you? A cuddle buddy?"

My hands fall heavy into my lap. I, the world's biggest jerk, have hurt the sweetest boy alive.

"Warren, you're my..." He's so much more than a best friend, but I don't know where that leaves us. While I've grown closer to him since the accident, practically *fused* to him, I'm not sure it means we push aside a decade of *just friends* to experiment with more. Wouldn't it ruin everything? My eyes search his, as though he'll somehow be able to answer all my unspoken questions containing endless, weighted variables.

He shrugs, smiling weakly. Almost darkly. "Am I only here to hold you up when you're too weak to walk? To remind you to eat when you get too sad to remember?"

"That's not fair," I screech, breathless. But maybe it is. I can't tell anymore. "Warren, you're my—"

"Best friend," he finishes, the words seeping with disappointment. Maybe even disdain.

"No," I whisper. My hands find the strength to travel upward, searching, until I'm holding his neck with trembling fingers. "You're *everything*."

I've often wondered what it would be like to kiss Warren. Lately, it's been a massive *what if* constantly circling my mind, especially whenever he's done anything exceptionally thoughtful or charming. Or sometimes, in the middle of the night, when I wake up in a panic only to discover he's still there, holding me. *Loving* me. And I love him. I'm just not sure that's enough to navigate this unmarked territory I'm leading us into.

Consequences be damned—I move in, my mouth searching for his.

"Are you sure?" he asks.

I nod, and his lips answer mine earnestly, his hands pressed against my spine. I'm not sure if it's so wrong, it's right, or the other way around, but I don't stop kissing him. How could I, when this is the most alive I've been in months? The most alive I've been in the *after*.

He's everything. This moment—this *kiss*—is everything. And while born out of grief, this newfound passion is rooted in a deep and durable love.

Chapter 19

April

"You alright, babe?" Warren asks.

My lips trill over an exhausted breath as I lift my gaze from the faux wood cafeteria table. "I'm fine." I offer the sincerest smile I can muster, pushing aside thoughts of Dale's most recent yelling campaign and last night's sleeplessness. "Promise."

"You're not fine," he says. "Something's up. Dale?"

Warren might actually be a legit mind reader.

"It's nothing," I say. "He's just..." Angry. Loud. Verbally and occasionally physically harsh. "He's sad."

"You realize you're eighteen, right? You don't have to stay there," he says, his hand reaching out for mine. "Come live with us. No sneaking in and out through the window at night. *Live* there. Free yourself."

I snort. "Be serious, Ren."

"I *am* serious. You're not happy there. You're not..." He searches for the right word, chewing on his bottom lip. "...*adored* there. My parents? They're obsessed with you."

"Creepy. Or flattering. I can't tell."

"Ha-ha," he deadpans. "They really love you, Gus. I love you."

"I love you, too." I've said it out loud so many times since we kissed, like I'm worried he doesn't believe me or he might forget.

"Move in with us," he pleads. "There's a spare room just begging for you to put your stuff in it."

"That's too much to ask of your parents."

"You're not asking. They're offering."

"Wh-what?" I stutter, the gravity of these words sinking in.

"I talked with them about it already. You shouldn't be living where someone yells at you for simply existing. He's mean, August. He's awful to you and that..." His eyes glisten. "That kills me. I hate it."

"You *talked* with them about this? Dale is my problem, Warren. Not anyone else's."

"He shouldn't be yours, either. He's the parent, August." He whisper-screams it through clenched teeth.

After a slow breath, I lean across the table and kiss him softly, briefly.

"I'm okay, Ren. I promise. I know he's harsh sometimes, but he's my dad. I can't stop caring about what happens to him. If I leave, who's there for him?"

"Gus..."

"Benny wouldn't leave him," I snap. "Not like this. Not like he is now. Benny would stay." I drag my hands across my face. "Maybe I *should* hate him and walk away. But I can't."

"Okay." He strokes my hand with his thumb. "Okay. End of discussion. I get it."

"I got a new phone," I say, desperate for a cheerful topic.

"*Finally*," he teases.

"I know. Now you have a way to reach me during the brief minutes of the day when we're not already together."

He chuckles.

"Sam's thrilled, too. Sent so many texts I thought he might break it. It's a cheap POS from the clearance bin. Don't look at it too hard; it might crack."

He nods, grinning. "Understood. Even so, we should celebrate. What about dinner after my game tonight?"

He casually suggests date night every week, and every week I convince him to stay in. Movies, snacks, making out—all of it better in private.

I shrug. "Maybe. If I can keep my hands off you long enough for a public appearance." He nearly spits out his last drink of milk. "It's true. You're unbelievably sexy when you play baseball."

"Ah," he says, wiping his mouth. "The real reason you've been to every game this season. I see."

"Hell yes. I'm still convinced EOU offered you a scholarship based solely on that booty." I bite my lip, wiggling my brows.

He rolls his eyes. "Sounds legit."

"Seriously, Ren, watching you play is the best part of my week. I love supporting you. Also, I have nothing better to do, so..."

"Girlfriend of the year," he says, smiling.

I scrunch my nose, shrug my shoulders. "I do what I can."

"You're so cute; it's not fair." He kisses me again.

"Alright, alright," I say, pressing my hand against his chest. "Let's go. Or we'll be late for our riveting discussion on *Crime and Punishment*." I gather my garbage onto my tray. "Such an appropriate name for the longest and dullest read in the history of time." Also appropriate, it was assigned by Mr. Bannerman, possibly the dullest teacher in the history of time.

"Right? It should be illegal for non-English classes to assign reading. Just sayin'." Warren stands, offering to take my tray. I let him. "Did you actually get through the whole thing?"

"*Ugh*, yes. I about jabbed my eyes out, but I finished it." I stand, turning toward the exit. A short auburn bob, ivory skin, and glassy green eyes are there to greet me. *Millie*. We haven't talked in the *after,* except our brief exchange outside the church in December. Something rises to the surface from that deep down, tucked away and buried place inside. Shame. Grief. Jealousy. More and more shame.

"Hello, August."

"Millie," I whisper, my mouth dry.

Warren discards our trays and returns to my side, sliding a protective arm around me.

"I'm on the yearbook committee."

Of course, she is. "Oh?"

"We'd like to do a page for him. For Ben. We wondered if you'd like to have final say on the content and layout. Maybe even put something in there. A message."

Benny. My Benny. Gone, and nothing for him here but a page in the yearbook. A message? What would I say?

His death was stupid and terrible. It's nice you're all trying, but what the hell good does it do?

We're all garbage humans compared to Benny, his selflessness, and the infinite love he carried in his heart.

No. I have no message.

"I'll send you a copy of the obituary," I mumble.

"Kay," she says, smiling faintly. "That's it?"

She expected me to be...what? Excited? Grateful?

As she turns to walk away, I blurt, "'Two Little Boys'." My voice is shrill. The rest of the cafeteria falls silent.

"I'm sorry?" she whispers, coming closer.

"It was his favorite lullaby, ever since he was... We sang it together. You should put the lyrics on the page. He loved music."

"I know," she says, remembering something lovely if the glimmer in her eyes is any indication. "'Two Little Boys'?"

"Yes. If you can't find the lyrics, let me know."

"I can show you the page when it's done?"

"I...I don't... Maybe?"

"It's okay," she hurries, and I realize I'm struggling to breathe.

"Excuse me," I whisper, breaking free from Warren's arm and turning to bolt away. I make it two steps before I run into something. Some*one*.

"August!" Warren calls. "You okay?"

I haven't even processed I'm in a heap on the floor with another human before Warren's pulling me up.

"Yeah, fine," I assure him. Pain is relative.

The victim of my unintentional assault stands from the concrete floor. Seth.

Warren's arm is back around my shoulder, nothing subtle about his stance. Seth straightens, then backs away. I'd always thought he was taller than Warren, but today, he looks shrunken—drained and hollow-cheeked. His eyes, once a beautiful ocean, have faded to a vacant gray. Where an ever-present, cherry smirk used to live, chapped, ashen lips press into a thin line, almost invisible against the paleness of his face.

"I'm, uh, sorry," I choke out. "Are you okay?"

"Yeah, sure," he stutters. We couldn't be more awkward if we were naked.

"Kay. Good," I say, swallowing.

"Yeah. See ya." Then he scuttles away, his head drooping as he goes.

Warren unnecessarily tightens his hold on me. "Are you okay?"

"Loaded question," I say numbly, my eyes still on the deflated Seth walking away. We're bonded by common tragedy, yet somehow strangers, miles of unspoken words between us.

I'm sorry.

I hate you.

I blame you.

I blame myself.

"Are you hurt?" Warren asks.

"Again, with the loaded questions," I sigh.

"Com'ere," he says, guiding my head to his shoulder.

Warren always hugs me as though he fears I'll fall to pieces if he lets me go. I think I'm afraid of that, too.

May

"One more!" Hannah pleads. "Gus with the Mitchells. All of you."

Warren and his parents gather around me as Aunt Hannah takes another dozen pictures. The grand total probably nearing five hundred.

With her phone *finally* pocketed, we all breathe a collective sigh of relief, and she attacks me with a fierce hug.

"I'm so proud of you," she says in my ear. "You look so beautiful, and I'm so *freaking* proud of you."

"Thank you," I whisper, surrendering completely to her hug, closing my eyes. My graduation cap slides off and falls to the ground.

"You know he's proud of you, too."

I cringe, my entire body tensing. The moment ruined, I pull away and pick up my cap.

The Mitchells and Fosters circle together for friendly conversation. Dale stands off to the side, disinterested in the whole affair. He showed up, though, which is more than I expected from him in the first place.

"I thought it was a lovely tribute," Mrs. M says.

"Absolutely," Hannah agrees. "I couldn't stop crying."

"Oh, not a dry eye in the house," Ryan chimes in, then they all pause to reflect.

I'd bowed my head and closed my eyes during the *In Memoriam,* refusing to peek. I know one day, somewhere, somehow, something will trigger me, and the dam will break, and the tears will fall. I don't know if a slideshow set to "If I Ever Leave This World Alive" (which Benny would have loved) would've proved the offending trigger, but I wasn't risking it. Not in a crowded gymnasium.

We gather in the Mitchells' backyard for a BBQ—everyone except Dale, which comes as a relief. The Fosters stay for burgers and dessert but leave for Hermiston before it gets dark. Hannah cries and takes twenty more pictures before making it from the backyard to the car. I send her away with a massive hug and a false promise to visit. How could I make that drive without Benny when we'd sworn to go together?

Long after Mr. and Mrs. Mitchell have gone inside, Warren and I sit near the fire pit, cuddled together under a blanket to keep the bugs away. *Congrats, Grad!* balloons bump together in the breeze. A brick of beef, potato salad, cake, and roasted marshmallows settles in my stomach. Wood smoke fills my lungs, and Warren's heartbeat provides a steady rhythm alongside the night music of crackling embers and crickets.

It's perfect. And it's perfectly horrid. The end of something I prayed would never come. But it's been nagging me for days, and I know I can't keep doing this. The longer I let it go on, the more the Band-Aid will hurt when I rip it off.

"I got you a present," Warren says.

An icy noose of self-loathing tightens around my chest. "You shouldn't have."

"But I *wanted* to." He kisses my hair. "Wait here."

He bounds across the yard with the athleticism of an Olympian, grabs a box from the picnic table, and returns, his breathing steady and controlled, as though he hasn't even moved. He hands me the box, beaming.

"Here."

"You're fascinating, you know that?"

"Just open it, Gus," he says, then plants a sweet kiss on my cheek before retaking his seat next to mine.

I bite my lip, reluctantly tearing into the gift. A new media player, charged and ready, sits inside. At my touch, the screen lights up, revealing already made playlists.

"Ren," I gasp, scrolling.

Angsty Gus

Cheerful Gus

Lyrical Gus

"For when you're ready to dance again," he says. "I think some of these will make killer solos."

"That ship has sailed," I say, meeting his heavy, hopeful eyes. "This is incredibly sweet. I can't even imagine the time you put into this. But I don't think..." I sigh, letting my forehead drop against his arm. "You're *so* sweet."

"There's more," he says, gently lifting my chin. "The last playlist."

My thumb swipes at the screen until I reach a dead end.

Benny's

Something balloons inside me, threatening to explode against the warm night air. "Ren? Wha...?"

"I found them when I dug around on your computer last month. There were some he uploaded from his phone, too. Poorer sound quality, but still amazing. You're singing with him on a couple."

I drop the media player back in the box, rub my hands against my forehead. "I said I wasn't ready," I say, my voice fading with every word. "I'm not..."

"Gus, listen." His hands envelop mine. "I know you aren't ready now. But one day, you will be. And you'll *want* those. Even if they hurt a little." I release a sharp, throaty laugh. "Okay, even if they hurt a *lot*," he revises.

I shake my head, looking at the box. "That's his *voice* on there."

"Yes, Gus. He's there."

I sit with this revelation for a long pause. Benny's voice is there for me to hear, should I choose to listen. Benny's *music* is there—something I've missed so intensely... No. Not missed. Something more. More than longing, more than desperation, more than agony. I've been wasting away without Benny, despite the love surrounding me. Despite Warren, his parents, Ryan, Hannah, Sam... They're all guiding lights in the darkness. But Benny was the sun. And the moon. And stars. And gravity. And without him, I'm floating away into a void.

"Warren, I..." I swallow, take a slow, deep breath. "Thank you. So much. You're seriously the most thoughtful person alive. And the best friend anyone could hope for." I swallow again, pulling my hands away from his. Readjusting in my seat, I wring my hands and close my eyes, trying desperately to summon even an ounce of courage.

It's been creeping up on me over the last few weeks. Why I say *I love you* so frequently, and why I don't feel completely right saying it. I hadn't been trying to convince *him*, but myself. Because while I love him as the same Warren he's always been, and it's even deeper and more significant now, it's not enough.

"Friend?" he asks, audibly offended. "I'm the best *friend* you could hope for. But not the best *boyfriend*."

I finally force myself to meet his disappointed eyes. That noose around my heart feels more like a grenade now, detonating inside me.

"What's happening here, August?"

"You have to know," I say, "I wanted to be her so badly. I wanted to be the *one* for you. I wanted it more than anything." My face flushes, and I press my hands to my chest. "I *prayed* for it, Ren. And I haven't prayed for anything since... And I *prayed* for you and me to be right together. For you to be the one for me. And you are, in so many ways. But not the right ones. I'm bleeding you dry, and I can't do that to you anymore. I have to let you save the good stuff for someone who will actually know how to be with you all the ways I can't."

I take a slow, deliberate breath, awaiting a well-deserved reprimand.

The fire pops and hisses as Warren's lips twitch. His eyes mist over. "How long have you known?" he asks.

"I've suspected for a while, but I didn't know—"

"How long is a *while?*" He sniffles, wiping at his eyes.

"Warren..." I reach my hand out for his, and it dangles in midair, waiting for him to accept it or shove me away. After a brief hesitation, he clutches my trembling fingers. "Ren, I knew today. I knew at graduation. And I've been fighting with myself ever since, because I love you, and I want to love you in *all* the ways. And if I'd kept my blinders on, I might have gotten there. But what the hell kind of person would I be if I held you back because I'm terrified of being alone?"

Warren wipes away more tears. "I wanted to believe it was finally happening. I wanted to believe it was real." He coughs, shakes his head. "Talk about blinders."

"No, this is my fault, Warren. All mine. I've been so selfish. You really have been—still are—my everything. I never set out to hurt you." An aftershock of self-loathing surges through me. "Ren, what I wouldn't give if it meant never hurting you. I would never have kissed you if it wasn't the strongest impulse I'd ever had in my life. I wanted it—wanted *you*—more than anything. And I'm so sorry I ruined it. Because, Ren..." I wait for his gaze to meet mine, then squeeze his hand. "You're the most important person I have now. And if I've driven you away..."

"Hey, now." He sighs, adjusting his chair closer. "You're not the only one who's been selfish. I knew. Deep down." He rakes a hand through his hair. "You can't take all the blame."

"Are we going to get through this?" I ask, knowing I don't deserve the answer I'm hoping for. "I mean, if you need some time away... If you're angry and need space, I'll understand. I swear. I just need to know we're not ruined forever."

"Not forever," he says, frowning. "But temporarily—I think—we might be a little...fractured."

Direct hits, every last word. I deserve them all and worse. "I'm so sorry. You have to know..."

He shakes his head, sniffling. "I do. Doesn't make it hurt any less."

"I'll give you time," I say, standing to leave. "I promise not to be crazy and needy for a while."

"Don't make promises you can't keep." I think he means this as a quip, but it comes out as an accusation—a fair one, at that.

I stand frozen near the fire pit, smoke burning my eyes.

"Don't forget this." Warren places the box in my hands. My little piece of Benny I'm not sure I'll ever bring myself to embrace. "Gus?"

"Huh?"

"Are you doing that thing?"

"Huh?" My legs are already wobbling. My head is fuzzy.

"You know, where you stop breathing instead of crying? I'll drive you home."

"No, I'm giving you space. Remember? No crazy." I wheeze between words, tucking my hair behind my ears with shaky fingers. "Go inside. I'll pull myself together. I promise." I feign a smile he probably doesn't believe and take a seat back in the folding fabric chair. He disappears into the house, and I watch as the fire fizzles and dies.

🎧

Isolate myself from everyone but Warren for months. Check.

Jump into a relationship I wasn't ready for...*with* Warren. Check.

Break Warren's heart—and what's left of mine. Check, and check.

I'm a one-woman shit show, and I don't think I can even begin to clean up this mess. Can I ever atone for these sins? What am I even doing with my life anymore? Didn't I force myself to go on living in an attempt to do the *right* thing? To be the person Benny would have wanted me to be? *Epic fail, Gus. Way to go.*

Ryan and Hannah begged me to live with them; I'd turned them down. The Mitchells offered me a home; I'd said no. I'd stayed behind in this broken house with my broken father to satisfy some self-manifested standard, needing to do as Benny would have done. But Benny wouldn't have just *stayed*. He would have lived. He would have helped. What have I done besides ruin the only friendship I have left in this world?

Help me, Benny. Help me do this.

I plug my earbuds into my new media player. I start with the playlists Warren's made for me. First *Cheerful*. The selections elicit something resembling amusement, and I can't help but bob along, tapping my foot to the beat. After a few songs, I switch to *Angsty*, and it hurts how well Warren knows me. I wonder if we'll ever be close again. These songs are exactly the kinds of melodies I'd blast at the studio when I needed to blow off steam. I can imagine I'm there now, and my body instinctively sways to the music. My movements grow fuller, more complex. By the second chorus of the second song, I'm turning and leaping around the room. My bedroom, unfortunately, isn't meant for expressive dance, and I smack my ankle against my dresser in the middle of a double attitude.

My eye catches the last playlist—*Benny's*.

I can do this. I should do this. I can do this. But at the mere thought of pressing play, my hands sweat and tremble.

At the slam of the front door, I jump, throwing the player and my headphones across the room. They land on the tangled mess of sheets and pillows atop my mattress.

Dale's fuming about a difficult client as he storms through the house, then roots around in the kitchen, finding any excuse to slam a door.

"August," he yells. "The hell are you?"

I take a calming breath before meeting him in the kitchen.

"You could have been there," he shouts, grabbing a beer from the fridge. "You could have helped. I can't do *everything* by myself." He takes a swig. "You ever go'n do anything useful, or do you expect to hold up in your room the rest of your life, contributing nothing to this family?"

"I can help," I say, almost eagerly. "I was gonna take a summer job, but I can come to the garage instead."

"Well, then." He coughs, belches, then disappears into his room.

I can do this. Help Dale. Work with him. Maybe, just maybe, patch things between us a little. Instead of hurting the people I love deeply, I could try to love Dale again, the way Benny did. The way he would have wanted me to. Working with Dale can be my atonement. My way to set it right.

Chapter 20

September

True to my word, I've given Warren space. We text, but our conversations are shallow. Every time I've suggested maybe getting together for a movie or a taco or a stupidly expensive coffee, he's had a reason to turn me down. Work. Baseball meeting. Training. Class. Under the weather. I'm sure he makes a constant, conscious effort to avoid me on campus; otherwise, I would have bumped into him by now.

I don't blame him, but I miss him. And every day without him in my life—*really* in my life—eats away another bit of my soul. I'm Swiss cheese, wobbling around aimlessly, desperate for my friend but too pathetic to fix it.

I still help Dale a couple of days a week, as my class schedule allows, but it's mended nothing. For a delusional minute, I'd thought we were leaving the darkness behind us. But by mid-July, he'd started screaming at me again. In early-August, he slapped me during a drunken lecture, and by the time classes started, I was back to skulking in shadows, afraid in my own home.

Today, when I show up to help with invoices, he throws me out, claiming I screwed up yesterday. A client stormed in upset because she was overbilled by hundreds of dollars. I wasn't even here yesterday, and I'm pretty sure he knows that. No way it was my mistake.

Rather than screaming at him openly—like I want to—I leave without a word and drive to the grocery store.

Chocolate. I want chocolate. The good, pure milk chocolate chips that cost three times what any reasonable person should spend on chocolate chips. I stomp toward the baking aisle an emotional, fuming wreck. I hate Dale's resorted back to punishing me for everything. I hate I've ruined things with Warren. I hate how Warren has taken such lengths to avoid me for over *three* months. I hate everything today, and I know chocolate won't fix it, but it'll make me momentarily satiated, and I'll take it.

Or not, because they are *out* of the good stuff. The nerve! My fingers run through my thick hair and clutch loose strands. "Are. You. Freaking. Kidding me?" The words muttered through clenched teeth, intended only for me.

"Can I help you find something?" An employee asks dutifully. I'm fully prepared to walk away without a response. "Oh. August. Hi."

With an irritated breath, I tilt my head, meeting his gaze. "You." Seth. Tall and blonde and in my way with no chocolate chips. Stupid Seth. "You work here, now?"

"Since graduation, yeah. Taking a *gap* year, or whatever."

"Good for you," I breathe, not bothering to feign interest. "Bye." I turn away, take a few steps.

"W-wait," he stammers. I halt. "Can I help you find something?"

I roll my eyes as I turn around, mulling over exactly *which* snarky comeback to use, but when I meet Seth's eyes, I freeze. He's not the same guy who asked me out on his first day of school or made cracks about dancing or Warren. Nor is he the empty guy who'd limped around for months after the accident. He's someone *new*. Why? Why does *he* get to change and do things like take *gap* years? What's so special about him?

"Hello? August? Is there something I could check on for you?" His eyes are soft, his brow puzzled. "What do you need?"

"I need my brother back," I spit coldly. "Can you do that for me?" He hangs his head, and I flee.

I'm almost to my truck when I hear him calling for me, his feet pounding against the pavement. "August, wait." *Nope.* "Please, wait! I'm begging you!"

"*What?*" I scream, turning around.

He stops a few feet from me. "Could you just listen for a sec? I want to tell you—"

I don't even understand what I'm doing until it's too late. I punch him. *Punch.* Not slap. My clenched fist pounds against his nose, and it hurts. So. Bad. *Ohmygosh, I think I broke my hand!* But on the outside, I stand stoic, my breaths only slightly exaggerated.

He stares, wide-eyed, his hand over his nose. I walk to my truck and drive away, numb.

❦

IT SINKS IN GRADUALLY, the gravity of what I've done. For a few days, I float around on a strange high. Then, little by little, regret gathers, looming over me. It pushes me down to earth bit by bit until, a week later, I'm a guilty mess.

I'm sitting in the student union building, ignoring a stack of assignments and wondering how I can ever apologize to Seth, when a tap on the table startles me.

"Hey, Gus."

Warren! Something like hope or joy swells inside when I look up to see his freckled face smiling down at me. I stand, asking, "Can I hug you?"

He answers by wrapping his arms around me. I squeeze back fiercely.

"You can always hug me," he says into my ear.

"Good," I whisper. He holds me tighter, lifting me so my feet hover above the ground. "Damn, I missed you."

He sets me down, breaking the hug. "I missed you, too."

"Do you still hate me?" I ask, almost panicked.

He gestures for me to sit, taking the seat across from me.

"I never hated you," he says. "I needed time to process, and I'm glad I took it."

"Are you okay now?" I suppress the urge to take his hand like old times.

"Yeah," he says, nodding. "Mostly. I mean, when I *really* thought about it, I realized I wasn't mad at you at all. I was mad at *me*. I shouldn't have ever let us go there. You were so vulnerable. But so was I, honestly, and I wanted it to happen, so I let it. I'm not sorry it happened—not even a little. You should know I regret absolutely nothing."

My cheeks flush. "I don't either," I admit. "Not really."

"Am I sad it's over? Well, yeah." He smiles, shrugs. "Gus, I won't lie. It hurt like hell. But I understand it better now, and I'm okay. And I miss you, and you're important to me, so can we just be over it? Please?"

My lips stretch until my cheeks hurt. "Absolutely."

He nods. "Excellent."

"I punched Seth," I whisper, my smile still stupidly wide. "It hurt. *So* bad!"

Warren squints, tilting his head. "I'm sorry, *what*?"

"I *totally* punched him. I jammed my finger." I point to a yellowing bruise on my swollen index finger. Unsure how to respond, Warren stares, his mouth gaping. "Time away was good for me, too," I admit, backtracking the conversation. "I leaned on you for so long; I needed to learn to stand on my own again. I suck at it, but I'm getting there."

"But clearly not there *yet* if you're going around punching people."

"Not people. A person. One. Seth. And sure, it was a bad call—"

"Oh, no, I think it's awesome. Honestly, I'm jealous. I've wanted to punch the dude more than once, myself. But it's not like you."

"Maybe not. But I did it. And that's not the point, anyway. I just mean I had to deal. It was good for me to have to deal. Alone. Without anyone grounding me. I breathe a little easier. You know?"

"Okay, then."

"What else is new with you? Still working at the movie theater?"

"Yeah, part-time now."

"Will you sneak me in for free midnight movies, sometimes?"

He shrugs. "Maybe."

"Do you work every flipping night and weekend?"

"Not necessarily. In the summer, I did. But they go a little easier on me now with my class schedule. We typically rotate taking night and matinee shifts on weekends."

"Meaning, the chances of hanging out this weekend are...?"

"I'd say it's looking pretty good," he says, grinning.

"Fan*tastic*." The ice thawed, the war over, I can breathe again.

Dear August,

I can't tell you what it means to me that you continue to indulge this old woman with your letters. Phone calls and texting are modern, thoroughly efficient wonders, yes. But there's something about a hand-written letter. It holds a certain magic, especially coming from someone I love so much as you.

If you ask Sam, letters are an unnecessary waste of time. Your texts, however, are everything to him. I can't tell you what an improvement I've seen in Sam since you two started communicating regularly again. He's a little more his old self. It's made my Mama Heart happy. I still long for the days before, but I'm grateful for the balance we are finding in the now.

Life is so unpredictable, and we never know what twists or turns await us, or what mysterious way God will choose to work in next. All we can do is hold on for dear life, thank Him for every day, and take nothing for granted. You, my love, know this more than anyone, don't you? Tomorrow is not promised, which is why I'm so thrilled to hear you've reconciled with Warren. I knew you two could figure it out. Breakups are so painful and confusing. The way you two have come back together is a rare and beautiful gift. I pray you treasure it always.

We hope you'll still come for Thanksgiving this year, but we understand if it's too hard. Maybe we should visit you? Please advise.

Thank you for being my pen pal. You are a bright spot in my world, August.

Love,
Aunt Hannah

HAVING Warren back in my life has been fresh air in my lungs. I'm trying to treasure every moment and view it like the rare and precious gift Aunt Hannah calls it. But something else in her letter troubles me. *Tomorrow is not promised.* I *do* know this. Better than many people ever will. It's why my previous encounter with Seth weighs so heavily on me. I punched him, walked away, and made zero attempts to reconcile. I've been cold. Heartless.

My media player stares at me from my desk, burning into my conscience. *Benny.* I've tried to listen to his songs so many times, but every time I go to hit *play,* my fingers refuse.

"What would you do, Benny?" It's a pointless question; I know exactly what Benny would do. And maybe I can't bring myself to listen to him because I know my actions have betrayed his memory.

I've given up on Dale. I nearly burned my bridge to Warren. I've not kept in contact with Millie when I know how badly he wanted us to be friends. And Seth? I've worn my hatred like a shield. Or worse, a badge.

Abandoning two Spanish assignments, one math practice test, and a three-page paper on *The Things They Carried,* I leave the campus library and start driving. I'm not even certain I'm doing this—really doing this—until I park in front of his house.

I'm frozen in the driver's seat, my hands permanently affixed to the steering wheel. My knuckles whiten. I watch the house for signs of life. "This is stupid," I mumble to myself. "He's probably not even here. What am I *doing*?"

I shake out my hands, reach for the key, and I'm fully ready to turn my truck back on and drive away when Seth steps out of the house. He walks down the porch steps onto the grass, eyes on my Sierra the entire time. *Busted.*

With a heavy sigh, I exit the truck and walk toward him. He holds his hands up defensively.

"I come in peace," I sigh. *I think.*

He crosses his arms over his chest. "Why are you here, August?"

"Guilt. Shame. I don't know. Something."

"Something?"

"Don't rush me! I'm growing a conscience, okay. It *sucks*."

His shoulders shake as he releases a quiet laugh. "Tell me about it."

"You recently grow one, too?" I ask, snarkier than intended. "Sorry. That sounded less horrible in my head."

"I think you're allowed to be a little horrible to me." His eyes downcast, his shoulders slumped, he kicks the toe of his sneakers against the grass. My heart plummets at the sight of this familiar gesture.

"It wasn't your fault." I yell the words across the lawn, desperate to expel them. They've been stuck so long, choking me. Closing a little distance between us, I try again, softer. "It wasn't your fault, Seth. This horrible thing happened to *both* of us. I've blamed you, hated you, and used you as a convenient target for my pain, which is just...despicable. I'm so sorry."

I search Seth for visible signs of shock, acceptance, anger, anything. There's nothing.

"Benny wouldn't have blamed you," I continue. "He would've

recognized a shared tragedy and *helped* you. Actually, he'd probably be your best friend by now." I chew on my lip, wringing my hands. "But me? I've shunned you. I've shunned everyone. I haven't *coped.*" There's that word again. "I need to move on, at least a little. Enough to see beyond a useless, undeserved grudge."

Seth stands before me a blank canvas, offering no readable emotion. He's not making this easy, which is no less than I deserve after all I've put him through. With a heavy sigh, I finish what I started.

"I can't claim to understand what you've been through, Seth. I've never even *tried* to put myself in your shoes. But if you're carrying any guilt over the accident, I hope you can let it go. I don't blame you. I never really did. You shouldn't walk around with the weight of this for the rest of your life."

I put my hand to my chest, drawing in a long, dramatic breath. It's done. I've said the words. Out *loud. Phew.*

"You," he starts softly. The thought remains unfinished as he shakes his head.

"What?" I prod.

He tugs at his face, licks his lips.

"What is it, Seth?"

"You're such a hypocrite," he says through gritted teeth.

"I'm *sorry?*"

"You want to talk about survivor's guilt? You've got it worse than I do." He clenches his fists, his voice growing in intensity as he continues. "Don't come here and tell me what *I* need to do when you can't even figure your own shit out."

Spit flies from his mouth with his last sentiment. I draw back, nearly tripping over my feet. The ever-growing pit in my stomach now tied in knots, I think I might vomit all over Seth's front lawn.

"Wh-wha...?" I stammer, never finishing the thought.

"We *both* lived. We *both* went to that funeral thinking, 'It should have been me.'"

My jaw slackens. "Wait. How were you...?"

"In a wheelchair." He rakes his hands through his hair. "I waited in the hall. But that's not the point. We both wake up every morning knowing we won't ever see him again. And if it makes me feel like hell, I can't even imagine how guilty I'd feel if I'd been in the same car with him. If he'd been my best friend. If he had been my family. If he had been my b-brother." His eyes swimming, he puts his hand to his chest, works his fingers back and forth. "You are *drowning* in it, August. You're barely alive at all." His first tears fall, and he wipes them away, clearing his throat.

"You know, everyone said such horrible things about you for not crying at the funeral. They called you *emotionless*—a robot. And every time I heard someone say garbage like that, my first thought wasn't, *wow, what an asshole.* It was, *what a freakin' idiot.* Tears aren't sorrow's only companion, August, and you're not as numb as you want everyone to think. While you've locked the world away, I've watched you. Anyone watching—anyone actually paying attention would see how you blame yourself and hate yourself every minute of every day. So why can't I do the same? Who are you to tell me to forgive myself? Couldn't we both blame ourselves and hate ourselves for the rest of our lives? Wouldn't that be fair? Wouldn't that be even?"

This unexpected outburst leaves me speechless, anchored to Seth's lawn, though there's no reason to stay. I spoke my piece, and Seth spat in my face. End of story. *Just go, August!* Yet, there I stand, jaw agape, stomach turning, chest tightening, struggling to process what just happened. I just poured my heart into an apology, and Seth had the gall to yell at me?

A fury rises inside, so intense I think my face has turned to literal flames. Maybe that's why my head is pounding so hard right now, why everything burns.

Seth steps forward, his mouth moving, but his words sound wrong, like I'm underwater. "August, *breathe.*" He squeezes my shoulders. "Breathe!"

Air stings my dry throat as I draw a sharp breath. I hunch over, resting my hands on my thighs, trying to find a steady rhythm again.

"Good," he says, a hand on my back. "How you doin'? You okay?"

I release a dark, abrupt laugh. "How am I *doing*?" I shove his arm away as I stand tall. "You're joking, right? I thought you could read me, Seth. I thought you knew *everything*."

He swallows, pressing his lips into a tight line.

"You have *no* idea what..." I grasp an invisible ball in front of me, strangle it, and release an ugly growl. "He wasn't my *brother*, Seth. He was my *twin*! A literal part of me. And he's gone forever. I'm *twinless*. Did you know that's an actual word? I didn't. But I do now. I'm twinless. And it's literal Hell. How dare you stand there and talk about *losing* him as if you actually knew him. You barely know me. And you *don't* get to lecture me on my feelings. No."

I shove my hands against his chest, and he stumbles into the porch railing.

"Of course, I wish it hadn't been Benny," I say, my voice fading in and out over the hot coals in my throat. "He was so much better than me—than *all* of us. You don't even know the half of his heart. But you're wrong about something, too." I take a single, shaky step toward him. "I don't wake up every day thinking it should have been me. I wake up every day *wishing* it were *you*." I shudder at my words, wishing I could pluck them from the air and shove them deep down inside me, where he never would've heard them. "Oh, gosh." I slap my hand over my mouth, turning away, staggering toward my truck.

"What happened to forgiving him, Gigi?" I freeze at the beautiful phantom voice. I know it's impossible, but still, I glance around. He's nowhere. It was a fluke—a trick of my cruel, stupid mind.

"He's right, August. You can't keep torturing yourself."

I shut my eyes, shaking my head. *No. This is* not *happening right now. I'm dreaming.* This must be a dream, or a full-blown hallucination. Yes. A nervous breakdown. I'm officially psychotic, and none of this is real.

"I love you, Gus Gus." The voice lingers, haunting me.

"Stop it!" I scream, my hands over my ears. "Stop!"

"Be happy," Benny's voice says conclusively.

Muddled, incoherent noises leak through my gaping mouth.

"August?"

"Stop it!" I squeeze my eyes shut. "Stop!"

Seth stands behind me, hands clutching my shoulders. I jump against his touch, shrieking.

"It's okay," he says. But it's not okay—none of it.

"Benny!" My hands slide from my ears and pound against my chest, attempting to beat back down all the feelings I've worked so hard to bury. They're all exploding to the surface, looking for air, thrashing against my skin and bones in a desperate surge. "Come back," I croak, looking toward the Heaven I hope exists.

"August, are you with me?"

"It hurts," I say, my hand still on my chest. And because it's true, and I have no other words, I say it again. "It *hurts*."

Unsteady on my feet, I sink my knees into the dewy grass. Cradling my head in my hands, I notice a foreign moisture on my face. "No," I mutter, touching both eyes. *Damp.* With my *tears. My* tears? No. "No! This isn't... I *never* cry!"

Seth kneels, taking me in his arms. "Oh, August," he says, his voice breaking.

Ten years of repression igniting at once, a mangled sob escapes my throat. Then another, and another, until I'm hysterical. Tears and snot coat my skin as I struggle to understand what's happening.

Seth cradles me back and forth. "You can let it out," he says gently, "but I need you to breathe."

I'm faintly aware of hands fumbling over me, reaching into my pockets, then Seth is talking again, but not to me.

"No, it's Seth," I hear. "I can't explain, but you need to get here. Now."

I don't know how long I've been crying. Probably hours, but it feels like days. I'm balled up on the Mitchells' living room couch, awkwardly leaning against Warren as I sob and sniff, gasp and wheeze, a mess of used tissues on the cushions and floor.

Anytime there's a lull in my hysterics, Mrs. Mitchell puts a straw in my mouth, urging me to take a sip of water. Warren asks, "What can I do?" Then I lose it again. About the fifth time this happens, Mrs. M brings me a pill.

"What are you giving her?" Warren asks.

"None of your business," she answers.

"I'm s-sorry..." I try. She shushes me, sticks the pill in my mouth, and orders me to swallow.

"Sleep, honey. We'll still be here in the morning, and we'll talk then."

It's still dark when I wake up with my head on Warren's stomach and a sharp pain in my neck. The longer I adjust to consciousness, the more *everything* hurts. My body's involuntary response to new lucidness—a long, drawn-out inhale and stretching of extremities—causes a slight moan of pain to break the silence of the early morning.

Warren flinches. "What's wrong?" he hurries, groggy but ready to spring into action.

I pat a hand against his chest. "Shhh. Go back to sleep."

He relaxes back into the couch, then stretches. I push myself to sitting, rolling my head and rubbing my neck. My legs are cramped and achy from sleeping in an awkward ball all night. I slide onto the ground into a side split. I gradually walk my hands forward, and my cold, tense muscles begin to normalize.

"Geez," Warren says. I can hear his grimace. "Save some flexibility for the rest of us, Gus."

"Get some sleep, Ren. I'm fine."

"You're not fine."

I shake out my legs before transitioning into a butterfly stretch. "No, I'm not fine. Not remotely. I had a full-blown meltdown last night, Warren. Psychotic break level meltdown."

"I know," he says, raising his brows. "I was there."

"Shut up," I grumble through a weak laugh. It hurts. I rub at my throat, then at my temples.

"Headache?" I offer a subtle nod in response, and he stands. "Hang on," he says, already out of the room. He returns with pain relievers and a giant glass of water.

"Bless you," I sigh, accepting the gifts. He sits on the end of the couch and stares at me intently. "What?"

"Gus, what *happened*?"

I down the entire glass of water before attempting an explanation. "So hear me out..." I chew my lip, then sigh. "I heard his voice, Ren. Like it was a real, tangible thing. Like if I stretched out my hand, he'd take it. He was *there*, but he wasn't."

Warren tilts his head, his doubtful frown looming over me. "Wait. *What*?"

I rehash my conversation with Seth and try again. "I said all these horrible things. And then, as I was ready to leave, not even bothering to try and apologize or take it back, there he was. Or at least, it *sounded* like he was there."

"Benny?"

"No, Kanye West. *Yes, Benny*! Keep up."

"Gus, I don't know what I'm even trying to keep up with right now. I mean, what you're saying..."

"Is certifiably insane? Yeah, I'm well aware. But you saw." I point to my eyes, no doubt bloodshot. "Niagara Falls, dude. Those were *legit* tears."

"Clearly."

"Okay, so... How would you explain it?"

"Explain *what*?" He throws his hands up.

"Any of it! I snapped, Warren. I'm broken, now."

Mrs. Mitchell comes into the living room, stares down at me, and winces. "Mercy, child. You wake up that limber? I need three cups of coffee before I can raise my arms above my head."

Warren and I both humor her with a grin, a chuckle.

"You laugh," she says, sitting on the couch. "Wait and see. It's all fun and games until you sleep on the wrong pillow and can't walk for a week."

"So," I start, my lips twitching, my cheeks flush. "I was telling Warren..." But now I'm staring at this sensible woman, and I can't say the words out loud. I'm an idiot. This is stupid. I'm stupid. None of this makes any sense, and I'll look like a lunatic. She'll have me committed. She'll never allow me in her home again.

"She heard Benny's voice," Warren says softly, still staring at me. "Anyone would have cried, Gus. Anyone."

"I'm not anyone," I say, my voice a high-pitched whisper, my eyes burning. "I *never* cry." The tears sliding down my hot cheeks make a liar out of me.

Mrs. Mitchell scoots onto the floor, groaning a little. She guides my head onto her lap, brushing my hair back from my face.

"Sometimes," I blubber, "I see him in my dreams. And I ask him —scream at him—if he's coming back. And he just *stares* at me. He can't be bothered to say anything. Then, last night..." I lose it again, wiping my snot away with my shirt. "What is *wrong* with me?"

"Nothing," Mrs. M soothes. "You're human, honey. And you're learning how to be human *all* over again since Benny passed. While also trying to become an adult. The pressure you're under..."

"So, this is me cracking under pressure?" I spit, then sniffle. Wipe my face again. "I'm pathetic."

"Stop it." Warren's voice is a contrast to the calm support of his mother. "August, look at me."

I sit up, wipe my face again, and sniffle as I push my raven rat's nest out of my face. "*What?*"

"You are *not* pathetic." His elbows propped on his knees, his eyes glowing, he leans toward me until his face is so close I can taste his breath. "You are strong. You are smart. You are a talented, fierce *badass*."

"Language," Mrs. M interjects without conviction.

"You've had to be strong for everyone else your entire life. Last night was Benny telling you to knock it off, and let it go, and take care of *you*."

"He was *scolding* me for being a bi—" I remember my audience. "For being horrible. I said some unconscionable things, Warren. If you'd have been there…"

"I wasn't. But clearly, someone else was."

"And what? He's been here this whole time and chose *then* to say something about it? Then floated away? Gee, thanks, bro."

"Maybe this was the push you needed to move on and finally do something besides walk around in your guilt bubble, hating yourself. It's been almost—"

"I *know* how long it's been!" Ten months now. Nearly a year.

"Okay, so you should also know that's a *long* time to walk on eggshells. You try not to talk about him. You rarely say his name out loud. You don't look at pictures or listen to his music. You're avoiding your grief, Gus. You're not—"

"Coping? Thanks for the reminder." Mrs. M puts her hand on my back, and my shoulders relax. "Sorry," I sigh, releasing some of my frustration. None of this is Warren's fault, and I need to stop being a total shrew. "You're right. This is karma. This is the weight…" I take a large, unexpected breath, shuddering as I release it. "This is the weight of all my lies catching up and crushing me." I've run from my grief too long, and now I'm paying for it. "Where's my truck?" I ask, standing. "Still at Seth's?"

"We brought it here for you," Mrs. M says. "But you shouldn't be driving right now."

"No. I shouldn't. I should be somewhere else entirely."

S<small>OMEHOW</small>, I remember exactly where his grave is. I'd planned to wander aimlessly until I found it. Because coward that I am, I haven't returned here since we buried him. And yet, wrapped in the old, faded comforter I keep in my truck, leaves on the dewy ground squishing under my feet, I walk directly to his place. My blanket providing a barrier between the wet grass and the jeans I've been wearing since yesterday, I take a seat beside his stone, which simply reads *Beloved Son and Brother*. That's it. That's all we gave him in death. I hadn't been aware, generous, or clever enough to think of anything else. What else could I have said? Something inspiring or spiritual? *Gone too soon. Didn't get a chance to peak. Died a painful death. Left his sister twinless, the jerk.*

"Geez, August," I mutter to myself. "Pull it together." Why is morbid humor so easy for me while legit emotions send me running?

My fingers trace the lines of the inscription. I brush away a few patches of caked-on dirt. I take a deep breath, wrapping the blanket tighter around me, despite its greasy, stagnant smell.

"So," I say, staring at his gravestone. "Hi. Been a while, I know. But here I am." My eyes swim. "I cry now. But you know this already because you're responsible. Even in death, you're crafty. You orchestrated this whole thing, wore me down until the flood gates opened. But did you have to choose that exact moment? Did Seth *have* to be the one to witness my meltdown? Seems rather cruel, man. Even for you."

I sniffle, wiping my nose with the dirty blanket. *Gross. Wash this thing occasionally, August.*

"I don't get it, Benny," I blurt, my breaths labored. "I don't understand why I'm here, why you're not. I hate it, and it pisses me off. You said you wouldn't leave me. *Did you think I would leave you crying?*" I choke on the lyrics, pause for a breath. "Remember? Wasn't it a symbol of something? How you'd never leave me? You went back on the deal, Benjamin! You cheated! And don't even get me started on *you*, God." I wipe my face again, blubbering at the sky. "Does it hurt you at *all*, knowing you ignored me and took him and left me here to deal with all of this by *myself*? Or am I collateral, meaningless damage?"

I muffle my cries into the blanket until I've pulled myself back from the ledge a little. Readjusting, I lie on the grass and rest my head atop a makeshift pillow. I place my hand on the base of his stone and caress it.

"I don't know how you expect me to do it, Benjamin. Especially not now, after this." I gesture to my wet face, cursing my tears. "I hate every minute of life without you." I continue caressing the stone lightly with my fingers. Then harder, and harder, until I've balled up my fist. I pound until my hand goes numb.

I rest next to him in silence, summoning the courage to pull out the tiny piece of technology tucked away in my pocket.

"I need your help, Benny," I whisper, putting my earbuds in and scrolling my thumb across the screen. "Help me remember how to breathe in and out every day. I'm suffocating here, man. I promise..." I pause, sighing. "I promise I'll visit more. And I'll listen to these. And I'll start..." a sharp cry releases, echoing through the graveyard. "I'll start talking about you again. I'll stop avoiding your name. I'll do better. But can you maybe help me out here?"

The sun is higher now, probably nearing noon; I turn my face to the warmth of the sky. Resting next to him, I force my finger to press *play* for the first time.

Chapter 21

OCTOBER

In the *before*, today was special. In the *after*, today is the literal worst. I visit Benny at his grave before the sun even rises. I stay for hours, crying openly, speaking with him when I have anything useful to say, and listening to his music on repeat. My favorite is his cover of Staind's "So Far Away". One of his favorites. *An oldie but a goodie,* he'd always called it. He's sped up the tempo and altered the time signature. His voice is smooth where Aaron Lewis's was gruff. It's perfect.

One of his original pieces, "Open Your Eyes", has a clear origin story.

> *What you're looking for, Old Man, you'll never find.*
> *So drunk and afraid, you can't open your eyes.*

Nothing subtle or veiled here. The more times I hear it, the more I question everything I ever believed about Benny's love for our father. Maybe it wasn't as durable or forgiving as I'd always thought. Maybe if he saw Dale as he was now... But he's not here to see Dale now, because of me.

It's well into the afternoon when I'm officially too cold and hungry to stay any longer. I leave Benny behind with a few parting promises and tears, retreating to my truck.

I turn my phone on to let Warren know I'm on my way over. We agreed neither of us was ready for any sort of "ceremony," but we could at least spend the day together, for whatever comfort that might be worth. The notifications on my phone go insane as it powers on and dread settles in. A multitude of texts, all from Warren.

I've tried calling... I screwed up, Gus. You're gonna hate me.

Got called into work. Left in a hurry and didn't leave anything unlocked. My parents are in Boise. I'm so sorry, Gus. I'm officially the worst friend alive.

You can come grab my housekey if you need somewhere safe. I'll be off by 9

Text me, at least, so I know you're okay

Happy birthday. For what it's worth. I'm so sorry, Gus. Really.

Somewhere *safe*. Whether he intended it or not, Warren has only sparked more conflict in my mind. Home hasn't felt safe in a long time. Not even before Benny left me there alone. But I could handle it; I *had* to handle it. Because otherwise, where did that leave Dale? And Benny always cared enough about Dale to try.

But then I hear that song, and I wonder if Benny had just been pretending all these years.

I text Warren—letting him know yes, I'm fine, and to let me know when he clocks out—before driving home. Dale's not there, so I don't hesitate to go inside and fix myself something to eat. I wander through the house as I take mindless bites of my grilled cheese, searching for any evidence a family once lived here. A few framed pictures of Benny and me, none of them recent. That's where it ends.

My heart and mind fight with my feet as I pad down the stairs toward the door that protects his sacred space. The room still smells a little like him. Just the faintest hint, but it's there. Enough to make me cry, enough to make me hesitate in the doorway before I force myself through it.

Despite his absence, I still sense his energy. Life abounds in this room—posters of his favorite bands on the walls. Song lyrics scribbled on post-its and scrap paper tacked sporadically around the room. Guitar picks and drumstick shards on the carpet. He's everywhere. And maybe that's the real reason I've never left.

Maybe more than anything, I couldn't leave him.

I trek back upstairs to my room, where the signs of life aren't so obvious. My dance shoes hang on the wall, the shadowbox from Benny still prominently displayed in the center. Beyond that, I haven't made a conscious effort to personalize my space in years. I've always just been *waiting* until I could move out and move on. Then, everything fell apart, and I gave up.

"What are you still doing here, August?" I ask myself quietly. "What is wrong with you?"

A slam of the front door reminds me exactly why I've stayed. What I've sacrificed, whether it's been worth it or not.

I make no noise but sit motionless on the bed, waiting to see where this goes. Heavy steps make their way to the kitchen. I catch snippets of slurred curses.

Sonofabitch...

Mind his own damned business...

Bastard...

No right to cut me off...

The fridge opens and closes, and the clinking of glass echoes down the hall. My tension eases as I hear his bedroom door slam, and I curl under the covers. I couldn't sleep at all last night, and I feel myself fading. But as soon as I close my eyes, my phone buzzes.

Warren: *Great news! The movies this week SUUUUCK and the theater was dead. I left. I've got something I need to do first, but then I can hang. Should I come get you?*

I feel almost giddy and have to remind myself not to make any sudden movements that might attract Dale's unwanted attention.

Me: *Yes. PLEASE! I'll be here. Park next door and wait for me. Dale's home.*

I can do this. I can get out of here. The window, maybe? But then

I remember I secured the old wooden-framed screen with about fifty nails over the summer. I binge-watched about twenty too many episodes of *Criminal Minds* during the dark period when Warren wasn't talking to me, then had a recurring nightmare someone snuck through my window and kidnapped me. The nails in the screen offered peace of mind, and the nightmares faded. But right now, they're keeping me trapped here in this real, waking nightmare where Matthew Gray Gubler is *not* about to burst through the door and save me with some well-timed psychological wisdom. Why not, Dr. Reid? Why not?

More importantly, why am I living somewhere I have to sneak in and out of at nineteen years old? *Seriously, August, what are you still doing here?*

An idea blossoms almost instantly. Maybe a stupid one. But it could work. The Mitchells had offered sanctuary once before. Though back then, it had been so different with Warren. He'd probably hate it if I moved in now. But I could ask, right? It wouldn't do any damage to *ask*.

"Dammit!" Dale's voice booms, then there's stomping, a clanking of keys.

He's leaving again? Already? It's go time.

This is my chance. I wait for the front door to close, wait for Dale to start up his pickup. But these things don't happen. There's a thud and a squeak. Then, after a long pause, muffled whimpers.

"Why?" he asks, over and over. "Why, God?"

Oh, Dale. Something inside me melts at the sound of this gruff old man sobbing through the wall. Wincing, I tentatively crack open my door, peering down the hallway and into the living room. He's a wrinkly, greasy lump on the floor, his tree trunk legs extended in front of him, feet limp inside his work boots. His hunched shoulders shake as he mumbles to himself. Bits and pieces reach my ears. *Stupid...selfish...why...makes no sense.*

I approach slowly, cautiously. "Dad?" He startles, then sobs, and reaches for my hand. "Oh, Dad," I sigh, accepting the gesture. His hand is rough and strong in mine, just as I remember it.

"He's gone, Goose," he laments. "My boy's gone."

"I know." I kneel next to him.

"It's his birthday today." Only *his* birthday.

"I know," I say. "I miss Benny so much."

This rattles him. He whips his hand back and meets me with venomous eyes.

"I don't just *miss* him! He was my son. Part of me! You couldn't possibly understand."

I know the smart move here. Leave. Get out, now, before this escalates. "You bastard," I exhale through clenched teeth. Guess today is not a sensible day. I stand, backing away from the broken man staring up at me with deer-in-the-headlights astonishment.

"*What* did you say to me?"

"What couldn't I possibly understand? Burying the one person in the world who understood me? Who loved me unconditionally? The person who *showed up*? It's no secret *you've* never been there for me. Ever. Benny was everything to me, and losing him nearly killed me, but I kept going. I may have sucked at it, but I've *tried*! What are you doing with your life, besides drinking it away and shouting bitter diatribes about the God who took your only boy when you've got a daughter right here in front of you?" My lips tremble. My teeth chatter. I know this was stupid, but it felt *right*, and it's almost a relief to have said it out loud.

The blind fury radiates from Dale. Giant warning lights and sirens practically whoosh around his head. I run for the front door, but his rage fuels his speed faster than my fear fuels mine. He catches me, grabbing my hair and pulling me back into a wall. I stumble into the entryway table, and my hand knocks the ceramic bowl full of keys, thumbtacks, and loose change onto the ground with a dissonant crash.

"You think we're done here?" Spit flies in my face as he threatens more.

"Let me go, Dad. You don't want me here anyway. You never have. I look too much like her, and I'm not good like he was, and you don't *want* me. So let me go!"

"Where would you go?"

"Anywhere. Anywhere else."

Dale runs a rough hand through his dirty, matted hair, turns, and shuffles a few steps toward his recliner.

"You'd leave me? Without a second thought?"

Oh, I've given it plenty of thought. But I keep still, silent, eyes shifting between the front door and my father fidgeting close by.

"You know, he used to at least pretend he needed me once in a while. He acted like I mattered. You've always shut me out."

"*What?* You're not even *remotely*—"

"I lost the wrong child!"

And there it is. I've imagined him saying it a hundred times. A million. I see it any time he looks at me. But this is the first time he's said it out loud.

"That boy," he sneers, "killed the wrong child."

I shake my head, squinting. "What boy? What are you talking about?"

"The accident. The other boy."

"Seth?"

He scowls. "You on friendly terms with the devil, are you?"

"Look, hate me all you want. But that truck put us in Seth's path. You *know* it wasn't his fault."

"Lawyer thinks I've got a good case for a civil suit against him," he grumbles, wiping his slobbery mouth.

"Lawyer? No, Dad. Don't. He's been through enough. *We've* been through enough."

He steps closer again. "*I* decide what's enough for me. I make the choices 'round here."

"You're unbelievable!" I shriek. "You're right; I can't tell you what to do. But I don't have to stick around to see how this plays out. I'm *gone.* Drink yourself to death if you want, asshole. I'm done caring about what happens to you."

I draw in a large, hurried breath, not sure it won't be my last. For a moment, in his stillness, I think I might walk away from this. But then his chest expands, and his eyes bulge, and I know I've dug my grave.

Reading the violence in his eyes, I flinch before the first blow lands. My fingers rub against my cheek, attempting to soothe the stinging skin, but he doesn't give me a chance to recover. Screaming indiscernible, drunken obscenities, he starts swinging his fists and doesn't let up until I've crumbled to the floor atop broken ceramic shards, hitting the corner of the table on the way down. I barely notice the jagged remnants breaking and burning my skin over the ringing in my head.

Though my body begs me to surrender, I force my hands underneath me, straining to sit up so I can hold my head high. Whatever comes next, I want the image of me facing him through tears and blood to haunt him forever.

Dale stands over me, hunkered down, nostrils flaring.

After a brief hesitation, his fist raised above me, he cries out—a deep, guttural howl—and runs away, slamming the front door behind him.

My hands give out underneath me, and I thud back against the hardwood floor. *Get up. Get up, August. Run.* Warren is waiting outside, and I need to *run*. But I'm paralyzed. Whether with fear or injury, it's unclear.

"August," a muffled, far away voice calls. "August, are you in there?" Gentle taps. The turn of a knob. "I saw Dale running like a bat out of hell."

"Ren," I mumble, barely audible.

"August?" The creaking of the door, then a thud. "*Gus!* No, no, no. *Shitshitshitshit.*" Hurried, urgent hands are under me, lifting my shoulders off the ground. "Open your eyes. Come on, Gus. You with me?"

"Warren?"

"I'm here. I'm here." He coughs, maybe to hide a cry. "For a second, I thought..." He sits me up, cradles my limp torso against him. "I'm calling an ambulance."

"No, don't. I'm okay."

"You're *not*." He readjusts to look at my face, examining the damage. He's blurry, distorted through my weary eyes. "Oh, August." His panicked voice jumps an octave. "What has he done to you?" He's gentle as he brushes his fingers over my cuts and bruises, but it hurts. Everything hurts.

"My head," I groan.

"I need to get pressure on this cut." He wriggles around a moment, then puts something against my forehead that smells of peanut oil and buttered popcorn.

"Don't ruin your shirt."

"There was already blood on it," he says coolly.

My eyes adjusting—clearing a little—can make out the crimson on his white undershirt where the blood had already seeped through. "I'm sor—" I start, sad I've ruined yet one more thing for Warren.

"Don't," he interrupts. "Don't, Gus. Don't tell me sorry right now." He sniffles. "You've done nothing wrong. Okay?"

Hot tears pool in my eyes. I whimper a quiet, "Kay."

Another minute's examination of my injuries makes way for a heavy sigh. "Nothing's broken," he says. "A miracle."

"You sure?"

"Like, ninety percent."

"Good," I squeak, trying to keep my emotional roller coaster in check. "So don't call an ambulance. Don't involve anyone else in this. Not now. Please. I can't...I can't l-let anyone else see me like th-this."

"Breathe," he says gently. "Breathe, Gus." I do. It hurts my head, but I take a slow inhale through my nose and let it out through my mouth. "Good. Now, I know you don't think you can trust anyone right now, but you can. I'll be with you. It'll be okay. Besides, you're gonna need stitches. This cut is pretty deep."

"No. No stitches."

"August."

"Just glue it shut or something."

He snorts. "You're kidding. Right?"

"Superglue it. Doctors do it all the time in hospitals; why not here? A little glue, a butterfly bandage, done. I can't see a doctor, Ren. Please don't make me. No one can see me like this!"

Warren rubs my back, attempting to quell my paranoia. "It's okay. Slow down. I won't make you go anywhere. I promise." He touches my face gently again, agonizing over every detail. "He could have broken you," he whispers. "August, he could have killed—"

He chokes on this realization, and his subsequent tears only accelerate my own, which sting my open wounds.

Warren wraps his arms around me, rocking us back and forth. "I'm so sorry I wasn't here, Gus. Forgive me."

"It's not your fault," I say through my sobs and slobber. "I was so stupid."

"No. This is *not* on you. Do you hear me?"

"If I'd kept my mouth shut. But I gave in. I yelled back. And..." Warren rocks me while snot and tears ruin what parts of his shirt I haven't already bled on. "I thought if I stayed, he might get better. I thought *we* might get better. I'm such an idiot."

"You're *not*."

"I am!" I wail. "Why does he *hate* me?"

"None of this was about you. He's a rotten son of a bitch, all right? You've done nothing to deserve this. You hear me, August?" I nod weakly. "Kay. We need to get you out of here, clean up these cuts."

"Not yet."

"Gus, don't—"

"I don't mean I can't leave," I assure him. "I just want to pack first. I don't ever want to come back here again. Please. I'll tough it out for now," I add, gesturing to my face.

"You can't tough out a head wound in need of stitches."

"Superglue," I correct. "And I can. I promise."

He sighs, his head bobbing in defeat. "A better friend would drag you to the ER against your will."

"Ren, *please*."

"Ugh, *fine*. Where do you keep the superglue?"

🎧

"My parents are in Boise until tomorrow. I left a message, but even if they left right now... We don't have three hours to wait around. We need reinforcements, Gus Gus."

I huff, knowing he's right. He forces me to lie on my bed with two ice packs over my face and orders me not to lift a finger. The problem remains: the task is grand, and he is one person.

"Someone with a truck would be preferable," he says. "We should do this as fast as possible."

"But Benny's stuff, too. I want his drums. And his guitar. Dale shouldn't get to keep hi—them."

A gentle hand lands on my shoulder. "I know. It's okay. We'll figure it out. I promise."

I'm not even sure where the image comes from, but I blurt, "I think Seth's dad has a truck. I saw one parked in front of the garage when I was there."

There's a long pause before Warren sighs, then coughs. "I saw it, too."

"Call him," I say.

"I don't have his number."

"Someone you know must have it. Or message him, beg him to call you. He's got Facebook or Twitter or something, doesn't he?"

"I hate the idea of *begging* him for anything," he grumbles, his thumbs urgently padding against his touch screen.

"Then give me the phone, you big baby. I'm the one here who has more reason *not* to want to see him."

"You're mean when you're in pain."

"You're forcing me to lie here and *not* help! It's pissing me off."

"Shh. Okay. Sheesh, woman." His phone buzzes. "Wow, that was fast."

"So answer it!"

"I'm leaving now, sassy pants," he calls over his shoulder as he walks away. "Seth, hey."

Warren is back fumbling about, packing what he can while we wait for Seth. I'm tired, and everything hurts. Maybe Warren was right to make me lie down and rest. Does he *always* have to be right?

"Hello?" a smooth baritone calls from the hallway.

"Here we go," Warren breathes.

I slide one of the ice packs off my face, adjusting my stiff neck so I can *almost* make out Seth's figure as he enters my room. Warren steps in front of him, further obscuring my view.

"What happened?" he asks.

"It's not pretty, but she's okay," Warren says. Memories of hospitals and waiting and heartbreaking news come in flashes.

"The hell?" Seth pushes past Warren. "August, what...? Who did this?"

I can't bring myself to answer, and Warren volunteers nothing. Seth looks between us, throws his hands up.

"Well? Who the hell did this? Where are the police? Why isn't she in a hospital?"

"I..." I start, but I can't answer him.

He kneels next to me. "Who did this?" His voice cracks. "They're dead. Whoever they are. I swear, August, I'll—"

"Look, can you help us or not?" Warren asks.

"What *happened*?" He puts a hesitant hand on my arm. "Who hurt you?"

"Now is not the time, Seth," Warren shouts. "Please don't make me regret thinking we could trust you."

"Please, just help me get out of here," I whisper, tears resurfacing and stinging my broken skin. "I can't stay."

"No. You're not saying...?" He stares, dazed. "Your *dad*?" He accepts my silence as confirmation, and his head droops as he curses through his teeth.

"This is time-sensitive," Warren interrupts. "Can you help us or not?"

"She needs a doctor." He leans in closer. "Did you *glue* this cut?"

"She asked me to do it!"

"And you listened to her? She's concussed! Why isn't she in the emergency room right now?"

"*She* is right here! And she is *fine*," I interject. "I can't go to the hospital, Seth. Superglue was a reasonable alternative, and you're wasting time. Time we might not have."

"We need to call the cops. Warren, tell her, man. We can't just—"

"Stop," I squeak. "Just help me get *out*. Please."

Seth gently, briefly, squeezes my arm, then retreats. "Where do we start?"

🎧

A GENTLE NUDGE stirs me from a murky dream.

"August. Wake up." Warren comes into view as I manage to pry one eye open a sliver. "Time to go."

I want to ask *why* and *where*, but my mouth won't cooperate with my brain.

"She shouldn't be sleeping for extended periods, anyway," Seth says, and I start to remember why everything hurts. Why he's here. Why it's *time to go*.

"Thanks, Sherlock, because I'm a total idiot who hadn't deduced that already."

"Dude, I'm just worried. Alright? Don't take it personally."

"Are you two done swinging those things around," I say, my voice scratchy and dull. "Or do I need to hide the breakables?"

Muffled laughs fill the echoey room. I try to lift my head from the rock it's on. No, it's a pillow. It only feels like a rock. And that's not a phone ringing, but a constant buzz in my ears. Warren braces his hand behind my neck and helps me sit.

"Mother of hell!" I whine.

"I'm so sorry," he says. "I know it hurts."

"Oh, my head. Amputate. Please." With a final adjustment, I'm sitting. I can barely open my left eye; the right is swollen shut. I almost reach up to touch it but don't.

"How long was I out?" I croak, clearing my throat.

"A little over an hour. We cleared out most of your room and grabbed Benny's kit."

"Shirley?" I ask.

"Yeah, we got Shirley," Warren assures me. "If we missed anything important, we'll figure it out later."

"Okay." I take a slow breath as my new reality—homeless—sinks in. "Thank you for this. Really."

"Are you emotionally attached to your sheets? Or the bed, for that matter?"

"No. It can stay."

"'Kay, then. You ready?"

"Not remotely."

He laughs quietly, reaching in his pocket. "It's my mom. Again. Let me update her real quick, so she stops sending panicked texts."

"Go," I say, my muscles twitching in a failed attempt to smile. Warren shuffles out of the room, mumbling into his phone. "Seth?"

"I'm here," he says, kneeling in front of me. His outline is there, but his features all run together.

"I can't imagine coming here was easy for you. Not after wh-what I..." I force a slow, ragged breath. "I'm grateful you came. And so sorry for the hateful things I said."

It's only when Seth's fingers brush my face that I realize I'm crying. He wipes the tears away, then touches my arm. He cringes with an audible hiss, turning my arm over in his hand.

"What's wrong?" I ask.

"There's something. Like glass. Hold still." He gets close, his fingers carefully picking out a ceramic shard. "We need to clean you up better," he sighs.

"Warren and I did the best we could under the time constraints."

"I know," he says gently. "Are you up for walking to the truck?" I manage a subtle head shake. "Would you be comfortable with me carrying you?" I nod. "Okay, then."

He carries me to the truck without another word. Without accepting my apology. Without a "you're welcome" for all the help he's offering. Not a sound. Just places me in the passenger seat of my Sierra, weighted down with the contents of my fractured life.

It's nearly midnight by the time the boys unload my belongings into the Mitchells' garage. Warren orders pizza only minutes before they quit taking orders, and Seth pays with his debit card after a prodigious battle of the egos.

Warren's phone still buzzes every five minutes with a text or call from his mother. I had to get on the phone earlier and convince them not to leave until the morning.

"She's concerned about whether to do your birthday dinner tomorrow," he sighs, putting his phone down and snatching another piece of pepperoni.

"What dinner?" I ask. "We agreed not to do it this year. It would be too..." Hard. Empty. Both. "We agreed," I finish lamely.

"Well, *now*, given the circumstances, she wants to do something for you."

"I thought your birthday was today," Seth interrupts. Warren and I both look at him. Well, Warren looks at him. I gape in his general direction, my eyes still a puffy hot mess.

"How did you know it was my birthday?" I ask.

"I see it every time I visit..."

Seth's voice trails off, but I hear the words he doesn't say, and they cut right through me. He visits Benny. I wonder how frequently, but I don't ask.

After a beat, Seth says, "I was trying to work up the courage to visit you when Warren reached out."

My head buzzes, and I can't process any of this right now. "We'll circle back to that," I murmur. "Ren's parents have held a birthday dinner for—" I swallow. "For Benny and me since we were eleven." Cough. "Benny let it slip our dad forgot about it that year. From then on, they always made dinner for us the day after. Like a precaution, to make sure we always celebrated, whether Dale remembered or not."

"Wow," is all Seth says.

"Ren, please tell her I'm not up for it. I can't do it. Look at..." I gesture to my face, choking over words.

"Hey, hey. Gus, it's okay." Warren rests a gentle hand on my knee. "We don't have to do anything."

"I need sleep," I say after a lengthy lull.

"Sleep," Warren agrees, offering his hand. "Mom says you get the master bedroom tonight, and you're not allowed to argue."

"Of course, she did." But that's the extent of my protest. I'm too tired. I say goodnight to Seth and let Warren help me between the soft, high thread count sheets. He places a fresh ice pack on my face and lies next to me atop the comforter.

"Some birthday, huh?" he grumbles. "I'm so sorry, Gus."

"Stop apologizing. You didn't do anything."

"I should have. I should have gotten you out of there. I should never have left you alone with Dale all summer. August, I failed. I failed you. And Benny. He'd be so disappointed in me right now."

"You don't believe that, Warren. And neither do I." We lie in silent, somber contemplation a minute before I speak again. "Today was so strange. I wanted to bury myself in the ground with him."

"I can only imagine. I stopped by to see him after work, and I almost couldn't get out of the car. I took him new drumsticks. Kinda stupid, right?"

"No." The thought of drumsticks resting against Benny's headstone makes my heart smile, even if my lips aren't up to it just yet. "It wasn't stupid at all, Ren."

"No?"

"It's beautiful. Like you."

"Happy birthday, August," he says. Then, reverently, "Happy birthday, Benny."

I reach for Warren's hand blindly. He takes it and squeezes.

"Happy birthday, Benny," I whisper. It's probably the pain killers I took, but I sense a phantom arm around me, holding me close. Like Benny is sending me a hug. Like he's gathered all my broken parts and started piecing me back together again.

Chapter 22

Once separated into *before* and *after*, my life now has a third segment. I just haven't named it yet. *Freedom*, maybe? But that sounds too...healed, which I'm not. Maybe this is merely an intermission. Yes, let's go with that.

Today is the first day of *intermission*, and I'm kicking it off with a headache of epic proportions. My entire body burns, aches, and throbs simultaneously, but at least I can open both eyes. Barely.

With my first stretch, an ice pack slides off my head and onto the pillow. Judging by how cool the pack still is, Warren must have brought me a fresh one during the night—probably several. I bring my fingers to my face, gently brushing over cuts and bumps. It all feels wrong, and a crusted, wrinkly residue on my forehead suggests I bled more at some point.

I push myself to sitting with a hoarse groan, the firm mattress unforgiving against the unhealed abrasions. My forearms and hands are a mess of red and purple polka dots. The mint green sheets and pillowcase I've slept on showcase scattered splats of blood.

"Dammit," I whine.

"What? What happened?" A distant voice calls. "I'm up. I'm coming." Warren bounds through the door in seconds.

"Geez, Ren."

"What's wrong?" Warren wipes his face, pale with sleeplessness.

"Nothing. I ruined your mom's nice sheets. I'm fine."

"She won't care. She texted earlier. They're heading home." He walks over to the bed, tilting his head at the mattress. I nod, and he sits.

I peel the sheets back the rest of the way, scooting to the edge of the mattress and sitting beside him.

"How you feelin'?" He asks, frowning.

"Like a train wreck had a baby with a dumpster fire."

"Gross."

"Very," I agree. "You know what really pisses me off?"

"Aside from the obvious?"

"Well, yeah." I laugh. Small and brief. "I was ready to leave. I'd already made up my mind. I was ready to start...*living* again. I reached out to Kali yesterday. I want to start dancing again. Teaching, if she'll let me."

"I'm sure she'll let you."

"I'm not. I bailed on her last year, right before competition season started. I let her down."

"She won't hold that against you, Gus. No one could expect you to get right up and start living again after everything you went through."

"Benny must be so angry with me for quitting." A thought I've swallowed so many times. "I let him down, too."

"No. Don't even go there."

"But—"

"August, do you think he would have ever been able to pick up a guitar again if things had gone the other way? Or a pair of drumsticks?"

"He was so strong. So much stronger than me. He would have struggled, sure, but he would have gone on. He'd never have gotten stuck like I did. I suck at life, Ren."

Warren turns his body toward mine. "He was always playing for you, Gus. He did everything for you." He puts a hand underneath my chin. "Look at me," he demands gently. "August, look at me." I do. "Something I always found amusing about you two was how each of you always insisted the other was so much stronger."

I shake my head, biting my cheeks. "No way. If Benny told you I was stronger, he was being modest. He knew better."

"Don't you dare go to that place. Just stop. Now." His eyes hold mine with an intense determination. I gulp. "I was there. Remember? And I saw you take care of him day after day, year after year. August, you fascinated me constantly. You're a force of nature."

"Come on, Warren."

"It's true, and you know it. Everything Benny accomplished, he gave you credit for. All he wanted was to make you proud." His voice breaks, and he coughs before continuing. "He told me about the night your mother left. How it was afterward. How you'd go to him every night and sit with him and sing until he fell asleep. You were *seven*! You were a *child*, working to fill all those gaps she left behind. You were both so young. And you both handled it well. But *you* grew up overnight and became, I don't know, superhuman."

"Ren." I swallow. "Stop. That's not—"

"I'm serious. He called you Gigi because it's all he could say when you two were tiny, and it stuck. Right?"

"Gigi. Then Gussie."

"Those were your 'baby names' to him. That's why he quit using them when she left. He told me you were a grown-up now, and we couldn't call you baby names anymore."

Hot tears run their silent course, converging with snot. I pull the collar of my shirt up, trying to dab the mess away. "I don't remember it that way."

Warren disappears for a moment, comes back with a wad of tissues, and helps me clean my puffy face.

"Benny told me every night after Liliana left, you made sure he practiced his reading and writing, made sure he brushed his teeth. You would make up a bedtime story, tuck him in and sing to him. Some nights you would just sit with him, guarding him until he was sleeping. You cleaned up after him—after *both* of them. You learned to cook and then taught Benny. He told me how you went to the store and bought him *medicine*?"

Memories continue leaking from my eyes; we've run out of tissue. Warren holds a hand under my chin again, forcing himself into view.

"Think about it, August. You always gave him credit for being the better student, but it wasn't because he was smarter. It was because you were always more concerned with how he was doing than how you were. You were too tired to be exceptional at certain things because you spent so much time making sure Benny was excelling at everything." He takes a deep breath. "And he spent most of his life trying to make it up to you."

"No," I protest. "That's not how I remember it. That's not how I dream about it. I was a scared little girl. I was always scared. He took care of me. We took care of each other. I wasn't the strong one."

Warren sighs. "Well, maybe it happened that way, maybe it didn't. But all I know is what I remember and what Benny told me. What I remember is this amazing girl who constantly looked out for her brother *and me*, relentless to ensure the people she loved were happy. And what Benny told me..." He pauses as his voice cracks and tears well in his eyes. "What Benjamin told me was you were his world. You were everything. He loved you so much—completely adored you. And he gave you credit for every ounce of good he had in him."

I fall against him, sobbing into his chest. "I miss him s-so much. I'm so," gasp, "so lost."

"Me too," he says, taking me in his arms. "Nothing seems right without him. I still go to call him sometimes. To see what he's doing because I'm bored and I miss him."

"Sometimes," I croak, "when I hear a new song I think he'd like, I go to show him. Sometimes I get to his bedroom door before I remember."

"When things happened between us and then ended," Warren says, sniffling. "The only person I could think to talk about it with—other than you, oddly enough—was him. That's why it was so hard to grieve you. Grieving you meant grieving him in a completely new and terrifying way."

"I'm so sorry I put you through that, Ren. If I could take it back..."

"I wouldn't," he says.

"Honestly, I wouldn't either," I admit. "It was pretty great while it lasted."

"Because I'm sexy as hell?"

"Yes, exactly." I laugh weakly at first, then again—a real laugh. So real it hurts, and not only because of how awkwardly my swollen head feels attached to my body.

"It's good to hear you laugh," Warren sighs. "I miss it."

"I miss me, too." I dab at my face with my shirt as Warren releases his hold on me. "I'm trying, though. I promise."

He frowns. "I know. And you can take your time. I'm not going anywhere."

I cringe when my stomach announces hunger with an obnoxious growl. "Oof."

"I'm sure you're starving. You ate like two bites last night. You want to get cleaned up while we figure out some breakfast?"

"We?" My facial muscles twitch, a failed attempt to furrow my brow.

"Seth," he says, eyes wide, lips twisted. "He never left. We took shifts last night in case Dale showed up drunk and angry. Nudging you awake every hour or so, making sure you weren't dead."

"Morbid. Also smart. Thanks, I guess." He shrugs in response. "So, my clothes? Any chance my dresser is accessible?"

Warren winces, then shoots finger guns. "We did *not* think that far ahead." He walks over to a dresser and points to a middle drawer. "I *think* this is where she keeps her pajamas. Godspeed." He salutes.

I glower at him. "Breakfast better be *good*."

Mrs. M's shampoo smells amazing. That's the positive I'm choosing to focus on while I acquaint myself with this unfamiliar reflection. I squeeze a soft gray towel around my torso, stepping closer to the full-length mirror in this bedroom that isn't mine. I'm an imposter, my nakedness an awkward intrusion, even with the door closed. The Mitchells might be taking me in, but this isn't my house, and these aren't my things, and this can't be my face. Or my body.

Nothing is right. My eyes are bloodshot, and the surrounding skin is purple and blue. A deep gash on my forehead has a fresh layer of superglue and three butterfly bandages holding it together. My lips are split and swollen. Warren's words from last night ring in my ears. *What has he done to you?*

What have *I* done to me? I don't recognize my extremities, muscle definition having slacked during these bleak months without the discipline of dance. If Kali *does* take me back, I've got my work cut out for me.

Crap. Kali! I rush to my phone, texting an apology that I definitely *won't* be meeting her for coffee this morning as we'd previously agreed. I can't see her right now. Not like this. I'm not even sure I can find the courage to leave this room and see Warren. Or Seth.

I squeeze the ends of my hair with the towel once more, then throw it in an empty laundry basket along with the remnants of my dignity. Dressed in a pair of Mrs. M's plaid pajama pants and a t-shirt that says, *But first, Coffee*, I take a final glance in the mirror. "Let's do this," I mutter, then abandon the privacy of the master bedroom for paralyzing uncertainty.

Warren and Seth stand as I approach the dining room. Each of them maneuvers to pull out a chair for me and awkwardly halt when they realize what's happening. They do a strange dance while I walk to the other side of the table and pull out my own chair.

"Y'all are cute when you're flustered," I say.

"Nice pajamas," Warren claps back, glaring.

I hold my hands up. "Truce."

"I got donuts," Seth rushes, gesturing to the spread on the table —a dozen donuts and a large fruit tray. "And fruit. Because, you know, balance." The lopsided grin he shoots me does something funny to my stomach. Why is he so gorgeous right now? Completely unfair when I'm sitting here in my mom-chic pajamas, messed-up face, and damp, unbrushed hair. And why is he looking at me like that?

I'm staring at him like an idiot—that's why. Get it together, August!

"Um." Blink. "Thank you. That was really...um, nice?"

Smooth, Gus. Way to go.

Breakfast is more awkward than Warren and Seth's side-shuffle over the chair. No one is sure what to say, and if we are, we're not brave enough to say it. It's not until the table starts vibrating I realize my heel is bouncing. *Whoops.* I cough, place a firm hand over my knee, and turn my gaze to Seth.

"So, at the risk of sounding like an ungrateful douche, why are you here? Still?" *Too mean, Gus! Too mean!*

Warren scoffs a laugh, and Seth fidgets in his seat.

"I," Seth starts, then winces. "I need to give you something." He almost trips backward, standing from the table. "I'll be right back."

I keep my mouth shut until the front door clicks. "He brought me something?"

"It would appear *he* brought you something." *He* comes out a dirty word.

"Be nice, Ren."

"I'll be nice if you stop acting like a psycho."

"You try acting normal around two attractive people when you look like a b-movie monster!" I pout, then regret it. "Ow."

Warren holds his hand up, wide-eyed. "Wait, what? Back up. You're attracted to him? Since when?"

"That is *not* what I—"

The front door opens and shuts. Seth returns to the table holding a faded shoe box. He slides it to me as he sits.

"These belong to you. I'm embarrassed I've kept them so long, and I'm sorry, but you and I..."

"Communication hasn't been our strong suit," I say. Seth nods.

"Exactly." He scratches at his hairline. "I hope they help more than they hurt."

With a gulp, I remove the lid. Something between a whimper and a gasp rises as the contents come into view—pictures of Benny and me together, sitting in the grassy courtyard at school. Benny's playing his guitar, and the two of us are smiling, singing, laughing. Warren is in a few of them, laughing right along. I remember this day. A perfect, beautiful day in late November. Not long before the snow fell and ruined everything.

"Seth, where...?"

"I took those."

I stare in stunned silence at the expertly framed and focused photographs.

"I used to do that a lot," Seth says. "Take pictures of people I thought looked happy. Or sad. Or lost. A little intrusive, I know. But it was a compulsion. The three of you were...glowing. I wanted to know why. I wanted to be in the circle, laughing with you. Honestly, I was jealous. I thought some of them turned out really well." They did. They all did—these are perfect. And painful. My chest hurts.

"Seth..."

"I took them for fun, but after I blew it with you that night at the studio, I thought maybe I'd show them to you after you'd had time to warm up to me again. Maybe for Christmas or something. But then— after everything—I couldn't. I'm sorry."

No words form on my trembling lips. Nothing can convey this billowing hope and simultaneous devastation inside of me. Ten months ago, I'd probably have buried or burned these, ensuring I'd never have to look at them again. I'd shut Benny out for so long— every memory, good or bad. Now, these are precious gifts. I hold them with delicate fingers, knowing their infinite worth. Benny and I hadn't taken a good quality picture together in years. Not on purpose, anyway. But here, right in front of me, there's an entire treasure box full.

"Seth," I try again, still unable to finish. My favorite image is one where Benny has his arm around my shoulder, and we're laughing. Mouths open wide, eyes squinting, teeth showing. It's a perfect moment, captured and preserved. My fingers gently caress Benny's smiling face. "Benny," I whisper, my eyes swimming. Warren's hand touches mine. I carefully slide the picture to him.

"This was..." My tears gather momentum. "I..." But there aren't words. Not for this. I stand, and Seth follows my lead. In a few quick steps, I'm against his chest, hugging his waist. He tenses a moment before wrapping his arms around me. After a few more breaths, he presses his cheek to the top of my head, and he holds me tighter.

"Thank you," I manage, low and throaty.

He begins shaking, choking on sobs.

"August," he says, "I'm... I'm s-so sorry." His fingers knead at my back, like holding me is what's keeping him breathing, what's keeping him rooted. Like it's everything. "Every day." He takes a deep breath. "Every damn day I wish..." He turns his head, presses his lips against my hair, and I don't hate it.

He's wearing yesterday's clothes, which he slept in after relocating everything I own from my house into the Mitchells' garage. Yet, I'm happy breathing in the smell of him. I'm even coming to terms with the warmth in my stomach at this intimacy.

But after a moment of melting into one another, the intensity skyrocketing, Seth releases his hold on me.

"I should go," he says. "Get some ice on your eye." He vanishes.

I stumble as the space in front of me becomes suddenly vacant. I brace myself against the dining table, my insides still humming.

"Well," Warren says, staring widely. "That was uncomfortable."

"What?"

"Never mind."

After a few slow breaths, I shuffle to the living room. *What the what? How did that happen? Or maybe I'm imagining things, and it didn't happen at all. I'm possibly concussed. So, really, I probably made the whole thing up.* I plop onto the couch.

"He's right, you know," Warren calls. "You should be icing that."

He joins me on the couch and helps me position a fresh ice pack across my face.

I pat his knee as thanks, letting my head relax into the cushion behind me. My eyelids droop until I relent, allowing them to close. I'm so tired; a nap won't hurt.

"I got you a birthday present," he says. I can hear pride dancing on his tongue.

"Ren, you shouldn't have."

"I wanted to. And it's literally perfect. Like, you won't even believe."

I open my eyes, sitting back up and facing him. He pulls a small, wrapped box from behind his back. Abandoning the ice pack, I take the package in my lap and peel back the paper. "Warren," I whisper, recognizing the logo. "New dance shoes?" The scent of new leather sends a shock wave through my body as I pull the new tan jazz shoes from the box. "They're too much."

"I'd hoped to persuade you to start again. But it sounds like you already did that for yourself."

I bring the shoes to my face, inhaling, inviting an aftershock of memories and longing.

"Call Kali," he says. "Get your job back. Get on a competition team if you can. Just *dance*, and don't let anything ever stop you again."

I nod, swallowing, carefully placing the shoes back in the protective box. "Thank you," I croak. "They're perfect. I love them almost as much as I love you."

He hands the ice pack back. "That's the head wound talking."

"Shuddup."

I slide to the arm of the couch as he pulls my feet up onto his lap.

"I'ma sleep, Ren," I whisper, my words slurring together.

"Sleep," he says, gently patting my leg. "I got you."

Chapter 23

NOVEMBER

Dear Fam,

There have been developments—many, <u>many</u> developments since my birthday. I know I ducked phone calls, <u>but I honestly knew</u> if I talked to any of you, I'd cry. And cry. And I might not be able to stop. That's a thing I do a lot now. Weird it took me nine months to break after Benny passed. Sometimes I wonder if I'm human or a malfunctioning robot.

I moved in with Warren...'s parents. Uncle Ryan about had a heart attack, didn't he? Psych! You're welcome. Please laugh. I'm hilarious. But seriously, I moved in with the Mitchells on my birthday. I'm in the guest room, and a good chunk of my belongings (and Benny's) fill the garage. I am a nuisance, but they claim to love me still. I think I believe them.

I have not spoken to my father since I moved out, and I do not wish to. The man has gone off the deep end, and I am not a strong enough swimmer to save him. I am saving myself instead. I will <u>never</u> return to his house, and I doubt we'll ever speak again.

I know it's tradition to visit you on Thanksgiving, but I made that drive with Benny last year, and we made a promise to always go back together. I'm not sure I'd survive driving there alone. Melodramatic as I may sound, I honestly can't bring myself to try. Maybe soon. But not for Thanksgiving.

Should you wish, the Mitchells have invited you to join us here. The food will be plentiful, and the company will be delightful. Tell Sam I know what he just said, and remind him I AM the most delightful person he knows. Sunshine and rainbows, all the way. You can bring Remy if you like. Unfortunately, there are no accommodations for Sadie. I'd give her my room if I were allowed, but Mrs. M has a strict NO HORSES INDOORS policy (her biggest character flaw, if you ask me). Please send Sadie my regrets. Take some time to digest the invitation, then give me a call. I'm here, and I'm waiting, and I'm 100% sure I'll blubber like an idiot when I pick up. So try to stick to simple 'yes' or 'no' questions if you can manage. Hope you can come. Can't wait to see you.

Hugs, and ALL my love,
August

🎧

The studio emptied ten minutes ago, and I'm still working up the courage to begin. I know no one can see me. No one is here to watch. But I'm nervous. So insanely, desperately nervous.

There's an adult category for solos this year, and Kali signed me up for regionals without my knowledge. "Better to ask forgiveness than permission," she'd said. "Get to work, sugar snap."

Getting back into the groove of teaching was one thing. Choreographing for classes is a creative process, yes. But listening to a song for *me*, finding the perfect moves to flow with the melody, progress with the emotional range of the lyrics? Completely different. I've danced a little for myself since the accident, mostly in the confines of my small bedroom and always to happier songs. I haven't dared to go where I'm about to go. Jazz solos are fantastic. I love them. But they're not where my strength lies, and I know it. Kali knows, too. She touched my arm before she left tonight.

"I'd love a contemporary from you. Somethin' raw. Gut-wrenching. Rip the judges' hearts right outta their chests, you know?"

She'd smiled, winked, planted a smooch on my cheek, and danced away, a purple bob bouncing behind her.

"Gut-wrenching," I say, scrolling through my media player. A lightbulb moment makes me question my sanity, but I go there anyway. *Benny's*. He's changed the tempo enough it could work as a contemporary piece. But can I trust myself to hold it together and dance to his voice?

"Guess we'll find out," I say aloud, selecting "So Far Away" and cranking the speakers. Regret is in my immediate future. I know it.

I close my eyes, inhaling the soothing guitar melody, letting my body move based solely on instinct.

These are my words.

I'm center stage; I pirouette, extend, hold. *Breathe*. This is good. I'm fine. Everything is fine. My switch leaps need work—yikes. I'm falling out of my fouettés. *Get it together, Gus. You can do this*. Extend to arabesque and hold, hold, hold. Better. *Control*. I am in control.

The music rises and falls, crescendos and quiets. Benny's voice strains as he reaches the final chorus, begging to be heard.

I'm not ashamed to be the person that I am today.

I fall out of a double attitude with a sharp cry. My hands slap against the floor as I crumble to my knees.

"August?" My head snaps up, my cheeks flush, and not merely from exertion.

"Seth?" He's in the doorway, slipping off his shoes. I can't tell if it's adorable or weird he remembers. "What...are you...?" My words trail off as I strain for steady breaths.

"Are you okay?" He's kneeling next to me, a concerned hand on my shoulder. The same subtle spearmint scent of his mouth—the memory of gum—breezes over my face.

"What are you doing here?" I ask, words coming easier this time.

"I've tried calling. And texting." He joins me on the floor, his legs crossing in front of him. "You're hard to reach. So, I cheated."

"You knew I was teaching again?"

"Warren mentioned it," he says, nonchalant. I raise a single brow. "Yes, I checked up on you. Can you blame me?"

"Guess not." I shrug. "I'm sorry I haven't answered your texts. Between diving in here, in the middle of the season no less, and classes, I've kept busy. Haven't had a lot of time to...process."

"The fact that I'm not Satan, you mean?"

I roll my eyes. "I never thought you were Satan. A CW villain? Maybe."

He laughs, rubbing his forehead. "That's fair."

I wince. "It's not, though. Really. I've been horrible to you. It's just, every time I saw you, I remembered..."

"I know."

"Some of the things I've said..." I shake my head, embarrassed at the recollection of my harsh words. "I honestly don't know why you keep coming back."

He tilts his head, offering a curious half-smile. "Don't you?"

"Why are you here?" I ask again.

"The dance you were doing when I got here? Intense. Was that...?"

"Benny? Yeah."

"Bold choice," he says. I nod, wide-eyed. "Is it for a competition?"

"Maybe," I sigh, frustrated with his constant deflection. "I haven't decided yet. I'm teaching two classes, and it's going well. But dancing for myself is strange now. I've got this sudden-onset imposter syndrome. I'm not sure I belong on the dance floor anymore."

"Something tells me you'll always belong here."

"Dancing to *that* song, though? Might be a mistake. I'm not sure I can..."

I rub my chest until the skin burns. Seth takes my fingers in his to stop me. Our hands dangle in the small space between our knees.

"It hurts," I whisper. "I mean, it's always been a bit like that, though. Even before... When I'd get overwhelmed by the stories embedded in my choreography. But those were unshed tears screaming to get out."

"Panic attacks?" He asks plainly. I flinch, furrowing my brow. "Sorry, it's just, from what I understand—and observed—you had panic attacks. Instead of, you know, crying."

"Geez. Sounds so dramatic when you say it out loud." Withdrawing my hand, I tuck wispy flyaways behind my ears. "What a piece of work I am, huh? It's a miracle I have any friends at all." I chuckle darkly as I shift positions, hugging my knees to my chest. "No wonder Warren couldn't stand me for so long."

"Wait, *what?* August, I didn't mean..." He scratches at his hairline, then throws his hands up gently. "Did you and Warren fight? When?"

"Graduation, and it wasn't a fight per se. We broke—*I* broke things off between us. It was awful, but it had to happen. He didn't talk to me again until September."

He winces. "Ouch. That's harsh."

"Me, or him?"

"Neither. The entire situation. It's amazing you've come through it still friends."

"There was really no other alternative. We've been friends so long, and he's so important to me. Honestly, I don't think I ever would have kissed him if I didn't know, deep down, our friendship would survive even if, romantically, we failed. And we failed hardcore." I click my tongue, pointing a finger gun. He laughs through a frown. "I was needy. And he never drew the line. I asked, he gave. I'd have bled him dry if we'd stayed together. We were both so damn broken and lonely. Mistakes were made. Mostly by me."

"You weren't broken, August. You were grieving. You've got to stop being so hard on yourself all the time for having human emotions. If dancing hurts, let it hurt. Don't try to explain it away or justify it."

"Who *are* you?" I shake my head, my shoulders tight against my ears. "Suddenly so insightful and concerned and always saying the right thing."

"Okay, ouch."

"Sorry," I mumble.

"No, you're right." He sighs, shrugging. "I'm not the same guy who made wise cracks and flashed his smile to get what he wanted. I was a different person when I moved here—a selfish, spoiled moron who said stupid things when all I wanted to do was take you on a date. Get to know you. My ego always got in the way." His features harden and grow dark. "My damn ego that had me driving too fast." He pauses, blinking back tears. He swallows down sobs, takes a calming breath. "I was within the speed limit, and they may not have convicted me in court. But it was my fault. If I'd been going slower, paying closer attention, I could have stopped in time. I killed him."

His words destroy me.

"It's my fault, August. And I'll never be able to fix it. Sorry isn't a big enough word."

I bite my lip as tears spill down my cheeks. After wiping my nose and face against the lycra fabric stretched over my knees, I scoot toward a sullen Seth until we're arm to arm, facing opposite walls. I let my head rest on his shoulder. His hoodie gives off earthy smells—something like cedar or sandalwood mixed with wildflowers.

"We can play the blame game all you want," I say. "But I promise you, I'll win."

"August—"

"You started it," I remind him. "If we'd been in the truck that day, he would have lived, even with the second impact. And we *should* have been in the truck, but the battery was dead. Probably my fault. I have no idea how it happened. But the battery was dead, and the jumper cables were in Dale's pickup. If I'd bought my own set of jumper cables. If I hadn't left the headlights on or whatever happened. If Benny had been with Millie instead of trying to protect me all the time." I sigh, wiping away a lone tear. "We can go in circles all you want here, Seth. But it happened. He's gone. And you may not have known him well, but I think you knew him well enough to know he wouldn't want us playing miserable *what-if* scenarios in our heads the rest of our lives."

"No," he sighs, his head resting atop mine. A single butterfly flutters in my stomach. "No, he wouldn't."

I clear my throat as though a tiny cough might expel the intruder. Instead, all its friends swarm to visit as Seth shifts even closer to me.

"I wish you could have known Benny," I say, ignoring the nervous excitement dancing inside. "Really known him. He was the most genuine person on the planet. He was a literal *light*. And when he was your friend, his light filled you up and made you think anything was possible. Anything always *felt* possible, because Benny loved me. He left a hole in my heart so big I couldn't even say his name without crumbling for a long time. But Seth, my life isn't ruined. And the messiest it's ever been—the hardest it's ever been—has never once been your fault. You've got to let it go. We've both got to move on."

His head nods against my hair. Sniffles echo in my ears, and his body shifts against mine as he wipes his face.

"The routine you're working on...is that part of moving forward?"

"Maybe. It would help if I could allow myself to have *feelings* and not panic attacks anytime the emotion gets real."

"You'll get there," he says. "I have faith in you."

I relax against him, unsure why he's so easy to be around when we share such a complicated history.

"Would you like me to leave?" he asks after a long silence. "So you can practice?"

I shake my head against his soft, cotton sleeve. "I think I'd like to sit here with you a while." It's strange how it comes out so easily, and I don't even try to hold it in. "If that's okay," I add.

"It's okay," he says, his happiness audible. We meld together as the minutes pass, as though if we sit here long enough, we might fill each other's gaps, if only a little.

Chapter 24

"August, honey, could you pass the gravy?"

Before I can process who is asking or where I am in relation to the gravy boat, Sam reaches over me and grabs it, passing it to Aunt Hannah.

"You okay?" he whispers. I nod, but I don't think I am.

I should want to be here, right? I'm sandwiched between the Fosters and the Mitchells, and I should feel good. Happy. Whole. But there's a disconnect, like I'm floating away from the dining room table and through the walls. I'm not even here anymore. Not really.

Uncle Ryan and Mr. M talk football. Aunt Hannah compliments Mrs. M on everything from place settings to the color of the walls. Warren is friendly with Sam, and they both attempt conversation with me. But I can't find anything worthwhile to say.

"That was absolutely delicious," Uncle Ryan says, wiping at his face with a Fall-themed cloth napkin. "I couldn't possibly eat another bite. Until dessert, of course," he adds with a wink. A wave of quiet laughter fills the dining room.

Dessert. Aunt Hannah brought me pecan pie. I should be thankful. Benny's favorite was chocolate cream. Did anyone even make a chocolate cream this year? Why didn't I? I stand from the table and leave, not even aware of what I'm doing until I hear the gentle clang of metal against glass. I've measured butter-flavored Crisco into a mixing bowl, and I'm cutting in the flour and salt.

Gentle fingers brush my arm. "Hey, Gus. Whatcha doin'?"

Sprinkle cold water. Blend with fork.

"Gus?"

Form into a ball. Where's the saran wrap?

A firm hand on my shoulder. "August?"

Warren's brown eyes radiate worry, maybe even fear.

"Saran wrap?" I ask. He squints. "Plastic wrap. Where is it?"

"Why? What's wrong?"

"Nothing's wrong. I need plastic wrap so I can chill the dough for the crust." He throws up his hands as though I haven't answered his question. "I'm making a chocolate cream," I sigh. "No one made a chocolate cream pie."

"Okay? And this is an urgent problem because...?"

"It's Benny's favorite," I say matter-of-factly. Only then do I freeze, exactly aware of what I'm doing. "Oh, gosh." My hand flies over my mouth, knocking the mixing bowl onto the floor with a crack. I shriek. The bowl has separated into four large chunks, with a few tiny shards surrounding it.

"It's okay," Warren rushes. "Don't move. I'll get the broom."

"I'm so sorry," I say through my fingers, searching for Mrs. M. Then I see them—all their faces—staring at me. Every one of them with pity. Aunt Hannah is crying. Sam's lip is quivering. *Dammit, August.* "I'm so... I didn't..."

"It's okay," Warren says, sweeping up the mess. "It's not a big deal, Gus. It's fine. Everything's fine."

We both know it's not.

"Excuse me," I say, fleeing the naked-in-a-crowded-room nightmare I'm starring in. I grab my coat and keys from a hook near the front door, slip my feet into heavy boots, and leave, knowing exactly where I'll wind up once I get behind the wheel. Warren calls after me and I know I should stop, but I slam the truck door and turn the key over. I'm shifting into gear when he hops in the passenger seat.

"You shouldn't be alone," he says.

"Yes, I should, Ren. You should go have a lovely Thanksgiving with your lovely family."

"You're part of my family. And half the people in that house came to see you. Not me. If you go, I go."

"Warren, I'm not good for anyone. And you shouldn't follow me everywhere. I'm bound to take you places you don't belong."

"What are you even talking about?"

"I'm not better, Warren! I want to be, but I'm not. I'm sad." My words come out squeaky and I realize I'm crying. I wipe my face, sniffling. "I'm sad *all* the time. Today is a *joke* without him; I can't stand it. And I don't need you to hear that because *all* you do is help me. I can't let *them* hear that," I say, pointing to the house, "because they've all been nothing but supportive. You've all been amazing. But I'm a mess, Ren. Benny should be here, and he's not, and it makes me furious. And I have no right to be furious because I'm so blessed. And all of this makes me feel like a garbage human. So, can you please let me go have a few minutes alone with my brother to wallow and talk to him like the lunatic I am, so I can feel a *tiny* bit better? Please?"

Warren breathes a heavy, single sigh. "Only if you let me hug you before you go," he relents.

I roll my eyes, laugh, and lean into a hug. He kisses the top of my head.

"I love you," I say. "You know that, right?"

"I do." He squeezes me, then releases his grip. "I love you, too. So be safe. And take this," he says, pulling my phone from his pocket. "Call if you need us to come get you."

"Promise."

Not without hesitation, Warren exits my truck, shuts the door, and watches as I drive away.

✤

My phone buzzes relentlessly as I sit on the frozen ground, shivering, having a one-sided conversation with Benny's headstone about why today is stupid and how he's a traitor for dying and leaving me here.

Sam: *Warren sucks at Smash Bros. It's embarrassing.*

Hannah: *Love you, honey. Chocolate Cream is chilling in the fridge.*

Mrs. M: *I hope you took your gloves. Be careful and come home when you're ready. Love you, sweetheart.*

"Home," I say aloud. "She called it home, Benny. I don't think I deserve these people."

Warren: *Your cuz is super sus. He's dominating every freaking game I own. Don't trust him. When are you coming back? Halp.*

Sam: *Warren's a baby. But his mom has good snacks.*

Ha! Yes, she does. Though how he's hungry after Thanksgiving dinner, I have no idea.

Seth: *Happy Thanksgiving, Gus. *Turkey Emoji**

*Is it weird I called you Gus? Did I cross a line? Do you hate me again? *grimace emoji**

I'm sure holidays are really weird now. I'm here if you want to talk.

*Or sit quietly & stare at the wall. *Wink Emoji**

I swear I'm not a stalker. I just want to know if you're okay.

"Not going to lie, Benny. He's super easy to sit with. And he's *really* pleasant to look at. And somehow, he always smells good. Like, unfairly good, under any circumstance." I tap my fingers against my phone, debating my next move.

Me: *Happy Thanksgiving. And you can call me Gus. *thumbs up emoji**

Seth: *Hey! How's it going today? Weird? Bad?*

Me: *Well, I got up in the middle of dinner & started making chocolate cream pie because there wasn't one & it's Benny's favorite. Then I broke a mixing bowl & ran out like a big psycho. So there's that. How's YOUR Thanksgiving?*

Seth: *Where are you?*

Me: *Where ALL the psychos hang out. The cemetery.*

Seth: *You like hot chocolate?*

I'M LEANED up against my Sierra, my gloved hands cupped in front of my mouth for additional warmth when Seth parks and waves me inside his car. The faded blue Ford Fusion is a far cry from the Audi he drove last year. The heat wafts over me as I hurry into the passenger seat.

"Heated seats?" I gasp for added enthusiasm. "So fancy."

"And cupholders," he says, handing me a tumbler. "Mind-blowing, right?"

The tumbler warms my hands, and the first sip sends comfort straight down to my stomach.

"Oh. My gosh." I sip again. "This is incredible."

"Claire—my stepmom. She makes it in one of those big pots that plug into the wall? You know?" He gestures with his hands.

"Crockpot?"

He nods, pointing. "That's the one. She does it every Thanksgiving and Christmas."

"Thank her for me," I say, then take another long drink of the deliciousness.

He twists his lips. "So, you wanna talk about it?"

"You mean why I was freezing my ass off talking to myself at a cemetery instead of in a warm house with amazing people who care about me and tried desperately to make today special, knowing how hard it would be for me?" I catch my breath. "Sorry."

He smiles. "Don't be. I asked."

I place the tumbler in a cup holder, pull off my gloves and hat, and pat down my now tangled mane, no longer the loose fishtail braid it had been this morning. "I thought I was getting better. But that's how it happens—I think I'm adjusting. I'll feel almost normal for a minute. Then I'll either be overwhelmed by guilt because I *felt* normal, or heaven forbid, maybe *happy* or at least content. Sometimes the sensation hits me that I'm watching everything from outside my body, and it's not real, and I'm not real, and I shouldn't be here. Or I'll feel so empty I'm not sure how I'm even standing. And it just..."

"Hurts," he finishes.

"So much," I say, a tear sliding down my cheek. "It hurts *so* much. And I do crazy, irrational things."

"August, nothing you've told me is crazy or irrational. Being left behind...it's traumatic."

I search his haunted eyes. "Who left you behind?" I ask, suddenly aware of how little I know about Seth and how little I've *tried* to know.

"My parents divorced when I was nine. My mom walked away. Didn't even fight for custody."

"Seth..." I reach for his hand before I realize what I'm doing. "I'm so sorry. That's awful."

"It's fine," he shrugs.

"No. It's not. Our mom left us when we were seven. She didn't even come to Benny's..." I swallow, wipe away a few tears with my free hand. "She didn't even come to Benny's funeral."

"That's messed up," he breathes.

"Divorce is bad enough without being discarded like a meaningless mistake your own mother wishes she could take back."

Seth looks at my hand covering his and places his other hand over it, fingers caressing my skin. "All this time, we've had more in common than you thought."

"I'm sorry I never took the time to get to know you. I never even *asked*..."

"You are now," he says, grinning as though he's won something.

I can't blame *this* warmth in my stomach on the hot chocolate. *Crap, how long have I been staring at him? We're still holding hands; is it rude if I take mine back? Is it weird if I don't?* I tug my hand away, using the hot chocolate as an excuse, taking a comforting taste.

"So," I say, "photography. Still a thing for you? Is it what your 'gap year' is all about?" I make air quotes with my fingers.

He laughs, tossing his hands in the air as he shrugs. "The gap year was more of an 'I have no clue what I want to do with the rest of my life' sort of thing. I really haven't gotten beyond that. I spent most of high school trying to fit in. See how well *that* worked out for me."

"I don't know what I'm doing with my life, either. I'm taking Gen Ed classes at college, and I'm not into them at *all,* which begs the question, why am I even going?"

"You're dancing. That's good, right? That's a direction."

I nod. "It is. It's great. But I don't know if I'm good enough at it to make it my life's work. I'm not sure I can be Kali."

"So don't be Kali," he says simply. "Be August. You're great at it."

Seth's fingers nuzzle my cheek, tucking a thick black lock behind my ear. I reach up, thinking I'll brush his hand away. A kind, *no thanks.* Instead, I weave my fingers between his. A nervous energy pulses through me, like a humming underneath my skin. He leans in, that sweet, spearmint memory intoxicating me as his lips inch closer. I'm frozen, unable to close the distance, yet unable to pull away.

He whispers my name, and I prepare myself for impact. I'm ready. I'm doing this. My lips brush against his with electric intensity. Another tiny movement, merely a breath, and I'll be kissing him. But I can't bring myself to close the gap. Sensing my hesitation, Seth pulls away, and his hands fall away from my face.

My fingers cover my lips as I mutter, "I'm sorry."

"It's okay," he says. "I get it."

"I'm not sure you do. I'm just not sure how this—us—could be anything other than...doomed."

"Gee, thanks." His words fall flat and heavy.

"No, I didn't mean..." I close my eyes, regrouping. "I'm such a mess, Seth. The last time I kissed my friend, it went entirely too far. And when it ended, I lost him. Warren couldn't even look at me for months. I can't survive that a second time."

"I'm not Warren," he snaps. "And you're not the same person you were last spring."

"I don't know *who* I am right now! Were you listening earlier? Less than two hours ago, I robotically started making a pie for someone who isn't even *alive* anymore. I cry *every* time I dance. Or see a Red Corvette. Or hear his favorite songs on the radio. And sometimes I sense Benny walking next to me, and I look over to talk to him because I forget it's *impossible* for him to be walking next to me. I'm a train wreck, Seth. And I'll drag you along with me until you're *crushed*. I'm barely living with myself as it is. If I screw this up, or hurt you, I don't think I could handle it."

"Okay, okay," he says, taking my flailing hands in his. "It's okay. You're okay." I hadn't realized I was crying. Again. Pathetic. "Take a breath."

I nod, reclaiming my hands and wiping my wet cheeks. "Sorry," I whisper.

"Don't be. I shouldn't have pushed you."

"You didn't." I release an exasperated sigh. "I need to get back. Thanks for the cocoa. Really. Tell Claire I loved it. Maybe she can teach me to make it sometime."

He nods, a sweet but faint grin on his lips. "I'm sure she'd love to."

I grab my hat and gloves and pull the handle on the passenger door. "Happy Thanksgiving, Seth."

"See ya around, August."

Chapter 25

December

Christmas music fills the Mitchells' living room. A mess of tubs and boxes scattered across the floor and couch. They have an artificial tree. It's not the same, even with Mrs. M's pine-scented wax melting in the decorative dish on the mantel. It is a beautiful tree. These are lovely decorations. And I am grateful. But this is not the same.

"*Mom!*" Warren shouts, entering the room, phone in hand.

"There you are," she says. "You're missing out."

"That picture you made us all take—you posted it online?"

"I always share something around the holidays for my Realty page. Is there a problem? I thought it turned out so well!"

I look between them, the tension palpable, at least for Warren. *Angst* practically scribbled across his forehead. He reads from his phone, "Happy Holidays from the Mitchells; Megan, Les, Warren, and our new addition, August."

My eyes grow wide in horror. "Oh, my hell," I say, but I'm already laughing. I'm mortified, but laughing.

"What's wrong with that?" Mrs. M asks, throwing her hands up. "I have a beautiful family. If it's a crime to brag about that—"

"*Mom!* I'm catching so much crap for this. You made it sound like August and I..."

"What?" she practically shouts, then her face stills. "Ohhhhh, no," she whispers, bringing her hands over her mouth. "Oh, Warren, honey. I'm so sorry."

"People think I eloped, Mom! They think August and I..."

He stops when I snort, then shriek, and keep right on laughing. My cheeks hurt, and I'm barely breathing, but I can't. Stop. Laughing.

"It's not *funny!*" he whines.

"I know, I'm s—" But I can't stop.

I fall onto the couch, holding my side, while Mrs. M and Warren stare, a blend of horror and amusement on their faces. Understandably shocked by my outburst, though no one saw it coming less than I did. I haven't felt free enough to laugh like this in so long, I wasn't sure I remembered how.

I laugh until I cry, everything hurts, and I've almost forgotten why I started in the first place. Then, it comes back to me, and I regain a little control. "What's her name?" I ask.

"What?" they both ask.

"The girl Warren's praying hasn't seen your post yet. What's her name?"

He squirms, shoving his phone into his pocket. I wriggle my eyebrows, and his mother slaps him across the shoulder. "Ow! Fine. Lauren. Her name is Lauren."

"The one with the cute pixie cut?" I ask. He blushes. "Ren! She's super sweet! Good for you."

"I haven't even asked her out yet!" He tugs at his messy hair, then throws his hands up. "And now I doubt I can even show my face at the theater this afternoon."

"Oh, you can, and you will," I say.

Mrs. M frantically taps at her phone screen. "I'm fixing it now," she says. "I promise. I'm so sorry, kids."

"This is what happens when you let a boomer have social media," Warren grumbles, checking a rapid series of notifications on his phone.

"Hakuna your tatas, young man. I am a tail-end Gen X-er, and I *will* cut you if you ever imply otherwise again."

Warren and I exchange baffled smirks and wide eyes before he falls dramatically onto the couch beside me.

"You're savage, Mama Mitchell," I tell her. "I love this side of you."

She bats her lashes. "Thank you."

"You laugh, Gus. What's *Seth* going to think about my mother insinuating you and I are some creepy teenage newlyweds."

"I insinuated nothing!" she argues.

"Why are you bringing Seth into this?" I ask. "We're not a thing."

He sputters a laugh. "Yeah. Sure, you're not."

"He's not even talking to me right now." Seth's lack of genuine contact bothers me more than it should. I scrunch my nose up, twist my lips. "He's all single syllable texts. Even when Kali offered him the gig taking pictures for the Winter Recital. Woman pays *well,* and he responded with a thumbs up and a 'cool.'"

"Very lame," Warren says. "Sorry, Gus."

I jut my chin out. "Don't be sorry for me! I'm fine, dang it."

"Clearly."

"What am I hearing?" Mrs. Mitchell wriggles in between us. "Warren and August *both* have love interests?"

"Mom," Warren groans. "Stop being weird."

"I take it back," I say, ignoring the spat between mother and son. "He sent something brief but thoughtful yesterday for the..." Anniversary? Is that what we call it? I always associated the word with celebration, which yesterday was anything but. "Whatever. It was kinda sweet. But other than that..."

"Well," Mrs. M says, "I think it's fair to say your situation is unique."

My lips trill over an exasperated breath. "Yeah. Every way you look at it."

"You're young, honey. Risk your heart a little—or a lot. Make mistakes. Try it on, put it back. Breathe. What's meant to be will be."

I hear Warren huff, and a fire ignites in my belly. We're probably both thinking the same thing: *bullshit*.

"Mom," Warren says through clenched teeth. "Can you not spout that crap today? We buried him a year ago yesterday. If that was *meant to be*, and nothing we ever did would have changed it, fine. But I don't want to hear about it right now."

"I'm sorry, honey. Really." Mrs. M puts an arm around each of us and sighs. "Life's a bitch, isn't it?"

I side-eye her, openmouthed. "Language, Mama Mitchell," I tease.

We all relax, chuckling.

"Have Yourself a Merry Little Christmas" rings through the speakers, and I close my eyes, absorbing all the haunting and too-close-to-home lyrics.

"Benny *loved* Christmas," I say after a lengthy lull.

"I miss how he'd make us go caroling," Warren says. "I pretended the only reason I went along was to appease him. But I really did love it. And not just because you always baked a million cookies."

"I loved it, too," I admit. "The retirement communities were my favorite. Those little old ladies loved him. He always left with a pocket full of butterscotch candies."

"Plentiful cheek pinching action, too."

"Maybe *we* can go," Mrs. M offers. "I know it won't be the same."

"Maybe next year," I say. "When it's not so fresh."

"Agreed," Warren says. "But you'll still make the cookies, right?"

"I'll think about it."

"You remember the bonfire last year?" he asks.

"The one I didn't go to?"

"Exactly. Benny took a plate of your cookies to Millie. Told her *he* made them for her."

I sit up, arms flailing. "What? He did *not*. He would never!"

"Oh, but he totally did," Warren says, stifling a laugh. "He wasn't as angelically perfect as we all liked to believe he was."

"That traitor..." I breathe, tugging at my lip. "I'm questioning *everything* I know right now. Everything."

Warren stands, tousles my hair. "Not everything, Gus. He loved you, and he was still annoyingly good. But he had it bad for that girl. He wanted her to think he was special."

"Can't fault him there." I sigh, contemplating. "He was special. Even if he was a filthy little liar."

Warren chuckles. "True story. Now, love you both," he says, leaning down to kiss his mother's cheek. "But I've got to get pretty for work." He bats his eyelashes, framing his face with his hands.

"Dork," I say. "More like you've got damage control."

"Ugh. *Yes.*"

"I'm off to the studio," I announce. "Tell *Lauren* your teen bride says 'hello.'"

Mrs. Mitchell laughs, burying her flushed face in her hands. "I'll never live this down," she says.

"Nope!" we answer in unison.

"You kids drive safe. And text me when you get there. Please! We can try decorating another time."

"Tomorrow," I say. "Maybe I'll be ready tomorrow." Probably a lie, but I grin convincingly and hug her before I go.

SQUEALS of congratulations and the ruffle of wrapped bouquets echo through the auditorium as parents and students reunite—another successful Winter Recital in the books. I feel ridiculous greeting parents and accepting their thanks in my full stage makeup, but the Instructor Showcase routine was not made optional to me, nor was my solo. "You need to get back on stage," Kali had ordered gently. "It's now or never."

I chose *now,* and my heart is still racing as I smile, shake hands, and pose for pictures. Every parent takes photos, even though Seth took legitimate portraits before the night began. He worked so well with all the age groups, even the little ones. I watched as he made goofy animal noises to elicit giggles from all the toddlers, snapping photos in rapid succession. My mind—completely uninvited—jumped to images of an imaginary future. Hypothetical white fences and fictional blonde children with ocean eyes.

The scenes were startling but not unwelcome.

"Gus Gus!" Warren hollers, and I turn to see his arms outstretched. "You were amazing!"

Surrendering to his hug, I ask, "You promise? You're not just saying that?"

He holds me at arm's length. I spy Mr. and Mrs. M approaching. "Are you kidding?" he squeals. "That was *epic*. You didn't tell me you were dancing to *him*. I legit wept. Openly. It was embarrassing as hell. He'd be so proud of you. *I'm* so proud of you."

"We all are," Mrs. M chimes in, touching my heavily hair-sprayed curls. Come competition, my hair would be in a tight bun and nothing else. But recitals allowed for a bit of flare. "I even got your aunt on a video call. She saw, too." Warren clears his throat, giving me a *look*. "Okay, *Warren* figured it out. I held the phone, though."

"So, your aunt probably got seasick watching it," he quips. Mrs. M smacks his arm.

"Thank you," I say. "All of you. You've all been so wonderful. I wouldn't be here without you." Moisture gathers in my eyes, and I use my fingers to fan it away. *Not today.* Not with all the mascara, eyeliner, and false lashes threatening to melt.

Warren wraps me in one more hug, swaying me back and forth a little too forcefully. "Dammit, I'm proud," he says. "My badass ballerina."

"Language," Mrs. M sighs.

"I'm not a ballerina," I say into his chest.

"I've gotta go, Gus," he says, releasing me. "Meeting Lauren."

"Have fun." I wiggle my brows. He rolls his eyes but grins as he breaks away, his parents waving and following him out of the auditorium.

I shuffle to my truck in my clunky snow boots, emotionally and physically exhausted. All I want is to wash this nonsense off my face, trade my full-body tights for oversized flannel pajamas, and crawl into bed for at least twelve hours. Between finals at school and recital prep, I've barely slept this week.

Then I see *him* braced against the door of my Sierra, and a second wind instantly engulfs me.

"Hey, you," I say, an idiotic grin on my face.

"Hi," Seth says, standing tall.

"Where have you been lately?"

He rubs the back of his neck. "Busy. Sorry."

"Don't be. I've just missed you." *Ugh, chill out, Gus! Geez!*

"I've missed you, too," he says, relaxing. "Look, I didn't want to steal you from your spotlight in there, but I wanted to tell you how great you did before you left, and I lost my chance."

He looks ready to shuffle away.

"You could always, you know, call. Or text. E-mail. Smoke signals. I'm not saying you need to communicate in lucid, full sentences or anything crazy like that. But occasional proof of life would be nice."

"You're right," he sighs. "I've been avoiding you."

"You think?" I spit, then wince. "Wow, that was mean. I can't believe I just said that."

He shakes his head. "It's not—"

"No, I'm sorry. Really. I know it's a lot being around someone like me. I'm a roller coaster. And not the fun kind."

"August, that's not it." He steps forward, his hand dangling near mine. If only I twitch my fingers, his will be right there.

"Then what is it, Seth? Are we even still friends? We'd barely gotten there, and then you pulled away."

"I didn't want to. I didn't know how…"

"How to what?"

"I don't want to be that guy who can't be your friend because of my own…stuff. I want to be there for you, regardless. But it's hard. And I haven't learned how to yet. I'll keep trying, though. I promise."

His breath forms a vanishing cloud as he sighs.

"What *stuff*? What's going on? You can tell me. That's how friendship works. You're allowed to be the one talking to yourself in a cemetery on occasion. You know, if that's your scene."

He rolls his eyes. "That's not what I meant. But thanks. I appreciate it."

"Then what is it? No offense, but it's cold, and I've slept a combined ten hours this week."

"Don't worry about it tonight. Go home and get some rest, Gus. We can talk more later."

"You'd actually have to pick up the phone in this scenario. And it would require more than a couple emojis and a single word."

"What do you want from me?" He squirms and throws his hands up. "I'm trying, but I suck at this, and it's hard."

"Suck at *what*?"

"Trying to be your friend when all I want to do is kiss you!" He holds up a timid hand, hiding his face behind it.

I'm frozen, unable even to breathe.

"I respect you don't want that with me," he says. "I even understand it. Logically, in my brain, I totally get it. And it's fine. But my heart is stupid and being around you... Sometimes it hurts. That's my problem. Not yours. And I'm trying. But I'll need a little patience, okay? Can you cut me a little slack until I get there?"

Words swim around in my head, but I can't catch a single one. I nod.

"Okay," he says, preparing to make his exit. He glances everywhere but at me and twists his lips, his body gradually shifting away from mine. I'm losing him.

"This isn't just hard for you," I blurt. Seth perks up at this revelation. *Well, that happened.* It's out there now, and I can't take it back. "It's not that I don't *want* more. But Seth, I'm still finding my rhythm."

He deflates. Yet even as his features soften, he reaches for my hand. I meet him halfway. Butterflies swarm at his touch, their rapid flutters generating a heat which rises into my chest.

"I'm not trying to be unfair or insensitive here, August. I get it."

"It's been a year," I stammer, tears pooling. "I still expect him to walk into the room or text me when I'm sad because he always sensed when I needed cheering up."

Seth takes both my hands in his, holds them to his chest.

"We were freakishly close, and learning to live without him is a never-ending struggle. I'm sure you—and everyone else—is sick to death of me making everything about him. But that's the point. I'm literally learning to breathe again. I still walk around with a hole in my heart. I can't handle more difficult-to-navigate things in my life right now. I'm not ready."

He holds my eyes with his, a subtle pout on his lips. "I hear you," he says, nodding. "And I don't want to make things harder for you. But I also have to take care of my own heart." He drops his head. "Damn. That sounded way less cheesy in my head."

My hand over my heart, I grin. "No. Please say cheesy things. I dig your honesty. It's kind of beautiful."

"Not sure about *beautiful*. You're beautiful. Up on the stage tonight, you looked at home. At peace. It was incredible."

I fidget at the flattery. "Thank you."

He drops his forehead to mine—exhales his sweet breath, the warmth ghosting over me.

"August," he says, and I'm nearly unhinged.

I know exactly how it will play out from here if I only move an inch. He'll take me—broken parts, leaks, and all. As-is, repackaged merchandise. But if we try, and we fail, and he leaves me, too… How many times can a heart break before it stops beating? How many holes can be carved in me before I collapse?

"I wish I were ready," I say, my voice pinched in the back of my throat.

"Me too," he says. "Goodnight." With the lightest kiss on my cheek, he walks away, taking all the warmth with him.

Chapter 26

Dear Millie,

I've wanted to reach out to you a million times, but I've lacked the courage. And the words. Forgive the old-fashioned pen and paper, but I've discovered over the last year that there's something special about a hand-written letter. It's meaningful, and you deserve something meaningful. Also, I hope it's not super creepy that I asked your mom for your college address. I'm not a stalker. Just someone with a lot of regrets.

I shut you out last year after the accident. But I want you to know it wasn't because of you. I blamed myself, and I hated knowing that if only Benny had allowed himself to be happy with you rather than babysitting me all the time, he wouldn't have been in the car with me. I couldn't stand myself, and I couldn't stand anyone else around to witness my dumpster fire of a headspace. Except for Warren. Poor Warren. That boy deserves a trophy. And Sainthood.

I don't know how much this means to you now, or if it means anything, but I wanted to say I'm sorry for shutting you out rather than allowing you to be part of my grieving process. Maybe we could have helped each other. Maybe we could have been good friends; I know Benny always wanted that. He loved you, you know. It was a new love, yes. And it was young. But that's what made it so beautiful. So full of hope.

Reach out to me any time. Maybe we could get together next time you're back home. I'd love to catch up.

I wish you the best, Millie. With all my messy heart.
August

⁂

Laughter seeps through my bedroom door as I sit cross-legged on the bed, my favorite picture of Benny and I clutched in my hands. I framed it soon after Seth first brought it to me. My fingerprints smudge the glass. I stopped cleaning it weeks ago. Why bother? The picture always winds up back in my hands, my fingers tracing the joy on his face.

My usual regrets play on a loop.

I miss you. You should be here. I'm sorry.

A subtle knock on the door disrupts my rhythm, and I clear my throat. "Come in."

Warren enters, closes the door behind him, and sits in front of me.

"I'm sorry for hiding," I start, "I just—"

"Shh." He pulls the sleeve of his sweater over his thumb and dabs at my face. It's both sweet and comical. "You're allowed to hide. No one expects you to be merry and bright right now, I promise."

I laugh, short and low. "Good." A lopsided grin greets me when I pry my eyes from the picture and look up. "Hey," I whisper.

"Hey, Gus Gus."

"This is hard."

"I know." He borrows one of my hands. Squeezes it. "We love you, though. And we get it."

I chew on my lip, nodding. My heart pounds in my chest. Somehow, I'm feeling everything and nothing.

My phone vibrates on the nightstand, but I don't flinch.

"Seth?" Warren asks.

"He's texted a few times today. I'm not sure what to say to him."

"You could start with Merry Christmas."

"I will. Tomorrow. Maybe. Right now..." Warren releases my hand as I start to fidget, my breath quickening. "I'm one of those sad songs Benny loved to play." I laugh, and it hurts. I pat my chest. "There's nothing... Warren, there's nothing... I have nothing..."

He frowns. "August, that's not true."

"It is, though." I sniffle, wipe my nose. "For now, anyway."

He leans in closer, not looking away even though I avoid his gaze, almost squirming under it. "I think—no, I *know* there's more left inside of you than you'd like to admit. It's okay if you're not ready. And it's okay if you haven't found it yet. But it's there. I swear, Gus. It's there."

I close my eyes, shaking my head.

"Trust me," he whispers. "It's there. Just waiting for you to let the right one in."

I scoot across the mattress until I'm close enough to lean into him, and he wraps me in a warm hug. His hand moves in a continuous, comforting circle on my back.

Cheerful music resonates through the walls. Laughter rises and falls. I'm not sure I'll ever be ready to brave the extended Mitchell crowd, despite their sincerity and best intentions.

"Would they hate me if I snuck out for a bit?"

Warren's chin brushes my hair as he shakes his head. "They won't even have to know. I'll cover for you."

"Don't lie for me, Warren. Just tell them I'm sorry."

"August is sorry," he breathes.

"A memoir."

🎧

M<small>Y FIRST COMPETITION</small> is in two weeks. Lunatic that I am, I've choreographed a combination slightly beyond my skill set. I will perfect it, though, or die trying. The music builds as I prep for my fouetté sequence with a quadruple pirouette in the middle and end. I nailed a triple at the recital, and I've been building my core strength. I know I can do this.

And one, two, three, person, crap! A blur at the corner of the room startles me, and I fall out of my pirouette with sloppy arms, fumbling into fourth position.

"Sorry," a familiar voice hollers over the loud music. "Didn't mean to scare you."

"What are you doing here, Seth?" I screech. Out of breath and panting, I wipe my forehead with the back of my hand. Ultimately useless, as my hands are also sweaty.

He slips his shoes off at the door, and I can't help but check myself in the mirror as I shuffle to the stereo, pausing the music. Flyaways everywhere, beet red cheeks, and moisture seeping through my tank. Lovely. I smooth my rebellious hair back against my sweaty scalp and tighten my ponytail.

"You really should remember to lock the door when you're in here alone," he says.

"I thought I had. Guess my mind was elsewhere." My breathing begins to regulate with a series of slow inhales through my nose, exhales through tight lips. "Why are you here? Shouldn't you be with family?"

"Shouldn't *you*?" he asks, his voice low. Accusatory.

I shrug. "My aunt and uncle aren't coming down until tomorrow morning. Christmas Eve is for the Mitchells. And I love them, but some of the extended family... It was too peopley."

He nods, a light laugh brushing past his lips. "I get it. I don't do amazing in crowded rooms either."

"Do you have family over?"

"Mostly my stepmom's family. It's not terrible. But if I'm being honest, I'm here as much to get a break as I am to see you."

I place my hand over my heart. "I'm flattered."

He smirks. "I tried texting, then calling. When it went straight to voicemail, I figured you'd be here. I have something for you."

Crap! Are we at the point in a friendship where we're supposed to buy Christmas presents?

"You shouldn't," I start, but he's already jogging lightly back into the hallway, and he reappears with a neatly wrapped package.

"You shouldn't have gotten me anything, Seth. I didn't—"

"You didn't have to. This...it already belongs to you, really."

I knit my brow, a crooked smile on my face. "Well, if I wasn't nervous before, I am now."

He grins, handing me the package. "Don't be nervous," he says gently. My heart races, regardless.

When peeled back, the hunter-green paper gives way to a beautifully matted and framed dancer's silhouette. Me. On stage at the Winter Recital. Midsolo, early on, before the tension builds. I'm standing tall with my leg in a full extension, foot pointed directly at the ceiling, arms in fourth, my skirt cascading around my frame.

"Who'd you get to model this?" I tease. He rolls his eyes. I hug the frame to my chest. "This is perfect, Seth. Really. It's gorgeous." I pull the picture back and stare at it a moment longer, then hug it to my chest again. "I can't believe it's me."

"It is," he says, smiling. "Told you, you were remarkable up there."

"Thank you. I love it." I reach for an awkward hug, the picture between us. "How are things?" I ask as we pull apart. "Haven't really talked to you since the recital. Not that I'm blaming you."

He nods, touching my arm. "Things are good." A grin spreads on his lips. "I signed up for some photography classes. They start in January."

"That's great! I mean, I'm not sure how much more you could possibly have to learn."

"Oh, plenty. I assure you. I'm barely an amateur."

I take the picture to the end of the room and brace it safely against the wall.

"What about you?" he asks. "Any more ideas about school? Or dance? Or any of it?"

"I'm taking the bare minimum credits next term. I'll be teaching four classes starting in January. It'll keep me busy. Plus, I auditioned for EOU's production of *West Side Story*. I'll be in the dance company."

"Gus! That's amazing."

"Thanks."

I sink to the ground, begin stretching out my tired muscles. Seth sits across from me.

"No, really. I'm proud of you. You're going to be a hard girl to get ahold of, though."

"I'll need an assistant to answer all my calls."

He smirks. "For sure." He tries to join me in stretching but quickly grimaces and gives up. I sputter a laugh.

"Here." I maneuver his legs into a simple v-sit and adjust his posture. "Hold this; don't be a hero. Flexibility is a marathon, not a sprint."

"I'm pretty sure it's a triathlon," he says, straining against the foreign movement.

"Well, you're cold, too, which doesn't help. Warm muscles are more pliable. Next time, run a few laps around the building before you come in and attempt to keep up with me." I wink, and his lips curl into a goofy grin.

"Noted," he says. "So, you seem good. Happy."

"Sometimes," I shrug. "I'm working on it. Varies day by day. Moment by moment."

"I get it," he says, nodding. "When's the big competition?"

"Two weeks."

"Can I come?"

I squint. "Sure?"

"Can I take you out to celebrate when you inevitably win first place? Or even if the judges are on acid, and you don't?"

"Um." I bite my lip. "I guess."

"So, it's a date?"

"Is that the one where a couple goes out in public and like...gets food?"

He tilts his head, wrinkling his brow. "I know you're being sarcastic right now, but please tell me you've been on a date before."

"Not even once," I admit, scrunching my nose.

"*What* am I hearing right now? Never? Not even with Warren? Weren't you together for *months*?"

"It wasn't for lack of trying on his part—poor guy. I wasn't up for it. I was more of a cuddle in quiet girlfriend. If you could even call me that. I was terrible at the whole relationship thing."

"I don't know," he says. "Cuddling in quiet sounds pretty great."

I tuck my chin to my shoulder, attempting to hide the width of my smile.

He stares, unflinching. "August, being around you is..."

"Me too," I admit.

His eyes gradually widen. "Yeah?"

"It makes me feel...*better*. Except for when it makes me nervous."

He laughs, his ocean eyes beaming. "I'd be lying if I said you never made me nervous. Mostly because I feel inadequate."

"Whatever." I shake my head, rolling my eyes. "Wait, do *I* make you feel inadequate? Because I never meant—"

"No, I just mean you're such a presence. You're so smart and talented. You're *funny*. You grew up with Benny and Warren, who are—and were—apparently the world's nicest guys. I worry I'm a letdown to you."

"You've never been a letdown, Seth."

Something in his grin doesn't trust me entirely. "Never?"

"Okay, *maybe* when we first met. You were a tad full of yourself. But that was a long time ago." I shrug, and his grin widens. "Besides, apparently Benny—while a great guy—wasn't above lying to get what he wanted."

Seth raises a single brow, tilting his head. "Oh, really?"

"I make—made—these cookies every year around Christmas. Amazing cookies. Put all Grandmas and Nanas across the globe to *shame* cookies. Apparently, he took some to the bonfire last year, gave them to Millie, and said *he'd* made them for her. The jerk."

Seth's shoulders shake as he laughs. "A betrayal of the deepest kind."

"Right? Pretty sure I bled internally when I found out."

"Don't let it burn too deep. He was just...smitten. Never underestimate how far a guy will go to impress a beautiful girl."

"When he's *smitten*?" I tease.

Seth stands, walks to the sound system. "You mock," he says, "but it's true." He connects his phone to the speakers and begins scrolling. "You see, a little over a year ago, I met this girl. A force of nature, really. She was like, blow-you-away gorgeous, with this dark, snarky wit. And she danced like it was her first, most fluent language." He looks up from his phone, staring at me from across the room with those beautiful blue-grays, and I'm melted butter.

Music in six-eight time fills the room. Ed Sheeran, I think.

"She told me this adorable story about how she learned to waltz with someone a long time ago. How she'd loved it and missed it." He walks toward me, holding my gaze the entire time. "So, I went home and watched videos on YouTube and asked my stepmom to help me learn to waltz. And I hoped to convince this girl to come with me to the Winter Ball, where I could show off my mad skills."

We're inches apart, my head level with his neck. Seth holds his left hand out, and timidly, I accept. He places his right hand firmly against the small of my back, and I straighten my posture against his touch. My left hand finds his shoulder.

"Unfortunately, on the morning I planned to ask this...*angelic* dancer to join me... Well..."

I close my eyes as a memory leaks out, sliding down my cheek. I take a single slow, controlled breath, and Seth leads us in a waltz.

I almost laugh, but then I realize there's absolutely nothing silly about this. Our eyes hold each other with an intensity rivaling the electricity of his hand on my back. No sooner is "Perfect" over than

The Lone Bellow's "Looking for You" starts, and we haven't stopped moving even for a moment.

"How many songs are on there?"

"Infinite," he says, smiling. "I can do this as long as you like. Or we can be done. But I'm not great at talking and keeping rhythm," he finishes. The focus in his eyes tells me he's not simply being cute.

"I'm impressed, Seth Davidson," I say, letting myself dance a little closer to him. My head nearly resting against his shoulder.

"I'll dance with you any day, August. I can't promise we'll win any competitions. But I would learn more than a waltz for you."

My fingers clutch at the fabric of his shirt, and his hips inch closer, igniting a fire inside me.

"You'll get sick of me, Seth," I whisper. "You'll get sick of my meltdowns and mood swings and how sometimes I can barely get out of bed to save my life."

He stops moving his feet, but he keeps swaying to the music.

"Shouldn't I get to decide when I'm sick of something or someone?" The confidence behind his gentle tone leaves me immobilized, breathless. I swallow and pull back enough to look up at him. "I love you," he says. "All of you. Not just the shiny parts."

In a state of near delirium, my hand travels shakily from his shoulder to his cheek. I study the softness of his features, all the while inching closer, until we're melding together—practically one person, sharing one erratic heartbeat.

"I'm all in," he whispers.

His hands gather at my spine, lifting me slightly.

"Bold statement," I say, grinning.

"I mean it," he assures me, his lips brushing against mine. "I'm in love with you."

Every part of me aching for him, I grab the back of his neck in full-force, guard down, wear-it-on-my-sleeves desperation.

"Good. Because I'm in love with you."

It's taken me so long to get here, it seems almost a waste how quickly I lunge at him. We're all hands and lips, exploring everything there is, hungry for more.

Minutes later, catching my breath, I whisper, "I don't want to lose you."

He brushes my cheek, his fingers soft and gentle.

"I'm here," he says. "I'll always be here. You won't lose me."

"No one can promise that."

He braces his forehead against mine. "No, they can't. But isn't that exactly why we should make the most of it now? I'd rather run with this, even if I crash and burn. Don't spend the flight so paranoid about the exit signs you miss the view completely. You know?"

"I've never been on a plane," I sigh, playfully jabbing holes in his metaphor.

"Why are you so difficult?" He swoops me up, spinning me around before letting my feet touch the floor. My involuntary, giddy squeal bounces off the walls of the studio. Seth steadies himself, then kisses me again. Lightly, but with intent.

"I'm *here*, August," he breathes. "I'm ready if you are. All in, remember?"

"All in." I kiss him once more, then rest my head against his chest, my hands relaxed against his shoulders.

The music plays on, a gentle acoustic guitar in three-four time. Seth keeps me close, his movement guiding mine as we continue to dance the floor.

"They'll be worried about you," he says. "Do you need to head back?"

"Not yet," I whisper. "Don't let me go."

He holds me tighter. "Not a chance."

I drink it all in—every detail of this perfect moment where I'm swaying slightly out of rhythm with someone who's seen me at my worst and loves me anyway. Someone who gives me hope that one day, all my broken pieces might stitch themselves back together. A patch-work heart; wounded, but still beating. Able to love again without reserve.

I may fall apart tomorrow. Or next week. Definitely by next month. It'll probably be years before I make it a single day without pausing to explore the emptiness Benny left inside me. Maybe when that time comes, Seth and I will have exhausted all our patience with one another, and he'll be gone. But he's here now. He's *here*, and I love him, and he's holding me in a way that makes me feel whole again, even if only for as long as this song lasts.

Acknowledgments

This book was a labor of love, and not just mine. While the concept and first draft belong to me, *Life After* would never have become a published, tangible book without the unfailing, unconditional love of my amazing support group.

To my husband, Brett. Thank you for your relentless encouragement through all the tears and doubt, stressful rewrites, and even all the years I put my writing on the back burner. You never stopped believing I could do this, even when I did. Your support is everything to me. I love you.

To my ride-or-dies, Karinna and Kate. You've been there through every disappointment, every vent session, every WHY DID I THINK I COULD DO THIS?! moment. You've helped me brainstorm, read my messy drafts, and offered invaluable input. Every victory belongs to you both as much as it belongs to me, because without you, I never would have kept going (and I don't just mean in regards to my writing). You are my people, and I love you. Friend is not a strong enough word.

To the amazing writer-moms I met along this journey who were instrumental in getting this manuscript query ready, and who helped me brainstorm problem areas throughout the process. Thank you to Andrea, who helped me with the dreaded synopsis. Not all heroes wear capes, my friend. I am so grateful. Carissa and Jenny, thank you for being my Alpha & Beta Readers. For cheering me on and being my sounding boards. You commiserated with me through every step of querying, including all the rejections. And when it came time to edit this bad boy, you stuck around and helped me make the words pretty.

Carissa, Jenny, and Kate held my hand through the final edits of this book. When I was ready to throw my laptop through a window, they talked me down and saved this book (and me).

To Julia, my editor, who fell in love with August, Benny, and Warren, and took a chance on a debut author. You helped me turn *Life After* into the best version of itself. Thank you for believing in me.

To the rest of the Immortal Works team who helped make this book possible, thank you.

I'm eternally grateful to my first cheerleaders, and the best parents in the entire world (I will fight anyone who says otherwise), Allan and Corean. First and foremost, you two let me be a super weird kid. You never snuffed out my quirks, or told me I *couldn't* write a book, even when my first attempts were so truly terrible. Thank you for introducing me to so much music. Thanks for years of dance lessons, costumes, and competition fees. For instruments and sheet music. For chauffeuring me to rehearsals, and all the other things that helped shape me into the delightful, well-rounded, moderately well-adjusted human that I am.

A heartfelt shout-out to Loren and Penny Arment, who I first heard sing their own hauntingly beautiful rendition of the song "Two Little Boys" by Theodore F. Morse and Edward Madden almost twenty years ago. Their voices, and that melody, imprinted on my soul. I love you both, and miss you terribly. Say hello to the midnight sun for me, will you?

Finally, to my children. Thank you for letting Mommy have spurts of alone time. Thank you for (mostly) understanding when I had to work, and when I was emotionally exhausted afterward. Thank you for being entertained with games, cards, music, PBS Kids, and the Wiggles as my deadlines loomed. I love you all so much, and I'm so thankful for you. You're amazing humans, and it's an honor to be your Mom.

About the Author

Genalea is an author, freelance editor, and full-time mom with an Associate's Degree in English Literature. Her work has appeared in *Gemini Magazine, Bookends Review, Grande Dame Literary, Writers in the Attic: Rupture*, and others. She resides in Southern Idaho with her husband, four children, and two dogs, where she enjoys small town living, playing music with her family, and occasionally getting caught behind farm equipment on the highway. *Life After* is her debut novel.

This has been an
Immortal Production